Nurturing Souls

Nurturing Souls

by
DS Bauden

Justice House Publishing, Inc.
Tacoma, Washington, USA
www.justicehouse.com

NURTURING SOULS

Copyright © 2003 by DS Bauden

All Rights Reserved, including the right to reproduce this book, or portions thereof, in any form whatsoever. For information, contact Justice House Publishing, Inc., 3902 South 56th St., Tacoma, WA 98409, USA.

Book Cover by Mark McHaley

Book Design by R. Paterson

All characters and events in this book are fictitious. Names, characters, places and incidents are products of the author's imagination or are used fictiously. Any resemblance to actual events, locales, or persons, living or dead, is entirely coincidental.

The typeface is Garamond, 10 point.

ISBN 0970887485

PRINTED IN THE USA

DEDICATION

For Nancy and John

I think of you both all the time
and I miss you terribly.
Take good care of each other,
just like you always have.

I love you.

#7

ACKNOWLEDGMENTS

To Lori – Thank you for helping me through the darkest point of my life. There are no words that I could possibly utter, that describe what you mean to me.

To My Sisters and Brothers – I can never thank you enough for the love and support you have given me. I love you all so much.

To Mark – Thank you for creating such a beautiful cover for my first novel. Having you a part of this has meant the world to me.

To Po – Thank you for being here for me when I needed to cry the most. You'll always be in my heart.

To Sonja – You are one in a million, darlin'. Always know that you are special. <gt>

To Amy – Thank you for being that ray of sunshine I needed so desperately. Your friendship means so much to me.

To Jen – Your belief in my storytelling is something I will never forget. Thank you from the bottom of my heart.

To Tri – You have the heart of a lion in the shell of a tiger. I am so thankful you are in my life.

To Robin and Rashidah - Thank you for believing in my story enough to publish it! This is something I'll never forget.

To Tee and Shari – Thank you for cleaning up my first diamond. She shines much brighter now.

One

The sun was beating down on the car transporting young Alicia McKenna to her new surroundings. The ride from the airport to her aunt's ranch was a long one. It had taken her some time to make the decision to leave home after her parents had passed away, but her aunt had offered and she had accepted. Her Aunt Edna was a very loving woman in her own right. Ever since Ally, as she preferred to be called, could remember Aunt Edna had been like a second mother to her. Most of all, Edna Petersen was Ally's friend.

It had been just six weeks since Ally had received the news of her parents' car accident. The loss had left her entirely empty and unsure of what to do with the rest of her life. She was a young nineteen and had just finished her first year of college. This was the worst pain she had ever felt. A new start was in order, and hopefully, that would begin with her aunt on her ranch. She raked her hand through long blonde hair, feeling completely numb as the car pulled into the driveway of the main house.

Here we go, she thought as the car came to a stop. Ally saw her aunt racing down the drive to meet her with open arms.

"Ally! Ally! You made it!" Edna cried, as she scooped her niece into a warm and full embrace. "I'm so glad you came."

"Hi, Eddi! I'm so happy to see you too! I've missed you terribly." Ally clung to the older woman as tears flowed freely down her cheeks.

"Let me look at you, darlin'." Edna pulled away and focused on the frail body in front of her. "Alicia, starving yourself won't bring them back," she whispered, moving back into the hug.

"I know, Eddi, I just don't have much of an appetite these days. Looks to me like you're doing well though." She poked her plump aunt in the belly and smiled, wiping the tears away.

"There's the girl I love. Let's see if we can keep her around for a while, shall we?"

"I'll do my best. Where's Jack?"

"He isn't here right now. He had some meeting in Phoenix. He should be back in a week or so. Don't you worry; he'll be back soon. He's excited about seeing you too."

"Well, good. We used to get together all the time when he was working near Chicago. What's it been, four or five years since we've seen each other? Anyhow, it's been ages."

"Let's get you settled in, honey, and I'll put on some tea. We can talk more in the kitchen, okay?"

Edna grabbed one of Ally's bags as she unloaded them from the car. Ally's eyes clouded with sorrow as she removed the last one.

"All right. I have my whole life in these bags. God, I still can't believe what happened."

"I know, sweetie, I know..." She draped her arm around Ally as they walked toward the main house.

The main house was an old country-style affair. The front door had an antique brass knocker and a thumb latch door handle. As soon as she grasped the handle, she was immediately flooded with memories of her childhood. Ally loved this house. She'd spent many summers here with her aunt, uncle, and cousin. Her Uncle John had died a few years earlier from a heart attack. One afternoon, he had been training one of the horses and had collapsed. Edna was out in the back and saw him go down. She ran to him, but he was already gone by the time she got there.

"That door always reminds me of John, too. It seems like a thousand years ago."

She left her bags and followed Edna to the kitchen. "I know, Eddi; I miss Uncle John so much. You two were my second parents. Now it's just the three of us," Ally said and squeezed her aunt's hand. Edna passed her a mug of tea to share with her free hand.

"I swore that I'd do anything to prevent anyone from collapsing from overexertion here again. I even hired a stable hand. Pretty nutty, eh?"

"That's not nutty, Eddi, you just want to be careful. I don't blame you. You can never be too cautious, believe me. I don't think that I've felt so unnerved as I did the first time I drove somewhere after the accident."

"We have extra sets of eyes watching over us now, honey."

"Yeah, we do. I can feel mom every once in awhile. I bet you can, too."

"My sister and I had a very special bond. I feel her around me almost every day. A part of me died that day..." Her voice trailed off as the emotions caused chills to run through her body.

Ally leaned over and hugged her aunt. The two women hung onto each other until the sobbing ceased.

"Enough of this. You came here to be free of this sadness, and what do I do? I'm sorry, honey."

"Eddi, I came here to start over, but I'll never be free of the sorrow. I do know that time will lessen that pain. I'm just going to take things day by day. That's all I can do right now."

"That sounds like a good plan, dear. Now, let's get you unpacked."

"Okay, will I be in my old room?"

"Actually, I had to give you the guestroom. Syd is staying in your old room. I didn't think that I'd ever get you here on a permanent basis, so I gave the room away when I hired Syd."

"Syd?"

"Yes, Syd is my stable hand. I'll introduce you two later. Right now, let's try to turn that old guestroom into something to your liking. I've been working on making it more homey, but I'm sure that you can put your own special touches on it." They went into the guest room and began working on it together.

"I'm sure it'll be great, Eddi, thank you for everything."

"Aww, honey, I'd walk through fire for you, you know that."

"I love you, too."

The two continued unpacking Ally's room and before long it looked quite comfortable. They just looked at each other and smiled.

The room was a soft emerald color, like Ally's eyes. Several old pictures graced the walls. Some were Edna's original paintings of landscapes and whatnot. There were also framed photographs along the windowsills showing the history of Ally's life. Many were of her with her parents. Her favorite was one of her with her mom and Eddi sitting along the edge of the Grand Canyon. They both seemed to be looking at that picture.

The room was as Ally wanted it to be for the time being. She would dig into the rest of the boxes later. Now she wanted to see her horse, Polka, before it got too dark. "Eddi, I'd like to go out and see Polka, okay?"

"She'll be happy to see you again. Syd will be out there to help if you need it."

"Thanks, Eddi."

Two

The stable was as she remembered it—two stalls for the horses and a loft that she and Jack used to play in. She saw an older man tending the field with Matty, the other horse.

That must be Syd. I'll go say "hi" after I find Polka. I can't wait to ride her. Maybe it'll take away some of this depression.

She walked out into the corral where she expected to find Polka, but what she did see was nothing short of awesome.

Ally's eyes could not break from the sight in front of her. Her long black hair was flowing through the wind as she and Polka came across the field. She was amazing. The woman had on black jeans, a white shirt, and a black vest. Her body was slim and quite flexible. Ally noticed that she flawlessly led Polka through a number of jumps and did a couple of tricks in the saddle. She seemed a million miles away and as happy as could be.

Ally's focus finally cleared and her heart skipped a beat as the mystery woman approached her.

"Alicia, I presume."

God I never thought I'd hear my name sound so incredible, Ally thought, marveling at the woman's accent.

"Hello? Anyone home?"

"Um, I'm sorry. Yes, I'm Ally. I see that I don't need to worry about Polka getting exercise while I'm away."

"Nope. Edna tells me she's yours. She's a great ride, and so beautiful."

"Yes, she is. I miss her when I'm away, but I guess that won't be a problem anymore. Do you mind if I ride her? I haven't ridden her in ages."

"Of course not. You probably should take it easy on her, we just did some drills and she may be a little tired. This heat doesn't help much either," the tall woman added, wiping her forehead with her forearm. Ally couldn't help but to stare. The woman had the most beautiful blue eyes she had ever seen.

"Are you all right?"

"Ye...yeah I'm fine. Sorry."

The woman slid almost seductively down from the horse and rose to her full height next to Ally's smaller frame. She stood about 6 feet tall and seemed all but angelic. Ally felt very safe standing next to this woman and experienced a closeness that she didn't quite understand.

"She's all yours."

Ally mounted Polka and noticed that the stirrups needed to be adjusted before she found herself on the ground.

"Could you give me a hand?"

"Sure..." The other woman reached under Ally's boot to raise the stirrup on the left side, then walked around to the other side. She raised the other one and held Ally's calf as she led her foot into the stirrup. Ally felt a jolt of energy course through her body. She sat waiting for the surge to end and when it was over she turned to thank the woman, but she was already gone.

Who was that? I didn't even get her name. My God, she was gorgeous.

She cleared her head of the thoughts raging through her mind and urged Polka into the field.

Riding Polka, a part of Ally's childhood returned to her. She felt more comfortable and secure at this moment than she had in two months. She still remembered the phone call the day her parents were killed. She was at the University of Illinois with only one week left for finals when Aunt Edna called. It wasn't unusual for her aunt to call, but the circumstances were more than Ally could possibly have been ready to bear.

☯ ☪

"Hi, Eddi! God, I can't even tell you how crazed I am right now with finals. I have four tests this next week. I'm totally exhausted. Thank God this will be over in a few days..." She could hear her aunt breathing heavily on the other end and began to suspect that something was terribly wrong.

"What's the matter, Eddi?" She waited for her aunt to find her voice amid the sobs.

"Ally..."

"W-what is it?"

"I don't know how to tell you this..."

"Just tell me, whatever it is, I can take it," Ally said, hoping that would be true.

"Honey, it's your mom and dad." That was all Ally needed to hear. A wave of panic crashed through her as her aunt told her that a drunk driver had killed her parents the previous night. They had been coming home from dinner, when a red Cadillac had swerved

into their lane, causing them to drive over the median, and into oncoming traffic. They died instantly on impact.

"They're really...gone, Eddi?" The tears on the other end of the phone confirmed that it was true.

"Ally, I'm so sorry. I don't know of any words that can lessen this pain any. I'll be in Chicago in a couple of days to take care of...arrangements for them... I don't want you to have to worry about... anything. Oh, Ally... I'm so sorry."

"I'll finish up with finals... and then I'll be home." Her mask of strength was showing through. She had to be strong...for her aunt's sake.

ಐ ಚಿ

The sobs wracking through Ally's body were almost as strong as what she had experienced at her parents' funeral. It was too difficult to try and understand why her parents were taken so horribly. She just needed to let it out and try to make the best of things.

"I just can't believe they're gone, Polka. They were taken way too soon." She nuzzled her horse and the mare seemed to know what her owner was going through. Polka nuzzled her back and they shared a moment of solace.

The sun was setting and Ally hadn't realized how long she'd been outside. She walked Polka back into her stall and gave her a couple of carrots. She said good-bye and made her way back to the house.

Three

"Eddi, I'm back," she called.

"In here, dear. I was just about to send a search party out for you. Have a seat; it's time for dinner."

"Let me go wash up, first."

"All right, darlin'."

"Mm, dinner smells wonderful," Ally said, as she slid into her place at the table.

"I can always count on you to compliment my meals."

"Hey, I come by it honestly. I believe it was one of your traits that I inherited."

"Yes, your mother and I were both cursed with healthy appetites. It's a good thing that you didn't develop the tummy that I have though," Eddi said with a chuckle.

"Don't think it won't happen. If I didn't work out, there'd be a lot more of me. Besides, I like the way you look."

"Dig in, it won't be that great if it gets cold."

"Okay, but let me grab a glass of milk to go with this."

"Don't get up, Syd's in the kitchen."

Directing her request to the kitchen, "Hey, Syd? Could you bring a glass of milk with you, dear?" Ally caught a glimpse of an 'OK' sign from the kitchen.

Ally took a bite of her food as her glass was placed in front of her. Not looking up she said, "Thanks, Syd."

"You're welcome, Alicia," came the sultry response.

Ally almost lost control of the food in her mouth. "Uh…you're Syd?"

"Yes, who were you expecting, Medusa?"

"I guess I was just expecting a man...sorry. I know that name can go both ways, I just assumed. Please excuse my lame stereotyping."

"You're forgiven." Sydney smiled, acknowledging the eagerness of her housemate's apologies.

Ally could hardly eat the rest of her food. She could not believe the woman she had seen earlier was the same woman her aunt had referred to as her stable hand. *My God! I can't even untie my tongue to ask for some salt!*

"Do you not like my cooking, Alicia?"

"Um...no I umm...it's very good. You cooked this?"

"Mhhmmm, I have many skills."

Oh, I can see that, Ally thought to herself. "So, how long have you been working for Eddi?" she asked brightly.

"I came aboard two years ago, I think. I arrived in the States about six years ago from Australia. My family had a sheep herding station there. My parents both passed away and I sold the station to my older brother."

"Why did you decide to come to the states? Australia is a beautiful place."

"Yes, it is. I went to school there for a year and ended up in a relationship that brought me over. When that didn't work out, I heard from some friends that your aunt here was looking for some help. It wasn't sheep, but I knew a lot about horses and stable work. I wanted to see what life might be like in the States, so I decided to stay. I love the work here, and Edna's a wonderful lady."

Sydney ended her tale, and when it appeared that no more of the story was going to be offered, Ally chimed in.

"Well it seems as though Eddi appreciates your work here. This ranch must seem pretty homey to you. Do you miss home?"

"Sometimes, but like I said, I like it here. Edna has been wonderful."

Ally studied the woman as she ate. *Sydney couldn't be much older than me*, Ally thought. *Maybe 25 or so*. Ally's appetite finally came back and she continued to eat everything on her plate and what her aunt didn't eat.

"I see it's a family trait," Sydney chuckled.

"You betcha!" Edna said with pride. "Anyone for some apple pie?"

"None for me thanks," Sydney replied.

"Count me in, Eddi. Do you have...?"

"Whipped cream is coming too, don't you worry." She smiled at her niece and walked back into the kitchen.

"So, umm, Syd. Is that short for Sydney?"

"Yes, that's where I was born. I guess my parents liked the name."

"It suits you."

"Do you think so, Alicia?" She smiled a very sexy smile at Ally.

"You can call me 'Ally'."

"I don't think so. I rather like 'Alicia'. It...suits you." She smiled at Ally.

"Well, I've never really been fond of my full name. It always meant that I was in trouble or something."

"Well, we'll just have to fix that now, won't we, Alicia?"

Ally sat there with her mouth slightly open. She just didn't know what to think about Sydney. There was something about her that she just couldn't shake. There was a silent mystery that was building. Ally wanted to find out everything there was to know about her. *But why?* she wondered.

"Thank you for dinner, Sydney, it was very good." *Two can play at this game.*

Sydney smiled at the younger girl's use of her full name. *Do you know what kind of game that's being played here, Alicia? I wonder...* Sydney's thoughts rolled through her mind as Edna walked in with two plates of apple pie. She couldn't hold back a laugh at Ally's child-like expression as the dessert was placed in front of her.

"Oooh, Eddi this looks fabulous."

"Dig in, child."

The rest of the meal was silent as Eddi and Ally ate their pie. Watching them eat this dessert was like watching Michelangelo paint the Vatican. Food, Sydney was learning, was an art to them. Never before had she seen two people 'oooh' and 'aaah' so much in her life. It made her smile in spite of it.

"If you two ladies will excuse me, I have to get the horses ready for the night."

"Sure, Syd and thanks again for a wonderful meal."

"You're welcome, Edna. See you later, Alicia."

"Being that we live under the same roof, you can count on it."

Sydney beamed a large grin and left the room, leaving Ally just staring in her absence.

"Ally? Is there something wrong?"

"Eddi, God, why didn't you warn me about Syd? She's not what I imagined. I really thought that 'Syd' was the older gentleman outside in the fields."

"Why would I warn you about Syd? She's nothing to be afraid of, Ally. I really like her. She's done a great job and she is really good company." Her aunt leaned in conspiratorially. "Quite a head turner, too. I guess it would have saved you some embarrassment though, eh?"

"Exactly! She's really beautiful. You'd think that she'd be doing something other than stable work, though. Not that there's anything wrong with taking care of horses."

"Alicia, my goodness, since when do you have to be ugly to work in a stable?"

"God, Eddi, I didn't mean it like that. I mean Syd isn't just pretty, she is drop-dead gorgeous! She could be a model or an actor, you know? I didn't mean anything by that."

"I know you didn't, child. You're quite the head turner yourself and, as I recall, we were just talking about how much you resemble my younger self. So, no offense is taken dear." She nudged her niece and smiled.

"I'm gonna head outside and breathe in this air that I've missed so much. Montana is a far cry from the Windy City. It's so peaceful and clean here. I'll see if I can help Syd with anything. That is, if she'll accept any help from a city mouse like me."

"I'm sure she will, dear. Go on now. I'll clean up here, don't you worry."

"Okay, Eddi, thanks for the pie, it was wonderful... and Eddi, thanks for bringing me here. I think I'm going to love being here."

"Bye now." Edna smiled at her niece. *I do believe that something or someone, will make sure of that,* she mused to herself.

Four

"Need any help?" Sydney started out of deep thought. "Oh, I'm sorry, Syd, I can come back."

"No, that's all right, Alicia. I just wasn't expecting anyone out here. This is the part of the day that I love. Take a listen."

Ally looked into the night's sky and listened, but didn't hear anything. "What are we listening for? I don't hear anything."

"Exactly, all you hear are crickets and the wind. It's so quiet this time of night. Sometimes I just sit out here or up in the loft and look out over the field. This place does remind me of home. Well, minus the sheep of course."

Ally sat and listened to Sydney speak. She felt intoxicated by her voice. It managed to be both soothing and powerful all in the same tone. She didn't notice that the taller woman had stopped talking; she just kept watching her expressions.

"I seem to keep pulling you from your own thoughts."

"I'm sorry. I have a lot on my mind. I didn't mean to be rude; I should just leave you alone."

"Alicia, wait..." Sydney held Ally's arm. Both women felt the tingle of that touch.

"Edna told me what happened to your parents. I'm truly sorry. No one should lose anyone they love to an accident like that."

Ally felt the tears welling in her eyes. "Thank you. I guess you know what it's like to lose your parents."

"Yes, but mine died of natural causes and I didn't lose them both at once. You've had to deal with a whole lot more than I did."

The two women studied each other in silence, both feeling an unusual closeness to the other that they were not quite willing to admit.

"So, um..." Ally started, faltering when she felt Sydney wipe a tear from her cheek. "Is there, anything that I can help you with out here?"

"That's sweet of you, but the horses have been watered and they're all set until 5 a.m."

"My God, that's early!"

"Well, that's what your aunt pays me to do."

"Do you like it here? I mean, being all alone and stuff."

"I like it very much. Alicia, I'm not alone here. I have Edna, and now, I have you." She winked at Ally and switched her gaze to the house.

Ally didn't quite know what to make of that last comment, but she was willing to bet, she meant that she had someone else under her roof now.

"Sydney?"

"Yes, Alicia?"

"Thanks for listening, I mean understanding what I was going through...I mean..."

"You're welcome, Alicia. Shall we go in and see what kind of mischief your aunt's getting into?"

"Sure." They smiled at each other and walked back up to the house.

Five

"Excellent, thanks Tony. I'll see you in a couple days. Bye." Edna hung up the phone as the two women walked into the family room. They plopped themselves onto the couch and waited for her to speak.

"Well, ladies, I'll be leaving tomorrow."

"What? Where are you going Eddi? I just got here," Ally said with a pout.

"Oh, honey, I'll only be gone a week or so. There's some new equipment for the stables that my friend Tony told me about. They are holding an auction in Indiana. If I want to update any of my old equipment I have to get there no later than tomorrow night. I've got to get my name in the hat."

"Ahh, I see."

"Come up and help me pack?"

Ally's face lit up and then she looked over to Syd. "You coming?"

"No, I think I'll just head up to my room and read before bed."

"Are you sure? You can probably get Eddi to tell one of her famous stories about my childhood. She loves to embarrass me."

"Really? How can I turn that down?"

"Good, come on." Ally smiled and unconsciously grabbed Sydney's hand and led her to the stairs, but let go before they proceeded to climb the steps and both women felt the loss of contact.

Sydney and Ally sat on Edna's bed and watched her rifle through her clothes to find the right ones to pack.

"Mustn't look too trendy. Ranch owners should look rustic, don't you think?"

Ally and Sydney exchanged amused glances.

"Eddi, just wear whatever you damn well want. Who cares what other people think? Life is too short. You gotta live your life for you and do what makes you happy," Ally declared.

"When did you become so philosophical?"

"About six weeks ago..." her voice trailed off and she dropped her head down.

Edna walked to the edge of the bed and put her hand on Ally's shoulder. "You'll make it through this, little one. I'll do whatever I can to make it easier for you."

"I'm sorry, Eddi, I didn't mean it to sound like that. It's still all so fresh."

"It doesn't go away, but it will get easier, Alicia. It hurts so badly because of how much your parents meant to you. That's not a bad thing. If it's of any comfort, whenever you need to talk, I'll be here for you."

"Thanks Syd, that means a lot to me."

"So, Syd, do you wanna hear about when Ally broke her leg falling out of the upstairs window?" Edna asked with a wiggle of her eyebrows.

"I wouldn't miss a story like that for anything."

Ally groaned. Looking back now she could laugh about it, but at the time it was none too funny.

ಬಾ ಲ

"Jack, hurry up! We're going to get caught!"

"Ally, just keep quiet! Mom is gonna hear you. Do you want to get out tonight or not?"

"Yeah, but damn it, can't we speed up the process?"

"Well, 'Miss-I-can-do-things-faster-than-anyone', if you'd help me instead of yapping, we'd be finished already."

Edna stared at the air vent leading up to her son's room. She heard voices that she assumed were Jack and Ally. They were conspiring about something, but she was unsure what it was. She thought it would be a good idea to find out why they were still awake when it was well past midnight.

"There, I think it'll hold," Jack said, looking proudly at his handiwork.

"It had better, otherwise you'll have to explain to Aunt Eddi what happened to me."

"Ssshhh! Tie this around you and I'll lower you down."

"Okay, but I'm more than a little nervous about this."

Jack had taken the liberty of stripping all the linens off of his bed and tying the sheets together. The 'rope' would get them in and out of the house without waking anyone. Jack had some buddies that they were going to meet up with. Summer was a time to hang out and drink with your friends, and at 13, Ally felt she needed to learn just how cool summer could be. She knew her older cousin was just the guy to teach her, too.

"Okay, Ally, just sit on the edge of the window and I'll lower you down."

"Are you sure you can hold me, Jack?"

"Come on Ally, you're just wasting time. Let's go!"

"Okay, okay."

Ally sat in the windowsill and lowered herself so that she was dangling by just her hands. She felt the sheets tighten around her as her body was slowly lowered to the ground. She grabbed the sheets and closed her eyes.

Jack was lowering his cousin to the ground without much trouble when there was a knock at his door.

Trying to sound sleepy he said, "Who is it?"

"It's your mother, who do you think it is? Can I come in? I can't find Ally, is she in with you?"

Sweat began to pour off of Jack's face as he decided how to deal with the other end of his 'rope.

"She's not in here, mom."

Edna opened the door and like a deer in the headlights, Jack froze in place, but not before letting go of the rope, causing Ally to fall the rest of the way down to the ground, breaking her leg.

"Well, I said she wasn't in here." Jack said, grinning weakly at his mother who shook her finger at him and ran outside to tend to her niece.

                         ☜ ☞

"It took over two months for my leg to heal," Ally said recalling the pain, but chuckling nonetheless.

"Oh, I'll never forget the look on Jack's face when I walked in! He never expected to see me there. Oh my... I'll never forget that as long as I live." Eddi did an imitation of Jack and the three women broke into peals of laughter.

"Me either..." Ally's laughter was quickly giving way to tears. It was, however, a pleasant change to be crying tears of joy.

"You were quite a little spitfire, weren't you, Alicia? My folks would've kicked my ass if I'd tried to break curfew like that."

"She's still a spitfire, so watch out, Sydney!" Edna flashed Sydney a knowing look.

"Well, I see a whole lot of packing is NOT getting done here, so I need to concentrate on the task at hand."

Ally walked over to her aunt and kissed her cheek. "I think I'm going to turn in. It's been a long day."

"Sleep well, little one, and welcome home."

"Thanks, Eddi. Good night, Syd."

"Good night," Sydney responded. A few minutes later, on her way back from the bathroom, Sydney looked into the room next to hers and saw the light still on. She stood in the doorway and saw Ally on her bed staring at a photo of her parents.

"Knock, knock."

"Come on in," she patted the bed next to her.

Sydney sat down and looked over the younger woman's shoulder at the photograph.

"You have your mother's eyes."

"She was beautiful. God, I can't believe she's gone." Ally stifled a sob.

"She isn't gone, Alicia. She's with you everyday. With every breath you take, she's there watching over you. They both are. I truly believe that." Sydney consoled her new friend by gently rubbing her back.

"I know, but it hurts."

"It does, but believe me, you're doing exactly what you need to do to let that hurt heal. If you didn't cry and left it all inside it'd eat you up into nothing. Believe me, I learned that lesson the hard way."

"If you don't mind me asking, how old were you when your parents passed away?"

"I was thirteen when my dad passed away and I was just about seventeen when my mom died."

"How did you handle that at such a young age?"

"Well, let's just say I became a very angry young girl," Sydney answered biting her lip. "I got into a lot of trouble, hung out with the wrong people, the usual rebellion."

"What snapped you out of it?"

"Right before I came to the States, I was involved in a relationship that eventually turned very bad. I had to change my life once and for all, just so I could feel again. I had been dead for a long time."

"I'm sorry. Were you in love?"

"Let's just say what I thought was love at the time, turned into something very hateful and hurtful. I don't want to feel for someone like that again. The loss is too big."

"You can't mean that. To deprive yourself of love just because of one incident when you were younger—that's silly!"

"I can't go through it again. Giving yourself entirely to one person just makes you too vulnerable. Showing someone every kink in what makes you 'you', gives them that much more to use against you."

"Sydney, that's not love. Love is something so much more than that."

"Are you an expert on the subject?"

"I'm not an expert, but I do know about love from watching my parents. They loved each other so much; anyone could see it. And FYI, I'll be twenty in a couple months," The words came out more bitterly than she expected.

"Excuse me, you appear younger. I didn't mean to presume anything. That's nice about your parents. From the passionate way you describe it sounds like they had the real thing."

"Yes," Ally said, quietly. She looked at Sydney shyly. "I'm sorry to have jumped into defense mode there."

"No worries." At Ally's yawn, she added, "I guess I should let you rest."

"I'm not really tired, but you have to get up early."

"You'll be all right?"

"I'll be fine. Thanks for the chat. It's nice to talk with someone that actually has an idea of what I'm feeling."

"Anytime you need to talk, let me know. I'll be here for you, Alicia"

"Thanks, Sydney. G'night mate," she teased in her best Australian accent.

"G'night mate," Sydney chuckled.

Ally turned down her bedding and climbed under the blankets. Tucking herself in she said a quiet prayer to her parents thanking them for giving her a home with Edna and for Sydney. She closed her eyes and settled into a restless sleep.

ଓ ଓଃ

Sydney awoke to a new noise in the house. She checked her clock and it glowed 2:37. *Must have been something outside*, she mused.

She lay down and tried to get back to sleep.

She heard the same sound again and decided that she wouldn't get any sleep without figuring out what the noise was. She put on a shirt and shorts and made her way towards the hall. She opened the door to the hallway and the sound grew louder; this time she could place it. Ally was crying and in the middle of a nightmare. Sydney quietly knocked on the door. There was no response except for the continued sobs.

Sydney opened the door and confirmed her suspicions. Ally was in bed tossing and turning as she cried.

"No... please... no!"

She made her way to the bed and slowly stroked Ally's hair. The small cries ceased and her new friend appeared to be sleeping more peaceful than before. Sydney got up and stood in the doorway. After another glance at the sleeping form, she closed the door and returned to her room.

She stripped off her clothes and jumped back into bed. Moments later, sleep claimed her.

ଓ ଓଃ

Sydney stirred in her sleep. A familiar, yet foreign scent wafted under her nose. She slowly opened her eyes to find Ally nestled in her arms. The clock read 3:45. *Perhaps Ally walked in her sleep and wound up in the most familiar room.* Sydney enjoyed the feel of the warm body next to hers. It had been a while since she'd shared her bed with anyone. Especially someone as beautiful as Ally.

I won't wake her, she needs to sleep, Sydney thought. *Hopefully she won't be too embarrassed in the morning. If she knew that she spent the night in the arms of a naked woman, she might feel a little self-conscious.* Sydney smiled. Yes, tomorrow indeed could wait—she relished the feel of Ally in her arms. She closed her eyes and waited for daylight.

Six

Ally stretched out in her sleepy haze and yawned. She felt rested for the first time in several weeks. As her eyes began to focus, she was surprised to find herself in her old room.

"Oh my God! How did I get in here? Great, just great. I can't believe you, Ally. This is the stupidest thing you've done in a long time! Stupid... stupid..." she spouted aloud, trailing off as she tripped on her way out of Sydney's room.

"Shit! Now how am I going to explain this one? I wonder if Eddi knows. Can't face this until after a shower...I look like hell," she reasoned with the image in her mirror.

Her aunt was reading the newspaper at the kitchen table.

"Mornin', Eddi."

"Almost good afternoon, child. I was hoping to say good-bye before I left."

"When is your flight?"

"I need to leave in a half-hour. I left the name and number of the hotel I'm staying at by the phone in the family room, but you two girls should be fine. There's plenty of food and Sydney can take care of the animals."

"All right, Eddi. Is there anything I can do for you before you go?"

"Promise me that you'll behave yourself while I'm gone."

She knows! Paranoid thoughts raced through her head as she grasped for a reply.

"You're worried about me?" she choked out with nervous grin.

"I know you better than you know yourself; just remember that." *We'll just see what happens while I'm gone.*

"Is that bacon I smell?"

"That's my girl. We'll fill you out yet."

"With all of this home cooking, I don't stand a chance."

"Help yourself. I'm gonna go out to see if Syd needs anything before I leave."

"Like a lock on her door?" Ally muttered under her breath, arranging several bacon slices on bread.

"What, hon?" Edna asked.

"Nothing, Eddi, I'm just hungry. I'll meet you outside in a couple of minutes." Ally finished her preparations and dug into her bacon, lettuce, and tomato sandwich.

༄ ༅

Edna found Sydney in the field with Polka and signaled for her to come in. Sydney made her way toward the stable.

"Hey there, Edna, what can I do for you?"

"It's what I can do for you, Syd."

"Hmm?" She shook her head at Edna not understanding what she meant.

"I just came out here to see if there was anything that you needed before I left."

"Oh, thanks, but I think that I have everything that I want."

"Yes, of course."

"I think we'll be fine, but thanks again for asking. Have a safe trip."

"Syd, there is one thing I'd like you to do for me."

"Name it."

"Please keep an eye on Ally. I thought I heard her crying last night."

"I will, Edna, I promise. She'll be in good hands while you're away."

"I'm sure she will be, thanks." Edna gave her a devilish smile and walked towards the main house.

"Now what was that about?" Sydney asked aloud.

༄ ༅

Back inside Ally was washing off her plate as her aunt walked into the house.

"Well, it looks as if everything is in order here. Take care, my dear. See you in about a week."

"Don't worry, Eddi, I'll be fine."

"I know, dear, just try to get yourself situated and make this your home."

"Right. I think I'll tackle the rest of my boxes today. Have a safe trip, okay?"

"Will do, honey. Come here." Edna pulled Ally in close for a hug. Ally needed to know that she was loved.

Seven

Sydney was in the stable tending to Matty and Polka when Ally walked in.

"Hey there." Trying to smile away her nervousness.

"So, the little sleepwalker awakens."

Oh shit, Ally thought. "You don't pull any punches, do you."

"No harm, no foul. Don't worry, it was kind of nice to share a bed again."

"Well good, glad I could help...I think."

"Talking last night got me thinking. Maybe I was too young when all of my emotions were ganging up on me." Sydney stopped what she was doing to look into Ally's eyes. "Maybe I will want to give my heart to someone...sometime."

"Just make sure that they deserve it. Don't waste your time otherwise. If someone was to hurt you, I can't promise that I wouldn't do some damage to them."

"Oh, darlin', I didn't know you cared," she drawled.

"You made me care. You have a heart of gold. I just couldn't stand to see someone walk all over it."

"That means a lot to me, thank you."

"You're welcome, Sydney." She liked the way that name dripped from her lips.

"What do you have planned for today?"

"I'm going to tackle the rest of my boxes this afternoon. The sooner I get settled in, the sooner I'll feel more at home. I hate living out of suitcases."

"Sounds like a good idea. Shall I leave Polka out of the stalls for you?"

"Yes, please. I'd love a ride later on. Maybe you could ride Matty and come with me."

"I'd like that. I'll see you later."

"All right."

As she walked back toward the house Ally could feel Sydney's eyes on her. She turned to see if the feeling had been right and found the warmest set of eyes looking back at her. Although her stomach crept into her throat, she managed to smile.

Eight

Ally started up the stairs. She walked past Sydney's room and a blush crept up her neck as the memories of where she had woken up came back to her. She shook off those feelings and moved to the task at hand.

There were four boxes staring at her and she stared right back at them before she finally gave in.

"All right, let's get this over with," she said to the inanimate objects.

An hour later, Ally sat staring at her last box, her boom box blaring out some old Prince tunes.

"The beautiful ones you always seem to lose."

"Isn't that the truth?" she said to the CD player.

Ally began screeching out her own version of the lust-filled lyrics. Sydney watched from the hall and smiled.

"Baby, baby, baby, I want you! Yes I do! Oh yeah, baby! Woohoo!" Ally was totally into it, improvising lyrics left and right when she looked up. Sydney was giggling in the doorway.

"OH MY GOD! Don't do that!"

"I'm sorry; I didn't mean to frighten you. I just didn't want to interrupt," Sydney explained between her fits of laughter.

"It's ok. Let me turn this down." Ally lowered the volume. "Well, are you going to lurk in my doorway all day or do you want to come in?"

"Actually, I was coming to see what you wanted for dinner," Sydney prodded.

"Dinner? Is it that late already?" Ally looked at her watch.

"No, but I need to prepare for it."

"You don't need to cook for me. I can just whip something up." Ally said.

"You whipping something up is a rather scary thought," the older woman quipped.

"I can cook, I'll have you know," she replied in mock indignation.

"I was planning some spaghetti if you're game."

"Ooh, that sounds great. Do you need help?"

"Yes, you can show up at the table at around six. I put Polka and Matty back in for now. Maybe we can get that ride after dinner. See you in about two hours?"

"Cool. Thanks. And Syd?"

"Yeah?" The tall woman turned.

"I'm sorry about coming into your room last night. I must've just gone there out of habit."

"Don't worry about it Ally. It was...nice."

"Okay."

Nice? Wow, definitely not the answer I was expecting. Maybe she's...no way. The way she looks, she could have anyone she wanted. Why would she look twice at me? I've got way too much baggage.

It was 5:30 when Ally finished putting away the last of her things. "Good, I have a half hour to clean up before chow," she announced to her room.

Nine

The stove was eliciting wonderful smells that Ally's nose discovered instantly. Her stomach chimed in and she made her way down the stairs to see if there was anything she could do to help with dinner.

The sight she beheld took her breath away. The table was dressed with candles and there were fresh flowers in the vase. *Boy, it's almost like a date.*

The wine was being chilled off to the side of the dishes and her chef/server/maitre d' was still standing at the stove watching the sauce simmer.

"Sydney?"

"Oh, hey, I didn't hear you come in. You startled me."

"Yeah well, paybacks are a bitch. And believe me, I still owe you after the singing thing."

"Ooh," Sydney grinned. "Sit down, dinner's just about ready."

Ally watched as Sydney put ladles full of the sauce into a bowl, set it down on the table, walked back into the kitchen, opened the oven, and took out what appeared to be garlic bread. She accidentally touched the baking sheet without a potholder.

"Shit! Ouch! I can't believe I did that."

Ally flew out of her chair and turned on the cold water. She took hold of Sydney's finger and let the water run over the burned skin.

"Thanks," Sydney said gazing into caring eyes.

"You're welcome." She took Sydney's finger and began to blow onto the injured digit.

Sydney noted that the younger woman seemed to tend to her so naturally. *God, would you take care of me like this forever?* Blowing on Sydney's finger caused a jolt of desire to wash over Ally. She seemed to hear the question floating through Sydney's mind. Both women were accepting the bond that was forming between them with open arms. The closeness felt so natural that trying to fight it was useless, and extremely futile.

"Better?"

"Much, thank you. You have such a warm touch. Very nurturing, thanks," Sydney answered quietly.

"Something my mom passed down to me."

"Remind me to say a prayer of thanks to her."

"You just did."

"I guess so. They say when the living thinks of the dead, the dead can hear their thoughts. Maybe they're right." Sydney grew pensive.

"I think so. Are you well enough to eat?"

"Absolutely, have a seat. The pasta and sauce are on the table. I'll get the bread."

"Oh no, I've seen what happens to you when you handle hot bread. I'll get it. You go sit down. You've done all the cooking, the least I can do is bring in a basket." The young woman smiled brightly.

"Okay."

Ally set the bread on the table and took her place. "Sydney, this is so nice of you. The table looks wonderful. If I didn't know better, I'd think that you were trying to wine and dine me."

"Heaven forbid." Sydney smiled innocently. "Glad you like it. I just wanted it to feel cozy for you. You know, like home."

"That's incredibly sweet."

The two ate in relative silence. The only sounds were Pachelbel's Canon and other Baroque classics coming from the speakers in the other room—Ally's ears perked up. "I really love this music. Great choice." Ally nodded toward the lilting sounds.

"Thanks, I've always loved Baroque music. I'm glad you like it, too."

"I love Pachelbel, especially the music from the Rhapsody on a Theme from Paganini. I absolutely love that piece. You know they used that in the movie 'Somewhere in Time.'"

"Yes, oh I loved that movie!" Sydney said. "God, I can't tell you how many times I've seen that film. Watching soul mates find each other after a lifetime. Their love transcended time. It breaks my heart and heals it all in the same motion. I'm just glad the ending was the way it was, I don't think I would've liked it otherwise."

"I totally agree! I even watch it when I'm feeling down," Ally smiled shyly.

"Why? Doesn't that add to your depression?"

"Not really, the way I look at it, as bad as things are, God, I couldn't imagine having the other half of my soul come into my life, and then disappear into nothing. That couple had it much worse than I do, so it makes me look at my problems differently. Things don't seem so bad, you know?"

"Well, that's something to think about," Sydney answered.

"I wonder if Eddi has that film. I'd love to watch it with someone that loves it as much as I do," Ally said, silently hoping Sydney would get the hint.

"Well, if she does, count me in."

"Note to self: Find 'Somewhere in Time'," Ally said with a wink.

They giggled. Soft conversation blended with the wine and dinner and it was a perfect meal for each of them.

"Thanks for dinner, it was wonderful."

"My pleasure. I enjoyed your company. I like you Alicia, I'm glad that you're here."

"I like you too. This was the best meal and conversation I've had in a very long time. Thank you."

Sydney started to clear the table, so Ally stood to help with the chore.

"How about you dry while I wash?" Ally said to Sydney.

"Sounds good."

Ally handed dishes to Sydney who was just staring at Ally's hands in the soapy water. Her mind began to fill with thoughts of desire involving Ally and a hot tub. She mentally kicked herself and dropped one of the plates.

"Earth to Sydney! Where were you?"

"That might be a better question for later," she said in a devilish tone.

"Uh-oh, I smell trouble."

"I do trouble best," Sydney said, cracking the towel against Ally's butt.

"Hey! You'd better cut that out or you'll be in for a fight you won't win!" Ally warned.

"Oooooohh, a challenge. Catch me if you can!" Sydney said landing another 'thwack' against Ally's thigh.

"You're a dead woman!" Ally yelled at the retreating form. "You'd better run, 'cause when I catch up with you, you're going to wish you hadn't started this!" She bent to pick the broken dish, which thankfully had split cleanly into two parts. She then armed herself with a towel and dipped it into the water. "She's going to be sorry she waged war with me," she said acknowledging the hunt was on.

"Come out, come out, wherever you are!"

"Aliiiiiiiciiiiiaaaaaaaaa, come and get meeeeee." Sydney taunted back at her in a singsong voice.

"You're toast!" Ally called. She walked over to the stereo and turned off the music.

Sydney smiled inwardly at Ally's attempt to track her. She began to move quietly from room to room following at a safe distance behind the younger woman. She decided that play time was about to begin. She quickened her pace so she was just a few feet away from Ally, at which point she was surprised by the younger woman turning suddenly and lashing the towel at her. It landed squarely on Sydney's upper thigh.

"Ow!" Sydney shrieked.

"I told you, I wouldn't lose this fight! Jack and I spent a good majority of our childhood doing just this."

"Oh yeah? I had an older brother too, missy."

Sydney whipped her towel only to have Ally grab it in mid air.

"Ha! I told you. You may be older, but I have more experience with towel warfare. Do you give or do I need to teach you another lesson?"

"More experience huh? How much experience? I bet Jack didn't teach you this..." Sydney said as she grabbed Ally's body and playfully tossed her to the floor pinning her arms above her head.

Ally looked into Sydney's eyes and found the home she had been looking for all of her life. She continued to stare as Sydney's expression changed from playfulness to something entirely more fervent. Ally wanted this badly, but Sydney, overwhelmed with emotion, let her go and retreated into the other room without another word.

"Sydney?" Ally's voice chased after her. "Hey. Are you all right?" Ally gently touched Sydney's arm.

"Please don't," was all Sydney could muster.

"Did I do something wrong?" Ally asked, her voice contrite.

"No, Alicia, it's nothing you did. I think I need to go outside for a while. Please, excuse me," Sydney said as if asking permission. Ally stepped aside.

She watched as the door closed and wondered what had happened that she missed. *Did she pick up on my feelings? Great, maybe she isn't attracted to me. Maybe she doesn't like me like that. Damn, I would've bet money after the dinner she prepared. God, I can't believe that I'm having these feelings. I've never looked at another woman this way, and now that I have, it's gotten me into trouble. Shit! God, what she must think of me!* She scolded herself for not thinking about Sydney's feelings. She contemplated going after her, but resisted the temptation.

Ten

"All right, sweetheart I'll see you when you get home. Don't work so hard. I love you," Sydney told her lover.

"I love you, too, Syd, I should be done with this project hopefully in about four hours. I'll be home as soon as I'm done here, I promise."

"Okay, Sharon, take care, hon," Sydney said, hanging up the phone.

"You too. Bye," Sharon said, placing the receiver in the cradle on her desk.

The tall redhead sitting across from her smiled wide as she approached Sharon like a hunter finding its prey.

"We've got four hours. You're all mine until then," she said as she straddled Sharon's lap.

"Oh, yeah, baby, we got a loooong time. I can do a lot to you in four hours. What are you wearing under that skirt, baby?" Sharon growled as she grabbed Tina's naked ass.

"You'd know better than anyone. Oooh yeah, I like that," Tina cooed into Sharon's ear.

ঔ ଓ

"My poor workaholic, I think I'll bring her a little picnic." Sydney grinned as she considered her plan. "She'll be so surprised to see me. God, I can't wait to see the expression on her face." Sydney packed up the dinner excitedly. She threw in a bottle of wine for good measure and made her way out the door.

ঔ ଓ

"Oh, God... yes... right there..." Tina panted from on top of the desk. Sharon had her head buried in between Tina's thighs trying hard to keep up with the body writhing above her.

"Yeah, baby...I can feel how close you are... come on baby...come for me," Sharon coaxed, as she thrust her fingers deep inside the redhead. "I love the way you sound, God, I love you, Tina...mmm..." Sharon moaned as she felt herself slipping over the edge. The two women found a rhythm between them and began to thrust their bodies for all that they were worth.

"Yes... yes... yes!" Tina shouted.

"Yesssss Tina...Oh, God! Yes!"

The two were oblivious to Sharon's door opening and Sydney walking in. Sydney's smile changed quickly to a fierce angry howl.

"NOOOOO!" Sydney shouted out as she witnessed the most serious betrayal of her life. Her heart was breaking into a thousand pieces and there was nothing she could do about it.

The two women climaxed simultaneously as Sydney walked in and couldn't stop their bodies until it was too late. Sharon tried to move from underneath Tina, but couldn't convince her body to budge.

"Syd...Syd, wait." Sharon panted.

"What, Sharon? Is this where you say 'this isn't what it looks like?' Too fucking bad that won't work in this case. Who's your whore?" Sydney barked, turning toward the young redhead still on the desk across the room. "Nice to meet you, I'm Sydney Thompson, Sharon's girlfriend."

Tina saw the six-foot, black haired woman approach her and began to get very nervous. She wasn't sure what Sydney had planned.

"So, Sharon, aren't you going to introduce us? We do have so much in common don't we?" Sydney spat out, whirling on her lover.

"Tina."

"Ahhh, Tina. Well, at least I know what name to shout out when I break your fucking head open!"

"Syd, No!" Sharon shouted.

"Oh, sticking up for your new fling? Too fucking bad. I gave up everything for you and this is what I get in return? You Bitch! You took me halfway around the world only to spit in my face? Fuck, Sharon, you couldn't have done this in Australia?"

"Oh, please, you act as if it never happens." Sharon said very coldly.

"It doesn't happen to me," Sydney growled, her voice shaking with rage.

"I'm sorry you feel that way, because frankly, Syd, it's happening to you, right now."

Sydney spit at Sharon and grabbed Tina by her hair.

"Give me one reason I shouldn't beat the shit out of you right now?" Sydney threatened.

"It wasn't my idea, it was Sharon's." Tina pleaded.

"Oh, you see, Sharon; your little puta can't even take responsibility for her own affairs. How old are ya, darlin'? Seventeen, eighteen? Robbing the cradle don't you think? God you're pathetic."

"Oh, Syd, look at yourself," Sharon mocked Sydney's pain. "You're the pathetic one. You're so gullible. Someone tells you that they love you, and you buy it without question. You leave yourself open for things like this. I saw what you were in school; I knew what you had done. I knew that I could have you if I made you believe that I loved the person you were." *She ignored the trembling in the tall woman's body. "All your baggage was nothing more than an invitation to have my cake and eat it, too. I've had more than just Tina here and I always had a beauty like you on my arm wherever we went. Every time I came home I had someone waiting for me in my bed. What a beautiful relationship."* Sharon said smugly, sliding nonchalantly into her chair and crossing her naked legs.

"So, everything was a lie?" Sydney asked, her voice stilted in fury. "So, I was a pretty plaything with a fucked up life, that you took control over? So I was just a hood ornament for you; a goddamn trophy? You fucking cu...no, I won't say it." Sydney let go of Tina's hair and less than gently patted her head. "I'll leave you to your pet. Don't come home tonight if you know what's good for you. I'll be gone by the morning. Don't come looking for me either, I don't want to be found by you." Sydney smiled as she offered that warning. She kicked the picnic food she'd brought against the wall and slammed the door to Sharon's office as she left.

೮ ೮

Sydney's thoughts drifted to the past. Her feelings for Ally brought the pain of her past relationship to the forefront of her mind. She sat in the loft of the barn that felt so close to home. Her heart was warring with her mind as she looked out the window. *I thought I was done thinking about her. Damn it, Alicia. I don't think I'm ready for this, yet.* She wiped the tears from her eyes and face and enjoyed the peace the colors of the night sky gave to her.

Ally fought with herself about going after Sydney. *If she wanted you out there, she would have invited you to come initially. Stay put, missy. Nope, can't do that.* Before she knew it, she was outside looking for Sydney.

She walked into the stable only to find Matty and Polka looking at her in wonder.

"Hi, girls, have you seen a tall, beautiful, brunette in here tonight?" she asked the horses only to get no response. Unless they were attempting to communicate something deeper in the munching of the carrots she'd fed them. "Okay, if I were out here and not wanting to be found, where would I go?" Ally looked around and decided that the loft would be a sure bet. It was rather dark up there so she fetched an old lantern from the house.

She lit the lantern and slowly crept up the ladder to the loft. Sitting with her legs draped over the edge of the window was her runaway.

"Do I need a secret handshake or can anyone play up here?" Ally said trying to lighten the mood.

"Come over here and look at this sky. It's just remarkable."

Ally joined her, and watched as the remainder of color left the sky. "Wow, I forgot how beautiful things were up here. You don't get colors like that in Chicago. There is a lot, actually, that I didn't get in Chicago." Ally thought that Sydney might catch the subtle hint thrown in her direction.

"I am sorry for earlier; I don't know what came over me."

"What do you mean? We were just having some fun. No harm, no foul, to quote a friend of mine," Ally nudged Sydney hoping to make her smile.

"You really amaze me, Alicia."

"What do you mean?" the young woman asked.

"I mean, most women I've encountered would have just let me sit out here and dwell on what almost happened tonight."

"So, I wasn't wrong about those feelings, you feel them too." It was more of a statement then a question.

"Yes, I just don't know what to do about them." Sydney turned to the younger woman. "Ally, did you know that I was attracted to women?"

"No, I just felt an overwhelming attraction to you and a familiarity that was only getting stronger. I know we just met, but I swear that I've known you all of my life."

"I won't deny my attraction to you, but I also told you how afraid I am of giving myself to anyone. I'm not sure I'm ready for this yet. Please forgive me." The dark head dropped forlornly.

"There is nothing to forgive, sweetie," Ally said warmly. "I'm sorry if I made you feel uncomfortable in any way. Friends?" Ally held out her hand.

Sydney stood and gently pulled the smaller woman into her arms. *Home, I'm definitely home,* was all that was going through the minds of both women. The embrace was so warm and so gentle that neither woman wanted to be the one the end the contact. The closeness came to an end when Ally felt Sydney's body stiffen.

"What's wrong, Sydney? Talk to me."

"I need to know something," Sydney said quietly.

"Anything." Ally felt Sydney's stare down to her toes. Whatever she needed to know, Ally knew that the truth would be the only way to answer.

"I... need to know..." her voice trailed off. The woman moved closer and closer until all Ally could feel was Sydney's breath against her mouth.

"What?" Ally almost pleaded with her taller companion.

"Kiss me... Alicia... please... I need to know..." Sydney's heart was racing with anticipation.

Sydney felt the soft lips touch hers for the first time. The kiss was so gentle and yielding she could have stayed there forever.

Ally had never felt the kiss of another woman. She'd never expected such softness. It was incredible.

They sank deeper into the kiss until Sydney finally pulled away. "God, I'm sorry! I don't mean to tease you like this. It isn't fair of me. I just needed to know. I couldn't bear not knowing what your lips felt like on mine."

Ally felt stung by this admission. "And what did I feel like?" the young woman sputtered. "Did I fulfill your curiosity? Is that all that was? A thirst for knowledge? Well, know this. I will not be played with; either you want this or you don't. I don't think I can handle any mind games right now, okay?"

"I'm sorry, I didn't mean to hurt you."

"That's always the case isn't it? Good night, Sydney." Ally spun on her heels, climbed down the ladder, and went back to the house.

"Well, that went well," Sydney muttered, feeling horrible as she stared into the night sky.

Eleven

Ally didn't realize what time it was, she just ran into her room, slammed the door, and locked it. She looked at her clock and saw that it was only around 9:00. She wasn't tired; she just needed to get away from Sydney. She lay on her bed with her face pressed into her pillow and wept. She cried for what could have been, she cried for the loss of her parents, but most of all she cried for a lost friendship with a wonderful woman—that would be the biggest blow.

"Why... why do I have such strong feelings for her? I just met her for God's sake! Why does life always have to be so friggin' difficult?" The tears overpowered her emotionally exhausted body finally letting sleep claim her.

Ally awoke to find her lights on, as well as her clothing. Sleep clouded her sight momentarily. She rubbed her eyes to try and focus on her room. *The guestroom. She even has my room.* Ally looked around at the progress she had made earlier and only then did she notice a small piece of paper sticking out from under her door.

ಀ ಛ

Dearest Alicia,

I am not sure how to apologize for putting you through what I did this evening. I mean how could you not pick up on my attraction to you? Look at the dinner we shared. It could have easily been a date. You hit the nail on the head when you suggested that I was trying to wine and dine you. I don't know if I can remember having had such a wonderful time as I did tonight. You're a beautiful woman. and if you let me get to know you better, I may get over my fears. I know I don't deserve such a chance, but I'm asking you as humbly as I can to please find it in your heart to forgive me.

It's been so long since I've known any warmth and affection that I guess I freaked out. What I'm trying to say is that I'm sorry. I'm sorry for using you, because essentially that's what I did. I did nothing less than that. I tried to have my cake and eat it too, I guess. I shouldn't have played with your emotions. You admitted your feelings to me, and that couldn't have been an easy thing for you. I don't know much about your past, but I'm willing to bet that you'd never kissed a woman before. I probably scared that notion from your head as well, and for that, again, I'm sorry.

I'd love to try and start over. If there is the slightest chance that this may happen I'll accept any punishment you deem fit for my behavior. I was wrong for treating you like that. It's little wonder that I haven't been with anyone for so long, it's probably a good thing for everyone.

Anyway, I just wanted apologize. If you want to talk about it later, come to my room, I'm sure I'll be up.

With much regret,
Sydney

☙ ❦

Ally put down the letter and sighed. *Well, what do you know? Maybe we can salvage a friendship after all.*

Ally made her way toward the light coming from her old room. Sydney had fallen asleep with her arms around a stuffed panda—the sight of her warmed Ally's heart. She lay uncovered. Ally pulled the covers over her friend when Sydney stirred slightly and whispered, "Thank you."

"We'll talk tomorrow. Sleep now," Ally kissed the top of Sydney's head. She rose to leave, but the look in Sydney's eyes seemed to warrant further conversation.

"What is it, Syd?"

"Your kindness—it amazes me. Even after what I did, you still came and tucked me in. I don't deserve you."

"Don't say that. Try and get some sleep and we'll talk in the morning. Jack should be home tomorrow, too. I think that's what his message said."

"G'night, mate."

Chuckling at their little joke, she echoed a "G'night, mate," in her best Aussie accent.

☙ ❦

Ally woke up in her own bed at around 10 o'clock. She was very thankful that her subconscious hadn't betrayed her. She took a quick shower.

"God, why does everything need to be so goddamned complicated? All I ask is that I get a good friend out of this. Sydney seems like a good person. I don't get any bad vibes from her. Well other than the fact that she likes to tease me mercilessly. I could see myself getting quite attached. I just need to channel my desire for her into our friendship; I can do that. I have no choice." She told the mirror.

Delicious smells from the kitchen filled her nostrils when she opened the bathroom door. *God, does she always cook like this?*

She went into her room and put on some clothes. She raked a comb through her long locks and headed downstairs. To her surprise Sydney was nowhere to be found, instead she found Jack seated at the table with one of his friends.

"Jack! You made it!"

"Hey, Squirt! Wow, look at you, all grown up," Jack said as she dove in for a hug. "I guess the 'squirt' thing still applies though, huh?"

She jabbed him in the side at his dig about her height. "I'm not a squirt, I'm just vertically challenged," she said noticing another handsome face watching her. "I'm sorry, you must think we're terribly rude, I'm Alicia, Ally for short."

He stood and extended his hand. "Peter, Pete for short."

"Short? I think not," Ally said.

"Yeah, I get that a lot. Once I reached six foot two, my dad said he would disown me if I didn't play basketball."

"And?"

"I sucked at basketball, but he eventually forgave me."

"Mighty nice of him. Who is responsible for the incredible aromas wafting through this house? It can't be Jack, I have never seen him pick up anything resembling a frying pan." Jack raised his brow at his cousin, and she immediately was taken off guard. "No way! You can cook now too? It has been a long time."

"Yes, it has, Squirt. What's it been, 4 years? I was so sad to hear about your folks. I was in Asia when I got the news. I'm sorry I didn't make it to the funeral."

"It's all right, Jack, I understand. It was so unexpected, but you were there in spirit, and I did receive your flowers and card. Thank you by the way. It helped more than you know."

"I just wish there had been something more that I could've done."

"You did plenty. Thanks for caring."

"I've always thought of you as the sister I never had."

"I feel the same way about you, Jack. It's different when you're an only child. I sometimes wonder what it would've been like to have siblings, you know? Would I be the person that I am now...that kind of stuff? Oh gosh... listen to me ramble on. Sorry, Pete."

"Don't apologize. You've been though a terrible time. Far be it for me to tell you not to talk about it in my presence."

"Have I told you that you have great taste in friends, Jack?"

"Yeah, at least this time you didn't have to break your leg to meet them."

"What?" Pete asked.

"Long story. Ask my mom when she gets back."

"Make sure that I'm far away when she tells that story again. I already had to sit through it again when she told it to Syd."

"Oh, so you've met. What do you think of her? I think she's great. What a looker she is, too." Jack elbowed Ally.

Ally rolled her eyes.

"So, are you hungry? I think I made a little too much breakfast. You think you can help me out?"

"You remember who you're talking to, right?" She gave him a dirty look, took a plate from the table, and rushed into the kitchen.

Ally loaded her plate with eggs, bacon, and bagels with jelly. She grabbed a glass of orange juice for good measure and made her way back to the table. Peter just watched in awe as this tiny woman packed a meal fit for an army into her small frame.

"Where do you put it?"

"In here," she patted her full tummy.

"Would have fooled me. You look as if you eat like a bird."

"Looks can be deceiving. Don't always trust your eyes, you might see things that aren't there."

"I'll try to remember that," Peter responded with a hint of a grin.

"How long are you here for?" Ally asked noticing how rich his brown eyes were.

"Only till the end of the week. Then Jack and I need to head back to Phoenix to see about our latest deal. We're partners, you see. The people were dealing with let us have a week to play while they made up their minds about our offer."

"Ah, a couple of tycoons!"

All three went out to the stables where they found Sydney brushing down Matty.

"Morning, Alicia," Sydney said.

"Mornin'. Jack's home," Ally said cheerfully. "Have you met Peter, Jack's partner?"

"Yes, Peter's been here before. We chatted for a bit while you were still asleep."

"Ah, sorry."

"No worries. How'd you sleep?"

"Like a baby. I didn't seem to wander last night either, so it was a bonus to wake up in my own bed this morning."

"I can imagine it was quite a relief." Sydney smiled despite the disappointment. She had almost hoped that Ally would stumble back into her room. She enjoyed holding Ally as she slept.

"Well, I would have hated to interrupt your sleep again."

"How about you? Were you able to fall asleep after I left?"

"I finally fell asleep. I also had a chance to really think about what happened last night. After reading your note, I found out that I have a wonderful friendship starting here with you. I'd be a fool not to try and keep that. I've lost the two people that were my life. I don't want to lose anymore." Ally's eyes filled with unshed tears.

"I'd like that too," Sydney agreed warmly. "Thank you and again, please know how sorry I am about last night. I don't want to hurt you anymore."

"It's forgotten – friends again?"

"Friends." Sydney looked up into Ally's green eyes and reached to brush away a stray tear that had fallen onto her cheek. She resisted the urge to caress her cheek. "You're so beaut…"

Jack horned into their conversation cutting her off and startling Ally. "So, what's up girls? Hey, Ally, Pete wants a lesson. You think you can teach him some of the finer points of riding?

"Um, sure. I'd love to." Turning back to Sydney, "We'll talk more later, I promise." She stroked Sydney's arm lightly, took Matty's bridle and lead her into the stable.

Twelve

Ally walked into the stable and saw Pete sizing up Polka.
"Ready for your first lesson?" Ally asked.
"You know, I've never stood next to a horse before, damn they're big."
"How else could they hold us, silly?" The fair-haired woman teased.
"Yeah well, I was just saying. It feels weird seeing them so close."
"Put your foot in the stirrup and climb aboard Matty. She's very gentle, so don't worry," she reassured him.
Peter did as instructed and then found the other stirrup.
"Okay, step one, hold the reigns at all times. If you want to turn left, pull slightly towards the left and she will turn. Same goes for the right," she instructed as she climbed onto Polka.
"What about walking, running, and whatnot?"
"To get her moving, just squeeze your legs around her belly. Like this..." she demonstrated the action with Polka. He did as she said and they were slowly making their way out to the fields.
"Now if you want to speed things up, squeeze your legs a couple times and she will start to quicken her pace." She showed him as she nudged her legs against Polka a few times until they were off into a slow canter. Pete did the same and caught up to Ally.
"Okay, my biggest question. How do you stop?"
Giggling, Ally replied, "Just pull on the reigns, but not too hard. You don't want to hurt her mouth. Let's go out a little further, there is a beautiful pond down there I haven't seen since I was a kid. I'll lead the way."
"Lead on!" Pete nudged his legs against Matty and they were off.
Sydney watched as the two disappeared from sight.

☯ ☪

Jack crept up on Sydney and spooked her. "Hey there! Anything I can help you with?"

"Jesus, Jack! You scared the shit out of me!" Sydney spat out.

"Sorry, you just looked kind of out of it. Are you all right?"

"I'm fine. You want to help, you say?"

"Sure, I need to do something. Those two won't be back for a while, and I'm sure you could use the help."

"Well, since you were kind enough to scare me to death, you can help me shovel out the stalls," she smiled wickedly and handed him a shovel.

"Me and my big mouth."

The two headed back into the stalls and began their glamorous chore.

"Man, I haven't seen Ally in so long, my God she's all grown up now. She's beautiful."

"Yes, she is," Sydney said not wanting to elaborate on the incredible lithe body, or the intoxicating fragrance Ally's body elicited, or the way her eyes made Sydney's heart melt, or the feel of her lips...

"Syd? Syd?" Jack said snapping his fingers in front of her face.

"Did you say something?" Sydney sputtered, more than a little embarrassed at being caught off-guard.

"Yeah, I asked you how Ally seemed to you. Is she doing all right?"

"Oh, sorry. Well, her first night here she did cry in her sleep but I think with a little help from family and friends, she'll be fine. I have to say considering that the cards she's been dealt, she's doing incredibly well. I don't think I'd be as together as she is. She's an incredible young woman."

"My partner thinks so too. I couldn't shut him up in the stables. It's like being school again, him asking me to ask her for a riding lesson. Jeez, how old are we?" Jack chuckled.

Sydney was not amused.

"So, how long are you home for?" Sydney asked wishing Pete's stay would come to an abrupt end.

"Well, it depends on the client. We have an offer on the table, and as soon as they make a decision, we have to go back to Phoenix to either pick up the pieces, or sign contracts and such."

"Let's just hope that it works out for everybody." She was including herself in that equation.

"Yes, let's," he replied.

By the time Jack had cleaned most of the stalls, they could see Ally and Peter walking their horses back from their ride. The two seemed very relaxed and were laughing and talking as they entered the corral.

"Hi, kids!" Pete shouted to them.

"Hey there," Jack replied. "How was your ride?"

"It was gorgeous! Ally took us down to the old pond behind those trees; you been there, bud?"

"Of course I have, dumbass, I lived here, remember? I think I got laid for the first time down there." Jack smiled at the memory. "Hey, Ally, remember the time we went down there with some of my friends and just drank ourselves into oblivion?"

"Ah, the good old days," she said rolling her eyes. The lecture she'd gotten from her aunt and uncle about responsibility had left a stronger impression.

"Seems to me you brought me there to play spin the bottle with your pals 'cause one of them made a bet with you that he'd kiss me."

"Ha! That's right! Steve I think it was. Man, that was a lifetime ago. Any bottles down there today, Ally? Hmmm," he said while wiggling his eyebrows.

"God, Jack!" She felt a blush creeping up her neck as she peeked over at Peter's smiling face.

"Well, if that's not a guilty smile I don't know what is," Jack said.

"For your information there were NO bottles where we were!" Ally defended, hoping to clean the grimace off of Sydney's face.

When she couldn't handle the frustration anymore Sydney made excuses to leave and walked towards the tool shed. Ally eyed her closely to see if she was angry. She couldn't quite pinpoint the emotion tugging on Sydney's face.

Is she jealous? The thought of Sydney jealous over Peter made her smile inwardly. *This boy doesn't hold a candle to you, my blue-eyed Aussie.* She looked up at Jack and Peter who were still talking about Jack's good ol' days at the pond. She rolled her eyes at them and they seemed to realize that this should be discussed in different company.

"Men," she said in borderline disgust. "Don't you think about anything else?"

The two guys just looked at each other and smiled at Ally. Ally sighed.

"Hey, Jack, we should probably check our email to see what's going on in Phoenix."

"Good idea."

"See you later, boys. Don't work too hard."

"Thanks for the lesson, I had a wonderful time. Perhaps we can do that again before I leave." Pete smiled at her.

"Sure, anytime."

Pete leaned over and kissed her cheek. She smiled shyly and turned to go find Sydney when her eyes locked with the raven-haired woman's. Ally smiled at her. When she got no response she approached her tall friend.

"Hey," Ally said.

"Hey, yourself," Sydney returned.

"Is something bothering you?"

"No, not at all? Is Romeo staying for dinner?" She asked sarcastically.

"Romeo? You don't mean Peter? Sydney, my God, are you jealous?"

"And what if I am?" Sydney answered testily.

"Then I believe you need to rethink our relationship. I thought you said you couldn't have this yet. Which means that I'm free to do as I please."

"Well, if you like that sort of thing, by all means, have at it," Sydney said bitterly, heading back into the shed in a huff.

Sydney couldn't help being cross with Ally. She wasn't going through that heartbreak again. She threw down the pitchfork she was holding and her mind screamed out. *I will not feel that pain again! I won't allow that to happen! I can't.* Sydney cursed her heart for feeling again and silently she cursed herself for letting it. She bent over to pick up the pitchfork and felt an agonizing pain in her ribs.

Ally followed Sydney not wanting to have their conversation end the way it had. When she walked in the shed, Sydney was holding her side in pain.

"Syd? What is it? You look like someone stabbed you or something."

"I jabbed my ribs earlier when I was fixing the front gate. I must have bruised them. I guess shoveling out the stalls wasn't the smartest of chores to do today," Sydney panted.

"Let me see," Ally said tugging on Sydney's shirt.

"Oh sure, now you want to see me naked."

"I'm serious! Come on, lift up your shirt," she commanded gently.

Ally let out a startled gasp. "Oh, my God, Sydney! We should have you looked at."

"You're looking at it right now."

Ally gently touched the bruised area and felt Sydney flinch. She watched the muscles contract down Sydney's strong abdomen.

"I'm sorry. Did that hurt?"

"No, it didn't, you tickled me. Come on, doc, just kiss it and make it better. It's not that bad," Sydney joked.

Not wanting to disappoint her patient, Ally thought she would see how far she could take this. She gently touched the area again and felt her body moving closer to Sydney's. She closed her eyes and kissed the bruise under Sydney's ribcage. Sydney's eyes widened with surprise as a tingling sensation ran through her body.

"Oh, Alicia, please stop. You don't know what you're doing to me." Sydney's voice trembled along with her breathing.

Ally kissed her again and let her tongue slowly circle the injured area. She wanted to devour every inch of this incredible woman. She needed her badly. Her heart was screaming inside, beating fast and full. She felt Sydney's body reacting to the stimulation.

"Oh... please... Alicia... please..." Sydney choked out. Ally, not hearing her pleas, wandered with her kisses and started blazing a trail over her stomach. Sydney grabbed Ally's head and pulled her into a heated, passionate kiss. Ally felt her soul grasping at her other half. Their tongues entwined in a powerful dance of desire. Unquenchable passion was surging through them when Sydney's defenses came back to haunt her again.

Sydney pulled away holding Ally's head in her hands. "I... I can't do this. I'm sorry," she whispered her name as the tears raced down her face. She smoothed her shirt back down and ran out of the shed, leaving Ally alone, shaking her head wondering what had just happened.

Thirteen

Ally found Jack and Pete in the family room talking. They noticed her entrance and smiled.

"Well, Squirt, it looks like we have to fly out tonight. There seems to be a mix-up in the contracts that we have to clear up. So, unfortunately, our visit will be cut short," Jack said sadly.

"Oh no. I'm so sorry that you have to leave. What time is your flight?"

"We gotta head out to the airport in an hour or so. I'll be back in a couple weeks though, I promise. Mom would have my head if I didn't come and spend some time with her as well. I know she was getting pretty lonely out here, but when Sydney came along, I think she really came out of her funk. I'm so glad that you'll be here for her, too. I know she was really excited that you took her up on her offer."

"You know, after mom and dad died, I didn't know my ass from a hole in the ground. When your mom talked to me at their funeral and let me know where my home could be, I knew I had someplace special to go. I wouldn't leave here now for anything. Although, it would be nice to actually spend time with her now that I am here."

"When is she getting back?" Jack asked.

"She said in a week or so, so I won't be alone long, don't worry."

"I'm not worried Ally, you have Syd here and you seem to like her so..."

"Yeah, I do, she's very nice. I like her a lot. I'm glad Eddi found her," she wondered where Sydney had run off to.

"All right you, Pete and I have some stuff we have to take care of before we go, so if you'll excuse us, we have to become boring again," he said ruffling her hair.

"All right, did you guys happen to see Syd? I thought she came in here." She tried to be nonchalant with her question.

"Umm... I think I saw her go upstairs a little while ago," Pete chimed in.

"Okay, thanks. I'll see you before you head out."

ℰ ℭ

Ally walked up the stairs and headed towards her room. She noticed Sydney's door closed and decided to keep walking. She just didn't get it.

*Why would she come on to me like that if she didn't feel something? I will not play these games any more; it's just too damn confusing. Next time, if there is a next time, I'll wait for **her** to make the first move.*

She cleaned up the clothes that were on the floor and made her bed. She tried to keep herself busy so she wouldn't think about Sydney in the next room. Thoughts flooded to her mind from that afternoon...the softness of the kiss they shared...the power in the lips kissing her...the desire that was building in her was overwhelming. She shook her head to clear those thoughts. Well, at least she tried to.

Ally decided that there was no more cleaning that could be done at the moment and wandered over to Sydney's room. She hesitated, then knocked on the door.

"Syd?" She waited patiently for a reply.

Nothing.

She knocked again and slowly opened the door. She looked in to find Sydney asleep with the same panda tucked under her arms. The sight made Ally's heart swell, but she knew this time to keep her distance. She quietly turned around and closed her door. *I'm still mad at you Sydney. I may have pushed a little too much today, but I don't think I deserved that.*

Ally walked down the stairs to see if Jack and Pete needed a ride to the airport.

"That's ok, I called a cab. They should be here any minute."

Pete walked up held out his hand to Ally. "It was a pleasure meeting you, Ally. I hope to see you again soon."

"Thanks, Pete, I hope so too. Maybe we can get to that second lesson the next time you come up." She reached up and hugged Peter's neck and he kissed her cheek as she pulled away. "Such the gentleman." Ally smiled.

"Who? Him? I think we need to talk," Jack said as Pete elbowed him in the gut. The cab driver announced his arrival with a honk.

"You're ruining my rep with your cousin here, man!" Pete joked.

"Don't worry, your reputation will be left unscathed, I promise," she reassured her departing guest. "Call me when you get to Phoenix, so I know you made it safe and sound, okay?"

"I promise," Jack said. He leaned down and hugged Ally.

"Bye!" Ally shouted as the car drove away. She waved her last goodbye and closed the front door.

It was close to dinnertime and Sydney still hadn't come down. "I guess I'll take a look at the horses to make sure they're fed and watered."

She walked outside and took to her chores without hesitation. It looked like there might be a storm later that night, so she made sure everyone was inside for the night. It was kind of nice taking care of Matty and Polka again. It reminded her of childhood summers with her family. Her aunt and uncle had taught her how to care for the horses and she loved every minute she had with them, especially Polka.

Ally's stomach reminded her that she still needed to eat dinner. She double checked the windows and doors in case of a storm and returned to the house. *I'm sure Sydney's awake by now. I'll see what she wants to do for dinner.*

She walked into the house to find it still quiet. She checked the family room and Sydney was nowhere to be found. She poked her head into the kitchen and noticed that nothing had been moved in there either. That could only mean that Sydney was still asleep.

"I guess I'll see if she wants dinner at all," she said as she walked up the stairs. When she reached the top of the landing, she heard the shower running.

"Well, at least she's awake now. I'll just wait for her to come out and see if she wants to eat. That's if she even wants to see me. Hell, I should be the one who's angry. She walked away *again*, and here I am. God, I must be stupid…or whipped, one of the two," she spoke softly. *My money is on the latter*, her mind chimed in. "Thanks a lot, you're a big help." She walked into her room, turned on her CD Player, and waited for Sydney to return from her shower.

ಙ ಜ

Sydney awoke from her nap more refreshed than she expected. She was grateful that her ribs were hurting much less than before. Her mind wandered back to the tool shed where she had experienced the most incredible feelings she had ever felt. Her body ached for that contact again. She could feel the moisture building between her legs. Her eyes welled with tears as she felt the longing to love Ally the way she wanted to be loved. Something kept her at a distance and she couldn't stop it. She knew her other half was right outside at the moment, but fear of hurt, rejection, and commitment stopped her from finding her. She wiped the tears from her eyes and cursed the throbbing in her core. Her body knew what she needed, but she was too stubborn to accept it.

"There's more than one way to skin a cat," she decided as she headed off to the shower.

The water beat down on her body as she let her emotions leave one by one. The tears returned and she welcomed the cleansing. Maybe this way, she would clear herself of whatever it was that was keeping her from her destiny. The tears slowed and she became more aware of her desire for Ally. Their kiss that afternoon had been incredible. The feel of the younger woman's lips and tongue on her torso was orgasmic. The loss that she had been feeling without her touch was continual. As she reminisced about their afternoon encounter, she found her hand roaming down her soapy body to fulfill a need that was overwhelming. Small, slow circles turned into fast, hard exploration. She braced her body against the wall of the shower as she released her frustration and longing in a matter of moments. Her thoughts of Ally were never ending—it was Ally she wanted to feel loving her body. As her breathing returned to normal, she rinsed her sudsy hair and washed the soapy water down the drain.

She stepped out of the shower to hear the faint sound of music. She felt her heart rate increase knowing that Ally was only a room away. *God, I wonder if she heard me. Oh well, nothing I can do about it now. If she knows, she knows.* She looked at her reflection through the steam on the mirror. "You can do this, Sydney. You know this is right. Just let it go. Be happy for once in your life. She's not Sharon, you know that," she reprimanded herself. She continued to dry off and geared up for another encounter with Ally. Living under the same roof made it inevitable.

ಬ ಇ

Ally heard the shower go off and a smile crept to the corners of her mouth. She knew that Sydney would have to talk to her and maybe after her shower, she would like to chat about it over dinner. This time, no physical contact.

The bathroom door opened and Sydney stepped out in her robe, her long wet hair dangling off to one side. Ally walked out into the hall and gasped at the sight in front of her. *My God, she's beautiful,* was all she could think.

"Hello, Alicia," the tall woman managed to get out.

"Hey there. Um, I know you probably don't want to see me right now, but I was wondering if you wanted to do anything for dinner. I mean it's no big deal, but if you wanted, I could cook something, or we could order something out," Ally rambled through her nervousness.

"Well, actually I am kind of hungry," Sydney replied nervously. "But I do have to go out and tend to my duties, since I kind of abandoned my job this afternoon."

"Oh, don't worry about that. I took care of it for you," Ally said proudly.

"You did?" Sydney said almost in a whisper. She couldn't believe the woman in front of her. *I'm a fool,* she decided in her mind. "Thank you, Alicia. That was very nice of you. And very unexpected. You didn't have to do that."

"I know, I just figured, well... It was kind of my fault what happened today and I do feel kinda bad for what I did." Ally told her.

Now she's apologizing for what I did! Sydney's eyebrows rose into her forehead as she listened to Ally take the blame from her.

"Wait a minute, Alicia. What happened today was NOT your fault. Know that right now," Sydney said, regaining her composure.

"Sydn..." Ally tried to get a word in, as usual.

"No! I shouldn't have responded the way I did. Ok, maybe you coaxed me a little, but I shouldn't have run out on you again. It was very childish of me and I'm sorry." The words came out faster than she could stop them.

"It's understandable. I know your position on this and I pushed, so for that, I, too, am sorry." Ally's gaze was gentle.

That said, dinner plans were still up in the air. Sydney told Ally to wait for her in the family room. She would get dressed and come down shortly. Sydney closed the door to her room and leaned against the door, exhaling with a sigh.

"She's too much. I have to do something before I lose this one for good. Take a deep breath, you'll be just fine," she coached herself.

She grabbed a pair of jeans and a baby blue polo shirt. She caught her reflection in the mirror and decided that tonight she would need to make the biggest decision of her life. That scared the shit out of her, but it was now or never. She knew Ally wouldn't wait forever. She took a deep breath, and made her way to the family room.

Fourteen

Ally waited patiently on the sofa for Sydney to return. She was nervously chewing the inside of her cheek. She didn't know what to expect from this woman. *On one hand she's incredibly beautiful, sexy, and an amazing kisser who oozes sensuality. On the other hand, she is surely the most frustrating woman that I've ever met. I don't think that I've ever felt as sexually crazed as I've been in the last two days.*

Shaking her head clear of her thoughts, she noticed that Sydney smiling at her as she entered the family room.

"Hey there," Sydney greeted her.

"Hey, yourself."

"Have you decided anything for dinner? Or did you want some input?" Sydney queried.

"Well, I really was waiting for you, before I made a final decision."

"I had a thought. Are you game enough to trust me?" the dark-haired woman asked with a raised eyebrow.

"Well, given our track record, I'm not sure I feel comfortable answering that question," Ally quipped, her words a bit more brittle than planned.

"Alicia, I know that I've given you no reason to trust me in any way, but I truly think that you'll enjoy my idea," Sydney pleaded, her blue eyes sincere.

"And if I don't?" the blonde woman prompted.

"Then you can tar and feather me if you like," Sydney replied with no small amount of sarcasm.

"Well, how can I pass up an offer like that?" Ally's green eyes twinkled.

"Good, give me a few minutes to prepare something and I'll meet you in the stable," the tall woman said.

"In the stable? It looks like its going to storm," Ally protested.

"All the better. I'll show you what living in the country is all about, my little city mouse."

"Your little city mouse? Hmm, 'my little country mouse,' are we getting a little possessive?"

"Well, let's just say that I've gotten used to having you around." She nudged Ally as she walked into the kitchen.

"All right, I'll meet you there, but if I hate whatever you have planned, don't think that I won't keep you to your word."

"Ha! I don't doubt that!" Sydney yelled from the kitchen.

Ally turned and went outside to meet Sydney at the stable. "I don't like this one bit. Just look at this sky; we are going to get soaked. She'd better not be jerking me around this time. I swear to everything holy that I'll kick her square...in..." Ally paused to gasp in surprise at Sydney's arrival.

Sydney was carrying a large picnic basket and a blanket in her arms.

"Are you game? I thought it would be nice to ride out to that pond that has everyone 'oohing' and 'ahing' and have our dinner out there. What do you think?"

"I think we're going to get drenched." She crossed her arms and started tapping her foot.

"Oh darlin', I've seen you eat. We won't be out there long enough for the rain to even think about hitting us. Come on, it'll be fun. We can take Matty and Polka. If it does rain, there's plenty of canopy out there under those trees. Will you have dinner with me, Alicia?" she asked flashing her best puppy dog baby blues.

"Oh my God, you are so not fair. Let's go Miss I-Can-Get-Anything-I-Want-With-Just-A-Bat-Of-My-Eyelashes," Ally said, taking the basket. Sydney laughed heartily and walked towards the stalls. It was music to Ally's ears.

Sydney climbed on Matty and took the basket from Ally. She in turn gave the blanket to Ally and then coaxed the horses out toward the field. The ride was quiet as both women contemplated conversation. They both wanted to share their feelings, but were unsure where that would lead. Settling for a quiet ride seemed to work best for them.

Ally led Sydney to the pond and Sydney couldn't believe that she'd never made it down there before.

"It's absolutely beautiful out here. I can't believe I'd never found this place. I could have filled so many nights here. You can really lose yourself looking at this landscape. I can see why you liked to spend time here," Sydney said in awe.

"Mmm, I know. I spent a lot of my summer nights here. I'd just sit at the edge of the water and think. I'd write sometimes or just veg out. I love it here. Over there, by that large rock, is where the infamous game of spin the bottle happened."

Sydney smiled and wondered what Ally had been like when as a teenager.

"I bet you had a ton of boyfriends when you were in high school, no?" Sydney asked the blond woman.

"Actually, no. I was kind of a loner in high school," Ally admitted. "A geek for lack of a better word. I had a few close friends and one very best friend, Tracy, but I pretty much kept to myself. I'd cut loose when I came out here though. I guess I felt much more comfortable here than with the people in my school. People are really hard in Chicago. They aren't the nicest of people. It's really hard to admit that too, since I've lived there pretty much my whole life. I mean I think city people are hard-hearted. I just see such a difference in people out here. They're much more willing to help out others, and that kind of thing. God, I'm rambling, I'm sorry," she apologized.

"Oh please don't apologize. I love listening to you talk. I bet you tell a great story. You have such a cute accent," Sydney grinned.

"*I* have an accent? You're the one from 'down unda'!" she kidded.

"Yeah, well, to me you have as much of an accent as I have to you."

"I guess that's true. This is great, Syd. You were right. Coming out for a picnic was a good idea. Thank you."

"It's the least I can do. I feel really bad about this afternoon. I shouldn't have left you like that. I'm sorry."

"Let's just start over and enjoy what we have now, okay?"

"All right. Let's eat. I didn't really have too much to work with, so I put some sandwiches together and a salad. I thought the wine would be a nice touch, as well."

"You thought right. This is really great."

"I'm glad you like it."

The two ate in comfortable silence, occasionally looking into each other's eyes and smiling. Sydney's mind was racing; time was running out as the sky turned darker with the storm's approach. They ate on the blanket-covered ground and then lay back watching the cloud movement with wineglasses in hand.

"Do you ever wonder what comes after life Syd? I mean, what do you think happens to us after we die?"

"I think about it every once in awhile, actually," Sydney admitted. " If there wasn't life after death, don't you think that this would all be a waste? I really believe that in living this life, we learn, our souls learn that is. We take all of that knowledge with us through our lives. After we die, our soul takes on another form and we start a new life, but with the same soul. Have you ever heard of people referring to others as being an old soul?"

"Yeah, I have. Is that what they mean? Someone that has had a few lives with the same soul?"

"Well, I personally think that's what they mean. I mean there is such a huge world out here. We couldn't possibly cover it all in one lifetime. I think we are given a chance to explore it all, but not necessarily in the same physical form. Now, don't laugh at me, 'cause I really believe this..."

"Okay, I promise not to laugh," Ally said, smiling.

"I think that in a past life, you and I may have been lovers," Sydney told her.

"What?" Ally's green eyes were round and wide.

"I mean it, Alicia." Sydney's tone was serious. "I've only known you a few days. But I also feel closer to you than I have anyone in my life, well outside of my family. I don't understand it, but I don't want to fight it anymore either. Alicia, after my childish tantrum this afternoon, I finally decided to stop being immature about my feelings. I need to look at the person who is willing to give me her heart, and know that she won't take mine and break it. That person is you, Alicia; I want to give you my heart. I know I have no right to ask that of you, but I want you to have it, that is, if you still want it." Sydney's eyes never left Ally's and she hoped Ally would see the heartfelt truth there.

Ally's mouth went dry; she couldn't believe what she was hearing. Her heart wanted to believe what Sydney was saying, but her mind kept thinking it was too good to be true. She downed the last of the wine, dropped her glass in the basket, and turned to leave. She ran to Polka and mounted her ride back to the stable. With a last look at Sydney's dumbfounded face, she urged Polka back to the house. Sydney grabbed the picnic items, jumped onto Matty, and chased after her heart. She chased Ally back to the stables and saw her head toward the house. She led Matty into the stable and ran after Ally. Ally turned around when she heard the urgent footsteps behind her. She saw Sydney running toward her and decided to face her fears once and for all.

"I really want to believe you, Sydney, but I just can't play these games," Ally said, her voice strident. "I have tried twice, unsuccessfully I might add, to show you I could love you, but you ran. Who's to say that you won't do that to me again? I have way too much going on in my life right now. I can't handle any more heartache. I'm sorry, I can't set myself up for that again," she said as the tears started to well in her eyes. She turned to walk away as the rain started to fall.

Sydney reached out in desperation to stop Ally from walking away from her. She caught Ally's arm. Ally turned around and fell to her knees.

"Baby, please..."

Crying, she pleaded, "Dammit, Sydney, please, just let me go."

"I can't do that," Sydney said. She pulled herself closer to Ally and held her face in her hands. She wiped away the raindrops that were falling against the young woman's cheeks as she leaned forward to meet the lips she so desperately wanted to feel again.

Ally's mind was racing with confusion. Her body, feeling the heat that was building inside, released a moan as the contact deepened. Sydney gently sucked on Ally's bottom lip and felt soft hands stroking her face. Ally was crying, but her tears were filled with an extreme happiness that consumed her entire being.

The kiss was very tender, as their exploring tongues tasted every ounce they were willing to share. Unwilling to break the contact, Sydney gently lay Ally down on the wet grass and continued their passionate baptism. The rain started coming down harder, but Sydney and Ally were oblivious to it all. Sydney moved her kisses down Ally's neck and shoulder. Nipping and biting as she made her way down her soon-to-be lover's body, Sydney heard Ally's sounds of desire.

"What do you want? Tell me…" she purred into Ally's ear causing a shockwave of electricity to shoot between her legs.

"You…I want you, please. I need you to touch me, feel me, taste me; I have to have you inside of me. I want everything."

"You'll have all of that, I promise you," she swore.

Fifteen

The two women lay on the wet ground ignoring the weather and relishing the feel of the other's body. Slowly Sydney raised Ally's shirt over her head and gently removed her bra. She knelt in front of Ally and pulled off her own shirt to reveal herself to her new lover. Ally watched in awe as Sydney continued to prove once again that she was absolutely beautiful in every way.

Their bodies moved slowly with the rhythm of their breathing. Sydney kneaded the round, fullness of Ally's breasts, gently rubbing her thumbs over the nipples. Ally's back arched in response. Sydney lowered her head to capture one of the nipples in her mouth. Slowly circling Ally's nipple with her tongue, Sydney made sure that Ally knew the depths of her desires. Sydney brought Ally's breast almost completely into her mouth and felt Ally's hand pulling her head closer.

"You feel unbelievable." Ally hissed rocking her head slowly from side to side.

The rain continued to fall on their almost naked forms, as the rest of their clothing was tossed to the side. Ally grabbed Sydney's behind and slowly massaged the muscles moving above her. Sydney's body was grinding into Ally's center and Ally found the passion that was building almost blinding.

The feel of Ally's naked skin against hers was the most amazing thing Sydney had ever experienced. Ally's body responded to her every touch, every kiss, every breath exhaled against it. She wanted Ally more than she wanted anything in her life before. She gently moved her hand down to Ally's lower abdomen and kissed the skin beneath her fingers. Ally and Sydney locked eyes knowing the act that was about to play out.

Sydney adjusted her body between Ally's legs and took a deep breath. She inhaled the sensual scent coming from Ally and wanted nothing more than to lose herself there. Ally grabbed handfuls of grass as Sydney's tongue gently touched her clitoris. A surge of desire poured out of her and into Sydney with one touch of Sydney's tongue.

" God, you taste incredible," she whispered to Ally, looking briefly into the electric stare of her partner.

Sydney moved her tongue in small gentle circles against the tender flesh beneath her. She held onto Ally's hips as she felt them begin to undulate against her mouth. Her mission was clear now. She wanted Ally to become nothing less than a weak, breathless, beautifully satisfied woman.

Ally couldn't keep her eyes open long enough to catch more than small glimpses of the woman bringing her to ecstasy. Her body was alive with every stroke of Sydney's tongue. Her thoughts went numb as the pressure building inside of her became almost too much to bear.

Sydney's tongue moved faster as she sensed the imminence of Ally's orgasm. She braced herself against Ally's body, feeling the beginning of Ally's release.

"Oh...my... God... Sydney... yes!" Ally moaned.

Thrusting her hips faster and faster, Ally's body fell slave to the intense touch of her lover. With the release, Ally felt a wholeness she had never known before.

Sydney rode wave after wave of unbidden passion and desire. Ally's body slowly recovered from the climax and her breathing once again became normal. Sydney climbed up the spent form of Ally and gently lay on top of her with both elbows resting on either side of Ally's head. Looking up into loving blue eyes, Ally spoke to her in almost a whisper.

"Oh, my God. That was incredible. I never knew I could feel this way."

"I'm glad that I could make you feel like that. I hope that you'll give me an opportunity to do it often," she said as she caressed one side of Ally's face.

"Do you see me trying stop you? Not gonna happen," Ally smiled and kissed Sydney tenderly on her lips.

The rain was still pouring down on them, and Sydney noticed a shiver run through Ally's body.

"It's time we went in an got you into a hot shower before you catch your death out here."

"Only if you join me," she said, causing an eyebrow to rise on Sydney's face.

"How can I refuse such an offer?"

"You can't, it's not an offer; it's a demand. I will not take no for an answer either, missy." Sydney laughed at Ally's mischievous expression sure that this night was only the beginning.

With Jack, Pete, and Edna away, the two reveled in the privacy they were given to explore their newfound love. They collected their clothing from the piles strewn on the lawn and made a quick run into the house. The brisk air from the air conditioning made their skin crawl with goose bumps.

"Damn, it's cold in here. I'll race you to the shower," Sydney taunted.

"Well, I don't know," Ally started to whine playfully. "Your legs are so much longer than..." Ally stopped and raced up the stairs knowing full well that retribution would be in order for her cheating.

"You're so dead, do you hear me, Alicia? You're mine," she yelled, reaching the top of the steps. She looked around the bathroom only to have Ally jump from behind her.

"Yah!" Ally surprised.

"Ahhh!" Sydney screamed.

"Gotcha!" Ally smiled in victory.

"That's what you think. I'll show you who's got who," she said, picking up Ally and throwing her into the shower. Ally mockingly put up a fight kicking and screaming, and laughing in-between limited gasps of air. Sydney turned on the water and watched Ally's eyes grow huge as the cold water began to warm.

"Come here, my little Aussie. I'd like to show you something," Ally said, wiggling her eyebrows at Sydney.

"Coming, my dear," she smiled, entering the shower and drawing the curtain closed.

Ally wasted no time; she grabbed Sydney's head and pulled her into a deep passionate kiss. The water cascaded down against both very aroused women. Ally broke the kiss and whispered into Sydney's ear.

"Show me what to do. I've never done this before."

"All right, baby, we'll make this a lesson you'll remember for a long time," she purred back into Ally's ear, causing a new outbreak of gooseflesh down her body.

Sydney reached up and took one of Ally's hands and placed it on one of her breasts. She held onto Ally's hand as they tenderly rubbed against the nipple with both their fingers. Sydney's body reacted to the stimuli of their shared movements. She exhaled deeply as the desire built between her legs once again. Ally's movements became more confident—she rolled the nipple with her thumb and forefinger. Sydney welcomed the feeling and let out a small moan.

Ally then took Sydney's full breast into her mouth. Her tongue circled over the nipple causing Sydney's breath to become more and more ragged.

"Yeah, I think you've got it, oooh right there. God, that feels good," Sydney gasped.

"Mmm. I like this," Ally purred.

Ally took her newfound courage and gradually moved her hand between Sydney's legs. The wetness she found increased her desire to explore this woman pressed against her. The water was beating down on Ally's head almost leading her to take the next step. She slowly moved her fingers around until she found a very sensitive spot on Sydney.

Sydney's body shuddered as she felt the touch of her neophyte lover. Ally pushed Sydney against the wall and increased the speed of her movements. Under the spray of the showerhead, Sydney began to quiver and her release started to build inside of her.

"You have no idea what you're doing to me."

"Oh, yes I do, sweetie, yes I do." She smiled inwardly knowing that she was the cause of her lover's shivering.

"You are very good at this."

"Yeah, well, I'm self-taught if you know what I mean."

Sydney smiled, thinking back to a few hours earlier in this same shower.

Ally quickened her movements as Sydney's breath became labored and her body stiffened with excitement. Sydney's tender flesh was swollen and slippery with arousal. Ally couldn't believe that she was making love to a woman, let alone a woman like Sydney. Her body was completely on fire with every sound that Sydney made. The sultry, deep voice humming into her ear was music Pachelbel himself would have been proud of. Sydney reached down to touch Ally's passion, when she felt herself go over the edge.

"Oh, Alicia! My God... that's it... Oh... There... Yes!" Sydney cried as the orgasm cut through her core.

Ally pressed Sydney harder against the wall as she felt herself crest once again in synch with her lover. Their legs slowly gave out and they melted down the shower wall and into to the base of the tub. Sydney wrapped her arms around the smaller woman as the spasms began to ebb. As their breathing reached a normal pace, they tightened their grip on one other. The sound of their heartbeats under the running water was all that could be heard.

"That was beautiful," Sydney sighed. "I've never experienced such an overwhelming moment in my life. I can't believe that I was willing to throw all of this away because of my fears. Can you forgive me for being such a child?"

"You don't have to apologize," Ally soothed. "This is all the proof that I need to know you're for real. Just don't get up and run this time." She pressed Sydney closer.

"I promise, I'll never leave you again," Sydney said, pledging her loyalty with a kiss.

The next few days were spent getting to know each other in-between their marathon lovemaking sessions. They talked and laughed about their lives and people in their past. They took many walks and rode tandem on Polka to ensure snuggle time. Their nights were filled with passion. Sydney was teaching Ally everything she wanted to know and more about what makes a woman ache for more. Ally showed Sydney a few things, too. Their hearts had found their home and weren't moving anytime soon.

☯ ☸

Edna walked in the door after spending five days with dirty old farmers and ranch owners. She was relieved to be home. She was even more relieved when she let her eyes roam over the two sleeping forms cuddled up on the couch. Ally had her body nestled against Sydney's longer frame and rested her head against her strong shoulder. Sydney's arms were wrapped around her young lover.

Edna quietly crept up the stairs and placed her luggage in her room. She passed Sydney's room and noticed it was immaculate and her bed was neatly made. She scratched her head as she walked over to Ally's room. Her lips turned upwards into a large grin. The sheets on the bed were strewn all over the place. Two sizes of clothing were in various places around the room, leaving a trail back to the bed. She knew that her niece would be well loved and taken care of.

She picked up the picture from the Grand Canyon and smiled as she looked toward the sky. "She's going to be just fine, Donna, I promise. She has someone to watch over her now, while you look down from up there. She misses you, but don't you worry. Between Syd and me, she's going to be loved and cared for until the day she leaves this place. And when that day comes, she'll have you, with your arms wide open for her to be cradled in once more. She's gonna be just fine," she repeated, with tear-filled eyes as she held the photograph close to her heart.

Edna placed the picture back on the windowsill and turned around to head back downstairs. With dinner approaching, she needed to get into the kitchen. From the looks of things, she was going to have a couple of starving women on her hands. And that was just fine with her.

Sixteen

"You're in such trouble when I catch you, Alicia." Sydney growled.

"Yeah, well, you have to catch me first," Ally teased and ran toward the house.

Sydney had been doing her best to wash down the horses with a large hose. Ally had slowly approached her friend without being noticed. Initially her intent had been to scare her lover, but once she saw the unattended hose, she lost all sense of control.

After dousing Sydney unmercifully, Ally had run to the main house to seek asylum with Eddi. She found her aunt asleep in her rocking chair in the family room.

"Damn! Now where can I hide?"

"Oh, no you don't," Sydney growled. "You aren't getting away this time, little missy."

"Now, Sydney, you know I was only fooling around," Ally croaked, holding her hands out in front of her. She laughed nervously, finding herself backing away from a drenched and mildly agitated woman.

"Fooling around, eh? Just what does 'fooling around' entail?" Sydney mocked menacingly. "You sneaking up on me, you grabbing a hose, soaking my skin, and then laughing and running inside to look for cover?"

Ally swallowed hard, having no idea what her Aussie lover was planning as revenge. "Umm, yes?" She winced.

Ally found herself being backed into the entertainment unit while Sydney drew nearer with every tick of the grandfather clock in the corner of the room. Sydney's breath tickled Ally's ear as she bent down to offer a warning.

"Paybacks are truly a bitch, my dear. And believe me when I tell you, I always get my revenge."

Ally realized she was short of breath and completely at a loss for words, a very rare event for her. She looked into the most challenging blue eyes she had ever seen, and knew she was no match for the tall raven-haired woman staring down at her. She just had to wait until her time came. It was exhilarating to her senses. Sydney, she had discovered, was a very creative person. *I wonder if everything she does is as imaginative as the things she does in bed.* Ally's thoughts sent shudders throughout her body, and her movements were not lost on Sydney.

"What's the matter, Alicia? Cat got your tongue? Hmm?" The taller woman smiled, and then gracefully exited the room, leaving a slack-jawed Ally slumping against the entertainment center.

"My God, what that woman does to me. Christ." She wiped her brow and made her way to the bathroom to wash her face and calm her nerves.

ಬಿ ಅ

A couple of months had passed since the two women had met. Ally's aunt had graciously opened her home and her arms to her niece. Living alone in Chicago with the emptiness that evolved around her had not been the life that Ally wanted. Her aunt's offer came as an answer to a silent prayer.

ಬಿ ಅ

The funeral had gone as well as could be expected. Most of Ally's family had attended both the wake the previous night and the funeral procession the following day. Everyone had offered their condolences to Ally, not wishing to trade places with her for anything in the world. To lose both of her parents the way that she did, they half expected her to wither away herself. These people didn't know the strength inside the young woman. At that time, neither did Ally.

Her Aunt Edna had arrived a week before the traditional formalities had begun. She had arranged the burial for her sister, Donna, and her brother-in-law, Tom. She knew that Ally wouldn't know how to handle the arrangements by herself. In truth, she hadn't even known for sure what she should be doing. How often do you have to plan such an event? Hopefully, this was the last time she would have to do it. Burying her own husband had been hard enough, but now her sister had been taken away, along with her husband. It had felt very surreal to her. "It's not nearly as hard on me as it is on her." Eddi had murmured to herself, watching her niece hugging estranged family members.

Finally, the day was coming to an end, and most of the guests had left Ally's home. The after-gathering was nicely catered, and the mood had been as light as it was going to get on such a tragic day. Ally just wished away her migraine as she forced herself to meet the sorrowful stares she received for the duration of the day. Eddi walked up to her just when she thought she could handle nothing further.

"How are you, honey? Do you want to call it a day? I can take care of the clean up down here."

"No. I'll help. It's the least I can do. You planned everything while I did nothing."

"Nothing? Oh, honey, you had to finish up school and move back here for the summer. You had plenty to do yourself. These things have a way of timing themselves very badly. Not that there would ever be a good time for this." She trailed off and found herself embracing a sobbing, scared little girl.

"Oh, Eddi...what am I going to do now? I've lost almost everything in a blink of an eye." Ally sobbed into her aunt's shoulder.

"I know, sweetie, I know. We just need to take things day by day. It's all we can do. But we have to keep going. Your mom would want that for you. I know she would," she said, cradling Ally's shaking body. "You want some tea?"

"Yeah... I think it may help my head...it's just pounding."

"All right, kiddo, go sit down at the table, and I'll get us some. I gotta let out the last of our guests and I'll be back. We can talk if you want to. Or we can just stare, cry, scream, or whatever your li'l heart desires. Okay?" She kissed the top of Ally's head.

"I love you so much. Thanks for being here for me."

"Oh, sweetie, there's no other place I'd be right now. Now scoot, I'll be in there in a couple of minutes."

"All right. I'm gonna say goodnight to Tracey," Ally said.

Ally's best friend, Tracey Miller, came in from the front room and embraced Ally. "God, hon.', I'm so sorry. I wish there was more that I could do for you."

"Thanks, Trace, I know. I just can't believe it. You know, two weeks ago I was just talking with mom about summer plans and I how much I couldn't wait to see her when I got home." Ally pushed back a sob.

"I know, honey, I know..." Tracey kept Ally in her arms until the fair-haired woman pulled away. Tracey's soft brown eyes looked into sad green ones, her heart breaking for her childhood friend.

"I'll be all right. Eddi's with me, go on home. I'm just gonna go to bed. I have the worst friggin' headache."

"Well, that's not surprising. Take care of yourself, darlin'; I love you, you know."

"I love you, too. Thanks for being here for me."

"What are friends for?" she questioned, running her fingers through her mass of curly ash-blond hair.

"Well, you're the best friend in the world. Good night." Ally hugged her again, kissed her cheek, and watched as Tracey left.

She padded to the dining room table and sat down.

Ally's eyes roamed around the room she was in. Every shelf on the bookcase held at least one picture of her or her parents. She scanned down to the roll-top desk and found a gift she had made her mother when she was ten. It was a picture frame that had My Favorite Mom etched into it, with a picture of her and her mother in it. "Like I had more than one," she said to no one. "Now I don't even have one..." She stopped and put her head in her hands and let the tears fall unhindered. Edna came in with the promised beverages and sat down next to Ally. She stroked Ally's back as she watched her niece down the healing liquid.

"Honey, I want to ask you something, and you don't have to answer until you're ready, okay?"

"What's wrong?"

"Nothing, I just want to ask you something."

"Go on."

"I want you to consider something for me," she said, taking one of Ally's hands in her own. "I'd really love it...if you came out to live with me...in Montana. I know it's far away from your friends and your school, but you make friends like bees make honey, and well, we got schools up in Montana, too."

Ally's face wrinkled up and she again began to cry.

"Oh, honey, I'm sorry. I should've waited to ask you that later on, I'm so sorry."

Sniffling, Ally finally found her voice. "No. Don't be sorry. I'm just so thankful to have someone like you in my life. Thank you so much for that. Please let me think on it, though. I have so much here; it would be such a huge change for me. I just don't know if I'm ready for more change. Is that okay? Can I answer you another time? I just need some time to really think it over."

"Of course, sweetheart," Eddi told her, stroking Ally's hair gently. "Take all the time you need. I'm not leaving for at least a week, so please, just think it over, and let me know. I would hate to think of you in Chicago, by yourself. I mean, I know you have school and your friends, but this house, well, I know how many memories you have here. I just want you to be happy, honey."

"I know," Ally said, sliding into her aunt's hug. "And I love you for it. Thank you."

"You're welcome, sweetie," Eddi hugged the slender form. "And I love you back."

‑ ‑

Ally was awakened from her reverie by a questioning stare.

"I'm sorry, did you say something?"

"Yes, Alicia," Sydney repeated, watching her young lover closely. "I asked if you were okay. You looked like you were a million miles away."

"I was, actually, I'm okay though, and don't you worry."

"When it comes to you, I worry. Just reflex, get used to it." Sydney smiled and opened her arms.

"I was thinking about the funeral...sometimes I still can't believe this happened. I'm just thankful I had Eddi. I don't know what I would have done without her. She's been unbelievable," Ally met Sydney's loving glance.

Sydney looked down into saddened eyes. "She's an incredibly giving woman. She's been a warm healing blanket...for both of us," she finished softly.

"I'm going to miss you so much, Syd," Ally said, moving into Sydney's arms.

"I know, I'm going to count the hours while you're gone." Sydney returned the hug with enthusiasm.

Ally had made arrangements to meet with her family's lawyer to finalize the paperwork for her parents' estates. It was a trip Ally was not looking forward to, but knew was necessary.

"It's going to be so hard to go back there without them waiting for me at the airport." Ally sighed sadly. "Sometimes it feels like this is someone's else life, and I keep hoping I'm going to wake from this nightmare."

"I know, baby, I know. I'm so sorry you're hurting so much." Sydney rubbed circles on Ally's back, trying to console her saddened partner.

Ally buried herself in Sydney's strong embrace. She loved when her partner let her guard down and was just loving, nurturing, and warm. The last couple months had been wonderful. She had met someone that truly felt like the other half of her soul.

There was trepidation behind the azure blues of her lover, though. Sometimes she would find Sydney lost in thought, looking frightened, but when asked, the dark-haired woman always had some way of explaining it away. Ally would let her think she was off the hook, when actually it saddened her to know she wasn't trusted enough to be let in on her lover's secret.

Sydney doesn't trust anyone, she thought. She had friends that she'd talked about and would go out with from time to time, but the only one with Sydney's full trust was Eddi. Ally was almost jealous of their relationship. They would have long talks that sometimes went deep into the night. Ally had tried many a night to stay awake with them, but sleep usually found her halfway through. Time and time again, she found herself in Sydney's arms being carried up to their room to bed.

Ally knew from the beginning that it would be an uphill battle to gain the trust of Sydney Thompson. It was, however, a fight the young woman had no intention of losing. Just to give Sydney a compliment, and not have her read too much into it, was exhausting. *She must've been hurt badly. I wish she'd talk about it; maybe it would help her. She's got to know I'd never do anything to hurt her,* Ally mused, pulling out of Sydney's arms.

"So, what do you want for dinner? I think I should cook." The blonde-haired woman smiled up at her lover.

"If you think that cooking dinner is going to get you off the hook, you've got another thing coming." Sydney smirked, placing her hands on her hips.

"I'm sorry about the hose thing, really. Please forgive me."

"Oh, I forgive you, my little city mouse, but I'll have my revenge. Mark my words."

"Revenge for what? What the hell did I miss?" Eddi asked.

"It looks like your innocent little niece here likes to play with water, Edna." Edna peered over to look at a very amused Ally. She then looked back to Sydney who seemed as though she were waging war inside her head.

"Now look here, girlies, if anything gets broken, I'll put the hose on ya both! Just calm yourselves, Christ Almighty, a girl takes a nap for five minutes and all hell breaks loose…" she trailed off, taking some juice out of the refrigerator.

"I swear to God, I don't know what gets into you girls," she said, drinking the juice from the container. She swallowed the liquid and looked up, finding two scrunched up faces staring at her.

"What? It's not like either of you will ever drink out of this!" she said, displaying the prune juice carton. "Can I help it if I like to be regular? Hell, on the other hand, you should try it, you may get rid of some of that hostility!" She smiled. "Then again, I didn't get sprayed with a hose, either."

"Hey! Whose side are you on?" Ally whined.

"The dry one. Now what are you making for dinner? This girl is hungry!"

Ally rolled her eyes and began opening cabinets looking for some ideas for dinner for her two best girls.

"Yeah, yeah, go on and sit down. I'll have something ready in no time," Ally said, looking into the cabinets and finding nothing she wanted to cook. "Eddi?" she called out, turning to face her aunt. "Can we just order pizza? I know how much you hate to cook, but I just don't have it in me right now."

"Sure, sweetheart. I haven't had a pizza in awhile. Tell me what you'd like and I'll have Moe deliver one over."

Ally looked gratefully at her aunt. "Thanks, Eddi. Cheese and pepperoni is fine for Syd and me. We always get that combo."

"Would you girls mind setting the table? I'll make the call and we'll be eating soon," Edna said, looking through her address book for the phone number to Moe's Pizza.

"Deal. Come on, Alicia, I'll help." Sydney said, walking toward the table.

༄ ༅

Ally stood at the terminal, her carry-on bag in one hand, saying goodbye to Sydney. "God, I still can't believe I'm going back home."

"I know, baby. Everything will work out just fine, I swear. Your aunt told me your parents had the best lawyers money could buy. They'll take care of everything. You won't have to do anything except sign on the dotted line."

"I know," Ally said, shrugging her shoulders. "This whole thing just sucks. The only thing I'm thankful for is that I'll be with Tracey."

"Oh, right. You didn't give me her information."

"Crap, I forgot. Do you have a pen?" Ally asked searching her bag and finding nothing.

Sydney checked the pockets of her jacket and came up with a pen and grabbed a brochure from a nearby car rental desk. "Here, I'll just use one of these. Okay, shoot."

"Okay, Tracey Miller, obviously, and her phone number is 487-555-5989. I'll try to call when I get in, okay?" Ally said, leaning in to hug Sydney one last time before boarding her flight.

Sydney replied, "Have a great flight, sweetheart. Try to get some sleep, okay?"

"I'll try." *I love you, Sydney.*

"Good. Now shoo, don't miss your flight," Sydney said with a smile. *God, I'm going to miss you.*

Waving again, Ally turned and walked through security toward the gate to board her flight for Chicago. Watching her walk out of sight, Sydney never heard the woman approach her from behind.

"Ah, parting is such sweet sorrow," Sharon said in a singsong voice.

Whipping her body around, Sydney stiffened while facing her ex-girlfriend. "What the hell are you doing here?"

Casually waving her hand in the air, Sharon replied, "Hello, my sweet. Eh, I was in the neighborhood and thought I'd stop by."

"The airport? Cut the shit, Sharon, what do you want from me?" Sydney's patience was just about gone.

"I want you back, Sydney. I've missed you," Sharon said, moving closer to Sydney.

Stepping back from Sharon, Sydney gruffly replied, "Are you out of your mind? Just stay the hell away from me. You've done quite enough to me for one lifetime. Are we done now? Because I know I have nothing more to say to you," Sydney's voice began to echo throughout the vestibule they were standing in.

She attempted to walk past Sharon, but she grasped Sydney's arm.

"You've got about two seconds to let go of me before I make you sorry you came here," Sydney snarled.

Slowly removing her hand, Sharon laughed softly. "Oh, Sydney, you were always beautiful when you were angry. I bet your little girl doesn't know how good she has it, does she?"

"Don't you go near her. Do you hear me? Just leave us alone! I'm trying to go on with my life. If you cared for me at all, you'd let me do just that."

Sydney stormed away from Sharon trying to rid herself of all the memories that came flooding back. In her whirlwind exit, she didn't notice the brochure falling from her pocket. Sharon picked it up and read the information quietly to herself. "Oh, Sydney, you can go on with your life, but I'm going to be there with you. I can guarantee that. Perhaps Miss Tracey Miller can help me with my plight."

Smiling, Sharon walked down the corridor and out of the airport with a renewed spring to her step.

Seventeen

By fall, Ally had decided that she would enroll in school for the upcoming spring semester. Edna and Sydney had been very supportive of her decision and agreed that she needed some more time to get used to everything that had so drastically changed her life. Starting a new school, in a new area, sharing a new home, with a new partner, and doing it all without her parents, was a little much for Ally to swallow at once. She was taking the days one by one.

Thoughts of her parents were very frequent and mostly came through dreams at night. Many a night Sydney had awakened to Ally thrashing about trying to fight off the demons in her head and in her heart while she slept. Sydney would always wrap her larger frame around Ally and instantly find the tiny woman relaxing in her embrace. Ally would then thank her in the morning for performing the exorcism, which she so lovingly called her bouts with the nightmares.

ಙ ಡ

Ally wanted Sydney to come with her to Chicago to see her home before it was sold. The house had been on the market for about a month. Deciding to sell it was hard for Ally, but it made sense. She was in no financial shape to maintain her parents' home, so she gave in and called the family lawyer and then a realtor. After her meeting in Chicago with the lawyers, it turned out her parents had left her quite a bit of money, but she wanted to use it to work on her journalism degree. Her cousin Jack had given her tips on some stocks and mutual funds for investing, but she was scared to death of the stock market. It didn't make sense to her. So for the time being her savings account had a little bulge to it.

Ally's mind was alive at dinner; she was in the defensive mode. Ever since the day she had showered Sydney unmercifully with the hose, she was nervously awaiting the turnabout. It was bound to happen sooner or later, she only wished it was sooner and then it would be over with.

She had decided she would ask Sydney to come to Chicago with her that night. *I think Eddi could handle things for a week. Hmm, maybe I'll ask Eddi first just to make sure.*

"You're awfully quiet. Are you all right?" Sydney questioned.

"Yeah, I'm fine. No need to worry." She looked up at Sydney with eyes that betrayed her. There were dark puffy circles under her usually vibrant green eyes, which made Sydney wish for more peaceful dreams for her.

"Alicia, as long as I breathe, I will worry about you."

"Hey, take it while you can, sweetie. It's hard to find someone that will do your worrying for you," her aunt interjected.

"I guess you're right. It means the world to me to know you care so much."

"I do care for you, very much. I think I always will." She said, gently stroking the inside of Ally's wrist with her thumb.

"Me too."

"Well, with that established, can I have some more of those potatoes?" Eddi quipped. "Ally, you outdid yourself. I love au gratin. They're my favorite."

"Thanks, eat up. Sorry for the mushy stuff," her niece said smiling.

"Not to worry," Eddi said, touching Ally's hand. "It makes me sleep better knowing you have someone in your life like Syd." The older woman smiled at them both. "I knew it was going to happen when I saw the first looks you two gave each other. It was priceless. It was loooove at first sight. You could barely eat and Syd kept staring at you during dinner." The two lovers blushed at the memories Edna was recalling.

"It was quite the entertainment," Eddi chuckled, spooning out more potatoes onto her plate. "I knew once I left for Indiana, I'd come home to some kind of news. I'm so glad I wasn't disappointed. Syd was just what you needed, Ally." She smiled at her niece. "And I think the same goes for you, my dear." She stated simply, pointing a finger at Sydney.

"Whoa...? I... Wasn..." Sydney started sputtering and looked at Edna, her eyebrows high into her bangs.

"Yes, you were and you did, so enough out of you." She waved her fork at Sydney. Ally marveled at how well her aunt could work Sydney. *God, I don't think there is another person on this planet that could get away with half the stuff Eddi does with her.*

"Hey there, we lost you again," Sydney said, breaking Ally away from her thoughts.

"I was just thinking, is all."

"Uh-oh!" Edna and Sydney said in unison and then laughed.

"Cut that out, you two! You know...oh never mind, I'll never win against you both."

The two women hi-fived each other and grinned stupidly at Ally, who in turn rolled her eyes and continued to eat.

ರಿ ಲ

"Hey, Eddi, can I ask you something?" Ally walked into Edna's room.

"Sure, hon, what do you need?" Edna replied, getting ready for bed.

"Well, it's not a need exactly. It's more of a want kind of thing. I was ahhh...wondering if...well, if it won't be too much trouble..." Her aunt was patiently waiting for her request and interrupted her ramblings.

"Sweetie, I'm not getting any younger here! Just ask me."

"I was wondering if I could take Syd to Chicago with me to pack the house up."

Edna pondered the question for a moment and realized this may be a good thing for both of them.

"It will only be for a week or so I swear. Tracey set up a service to help with the whole process," Ally continued again, talking fast. "I won't take her away from her chores for too long. Do you think we could?"

"I think it's a wonderful idea, dear. It might do you some good to go back there with her. Sydney tells me you haven't been sleeping all that well. I know you're heart is troubled. Have you asked her yet?"

"No, not yet, I was waiting to hear what you thought, and she is your employee after all, so I wanted to make sure that it would be okay. I would hate to take her away while you needed her, but I missed her so much when I was gone last time, I'd hate to go through that again. I mean I had Tracey, but it's not the same, you know, so if you wouldn't mind..."

"My goodness girl, you can talk at the speed of light. I'm surprised I can understand you at all when you get going like that." She chuckled.

"I'm sorry," Ally giggled. "I'm very excited about this. I want so much to take her with me. I want Tracey to meet her, too."

"How's Tracey doing?"

"Pretty well. I talked with her last night, actually, and she wants me to stay with her again when I go back home. I'm gonna stay at the house though. I think I need to say good-bye." Pushing her sadness down, Ally continued. "Anyway, she said to say hi to you."

"God, how long have you two known each other now?"

"We've been friends since I was five. I really missed her this past summer. The weekend I was there it wasn't the same. We hardly got a chance to talk at all! We usually sat poolside all summer or hung out on the roof of her house and stuff. I missed that..." Ally's voice trailed off and her aunt took her hand and squeezed it.

"How did she take the news of you and Syd?"

"Oh, my God," Ally said. "Tracey was the one who told me I was gay."

"What?"

"Yeah, about two years ago she told me that I was going to get fed up with not getting what I wanted from men. Then she said to make sure that dinner plans, on me of course, were arranged when I figured it out. I guess an 'I told you so' kind of celebration." She giggled.

"That girl is too much. So, she was happy about it then?"

"Oh please, my ears are still ringing. She's very happy for us though, and she can't wait to meet her."

"Who can't wait to meet who?" Sydney poked her head into Edna's room. "I was wondering what was keeping you," she said. "All right, what's up? You look as though you're conspiring against someone. It's not me is it? 'Cause I can outrun you both."

The two women laughed, and Ally moved and wrapped herself around Sydney's waist. "No, hon, we aren't conspiring, I promise," she reassured her.

"That's a relief, I can't be too sure around you two. Are you ready for bed, sweetheart?"

"Mmm, yes I am. Good night, Eddi, we'll see you in the morning." Ally reached over and gently squeezed her aunt's arm.

"Good night, you two." They were almost through the doorway when Edna's voice picked up a bit. "And could you keep it down tonight? I almost called an old friend to keep me company last night."

Ally couldn't keep the blush from flooding her entire body, and Sydney could do nothing but wink and smile at Edna as she closed her door.

"Oh my God, I never thought she would hear us!" A completely embarrassed Ally spouted.

"Alicia, you could wake the next county if you wanted to." She wiggled her eyebrows. "Not that I'm complaining, I rather enjoy your vocal skills, amongst your other ones."

"Good answer, mate." They laughed and closed their door for good measure.

Ally walked to the bed, folded down the blankets, and fluffed Sydney's pillow as she had done every night for the past two months. She tossed her socks into the hamper and got under the sheets. Sydney followed suit and assumed her position. Ally immediately snuggled into Sydney's shoulder. It was a routine.

"Syd..."

"Yeah, baby?"

"I need to ask you something." Ally stroked the smooth skin on Sydney's stomach.

"Do I need to get up?"

"Oh no, nothing like that."

"Okay, then ask me. Ow!" Sydney giggled at Ally's small jab to her ribcage.

"Okay, well, I've been thinking lately."

"So, I've noticed. Is anything wrong?"

"No, honey, just listen, please." She paused and took a deep breath. "I want to go back to Chicago."

Sydney's body stiffened and she sat up to look at Ally, willing the tears away from her eyes. "Chicago? Wait, Ally, what are you saying? I thought we started something really great here. You want to leave now? I thought…"

Ally gently pressed her fingers to Sydney's lips. "Sshhh. You didn't let me finish, honey. I need to pack up my parents' house and I want you to come with me. That's all, I swear."

Relief swept through Sydney and she thought she was going to pass out from the sensation of it all.

"Sydney? Are you okay? You look as pale as a ghost," Ally remarked, feeling Sydney's forehead and wiping away a thin layer of perspiration.

"I… uhm… I… would love to go with you. I need to ask Edna if it's all right, though. She does depend on me to tend to the horses."

"She said it would be a great idea. So… what do you think? Next week all right with you?"

Sydney gazed into the hopeful green eyes of her lover. "Sounds great to me. I think I need a vacation anyhow. I missed you when you went for that weekend. It'll be nice to accompany you this time." She smiled, the pounding in her chest slowly receding.

"Oh, you don't know how much this means to me," Ally told her. "I can't wait for you to see the house. And, I want you to meet Tracey. You guys are going to get along great. Thank you, I truly mean that."

"Honey, I'm excited too. I've never been to Chicago."

"Well, we don't actually live *in* Chicago; we live…lived…in the suburbs about 30 miles or so north of the city. But we can go down there if you want. It's quite a different scene from here. It's much louder and so much more is going on all the time. I don't miss that part of it."

Sydney's senses picked up on the pretended enthusiasm in her young partner's voice. "Is your school near there?" she asked, keeping her tone even.

"No, I went to the University of Illinois, which is in Champaign. That's about 3 hours from my house. It's kind of in the middle of Illinois," Ally said, a sad expression coming over her.

"You miss it already, don't you?" Sydney asked gently.

"Am I that transparent?" Ally asked with a fragile grin on her lips.

"Like glass, baby." Sydney slowly sunk back to the bed, dragging a teary-eyed Ally with her. She kissed the top of the blonde head and began to stroke the soft, golden hair.

"I'm sorry," Ally murmured into Sydney's shoulder.

"For what?"

"It seems I'm always crying lately."

"Honey, it's okay. I'm glad that I can be of some comfort. You know how much I care about you. When you're sad, I'm sad. I'll do what I can to make sure that beautiful face carries a smile whenever possible."

"You're so good to me," Ally said, snuggling closer to the lean body next to her. *How did someone ever leave you?*

Ally turned to face her partner and gently kissed her lips. Sydney deepened the kiss. Ally was soon offering her mouth to Sydney and was rewarded with a hot probing tongue. The stayed like that for a long moment and then pulled back to stare into each other's eyes. They were both breathing heavily.

"God, baby, you make me so crazy," Sydney purred into Ally's ear.

Shivers went throughout Ally's body as she pulled at her shirt to free herself of any obstacle from being able to be against Sydney's bare skin. *Just another advantage of Sydney sleeping naked; there isn't much to take off.* Sydney helped Ally with her shirt, her underpants following shortly afterwards.

"I don't understand why you still dress for bed. I never let you keep anything on anyway."

"I'm beginning to see your point," she giggled, pulling Sydney on top of her.

"God, sweetheart you feel so good."

"So do you," she said with a smile.

Sydney brought one of her hands to Ally's breast and began to tease her nipple. Sydney slowly began to grind into Ally. Ally's moans grew louder and her body began to rock against Sydney's. Sydney could feel her companion's desire building as she slowly moved up Ally's body.

"You know what, baby?" Sydney said, licking one earlobe.

"What sweetie? Tell me..." Ally panted in response.

"Paybacks are truly a bitch." She smiled and gently rolled over to her side of the bed, leaving a thoroughly aroused and confused Ally to her musings.

"Whoa...you can't be serious?" the younger woman managed to squeak out.

"Good night, sweet dreams." Sydney chuckled, feigning sleep and quietly waiting for the explosion she knew was coming. She worked hard not to let the laugh that was bubbling within her escape.

"Sydney Elizabeth Thompson! You aren't going to leave me like this are you?"

"Like what, honey?" Sydney finally erupted in laughter.

"OH... MY GOD!" This is about the hose isn't it? You're going to let me sit here and stew in my totally 'I want you now' state because of the hose, am I right?"

"Uh huh...that's right."

"Oh, no you don't!" Ally screamed with determination. "You can't raise my heart rate like this then simply roll over knowing that I won't be able to sleep for at least a week..." Ally stopped when she heard Sydney's laughter. "You're laughing at me, aren't you?"

Trying to regain her composure, Sydney sputtered, "Yyyes... As a matter of fact... I am..." The fits of laughter continued and slowly she turned over to see bright green fire looking down at her. *Uh oh, I'm in trouble.*

"Now, Alicia, you know you had it coming. I told you I always get my revenge... and I did." She tried to be stern as she spoke with a grin. "Why are you smiling?" Sydney asked.

"Well, you've had your fun, and now it's my turn." Ally said very suggestively claiming her lover's lips with her own.

Down the hall and in her room, Edna threw her pillow over her head, again.

Eighteen

The sun always came up earlier than Ally liked. This morning was nicer than most though. She knew that in only hours, she would be back in Chicago, this time, to the house that she grew up in. She wanted to show Sydney her home. She was also excited for Tracey to meet the love of her life. The only thing that would be missing would be her dad and mom. She knew going back was going to be hard, but she was also hoping that in some way, it would help with her demons. She was so grateful that she had someone like Sydney to understand what she was feeling and to accept her.

While Sydney was looking forward to this trip, her mind was reeling from so many conflicting emotions. She was terrified by her feelings for Ally, yet at the same time, she was so happy and tingly whenever Ally was around. Unfortunately, this brought her back to a time in her life when she was the most vulnerable, and that scared the living shit out of her.

☙ ❧

"*Come on love, come to the States with me. You will love Montana. Please, think about it, Syd, for me. You know how much I love you. Let me erase of all the painful memories from here. We'll be so happy together.*" Sharon pleaded.

"*My entire life is here, babe,*" Sydney answered. "*I grew up here. My family's station is here; you know how much that means to me. It's the only thing I have left of my family, well other than Tim. I don't know if I can up and leave it.*"

"*That's what I'd be doing, though, hon,*" Sharon countered. "*School isn't for me, you know that. I can't stay here; it's simply not me. Montana is my home; I need to go back there. I'd really love it if you'd come with me. I guess it's a test of our love. After everything I've done for you, I can't believe that you wouldn't come with me.*" Sydney was torn.

"Don't doubt my love for you, babe," she pleaded with her lover. "You know I love you. I'd do anything for you; you know that. This is a huge step for me. Let me talk with my brother about the sheep station. If he gives me a proposal for it that I can live with, I'll take you up on your offer. I promise."

"Oh, love, you don't know how happy that makes me," Sharon gushed. "I know you'll make the right decision."

'I hope so.' Sydney thought as she hugged her lover.

Ᾰ ◓

"So Timmy, do you seriously want it? I mean is this something that you know you truly want? I know you know how to run it, you basically showed me everything I needed to know. I only want to make sure that this is something that you want for your life, for your future." Sydney said to her brother.

"Syd, when you took over the station, I wasn't very happy about not being a part of it," Tim told his sister. "It's the last thing mom and dad had together. It was always a part of our family: Dad, Mom, and Bi..." Tim paused at his own words.

"You know you can say his name, Tim. It won't bother me, unless it bothers you to say it." Sydney paused sadly. "I seriously hope that's not the case though. He was a good kid, Tim. Unfortunately he was in the wrong place at the wrong time. If anyone should be silenced from saying his name, it should be me. I know what the courts said, but it doesn't take away the fact that I was a part of what happened to him. I can now say that I've forgiven myself. But that's only because you forgave me too." Sydney took a breath. "So for the hundredth time, thank you for that. I'd hate going through life without my older brother. I know that you'll be a great foreman to the station, too. Please know, Tim, that I never thought you had any desire to have it, otherwise you know that I would have shared it with you. It would've been great to run it with you. I only figured since you didn't say anything that you were okay with it. I'm so sorry."

"Please, don't apologize." Tim assured her. "I'm happy you thought of me before you sold it to some bloke off the street. Consider it sold, to the best and highest bidder." Another pause. "About Billy? I do forgive you. Sometimes it's still hard to hear his name though. He'll be around though, I'm sure of it. Mom and dad, too. I think I'll be surrounded by them everyday that I'm there."

"I think so, too, Tim. The only thing that I hate about this deal is the fact that I'm going to be leaving now. I'll miss you. We've finally come together, you and I. I'm so sorry for all the years that we didn't speak. I didn't understand death and why it happened. I didn't want to 'get it.'"

Sydney took another deep breath. "You saw what I became: I was a monster that didn't know what love actually was. God, and after Billy and mom died, I wasn't sure that I wanted to live at all. I'm out of that hell now, and I finally know the value of family and loved ones. You're all the family I have left now. Well, besides Sharon that is. I love her with all my heart, Tim. She believed in me when I didn't believe in myself. Even after everything that's happened in my life, she's willing to take a chance on me. I don't want to disappoint her in any way. There isn't anything I wouldn't do for her."

"I know, but..." Tim began.

"But?" Sydney prodded, a little annoyed.

"Yeah, but...why couldn't you have fallen for a woman who lived on this side of the planet?" Tim grinned at her and they shared a smile and embraced each other. "I'll miss you too, baby sister. I love you, ya big softy...God, she has you so whipped doesn't she?"

"Yeah well, love makes you do the strangest of things, Timmy. Let's call dad's lawyer and legalize all of this eh?"

"You betcha."

ಬ ಏ

"Sweetheart? Are you packed?" Ally broke into Sydney's reverie.

"Hmm? I'm sorry, hon, what did you say?" Sydney asked.

"Sydney, are you all right? You looked kind of out of it when I walked in." Ally walked over to Sydney and placed a hand on her arm. She felt the tall woman flinch under her touch and slowly pulled away.

"I'm sorry, I didn't mean to..."

"Look, I know you're bothered by something, I only hope one day you will feel you can trust me enough to talk about it," Ally said comfortingly. She picked up the rest of the bags and went downstairs.

So do I, love, so do I. Sydney wrapped her arms around herself for comfort.

Nineteen

The flight into Chicago was a quiet ride. Ally sat next to a very silent Sydney. As they exited into Chicago's O'Hare Airport, Ally immediately felt exuberated at being home again. Sydney remained quiet, other than basic small talk, as they waited for their luggage. It worried Ally that Sydney hadn't spoken much since they'd left Edna in Montana.

"Honey, are you sure everything is all right? You haven't said more than two words since we boarded the plane."

"Of course, I'm fine," she lied, thinking about the last time she had been inside an airplane.

Sydney had been on her way from Sydney, Australia to the USA with her love, Sharon Harris. This was supposed to be the next step towards eternal happiness with her partner. Too bad Sharon's extracurricular love life took precedence over a longtime commitment. Sydney shivered at the thought of Sharon and what she had sacrificed for her. She swore she wouldn't let the bitter memory interfere with her relationship with Ally, but right now it was all too familiar. Sharon was making it very difficult for Sydney to forget. Sydney knew that Ally was going to ask her about what was bothering her. She had to build up the strength to share the pain that she'd never voiced to another person other than Sharon.

Sydney knew that she loved Ally, but every fiber of her being was scared to death of sharing this painful information with her lover. Once she did that, she would be setting herself up for heartbreak. She couldn't handle that kind of pain ever again.

"There's Tracey, come on! " Ally said excitedly spotting her longtime friend waving from the arrival drive-up.

"Tracey!" Ally screamed with joy, embracing her friend.

"Hey, girlfriend! Long time no see," Tracey said as she extended their entwined arms and eyed her jovial friend. "And who do we have here?" she asked, looking Sydney up and down with appreciation.

"Tracey Miller, meet the love of my life, Sydney Thompson. Sydney this is Tracey." Ally introduced.

"Hello, Tracey," Sydney said politely, taking Tracey's hand. "I've heard so much about you. It's a pleasure to finally meet you," Tracey shook the tall woman's hand.

"Right back at'cha. It's a pleasure to meet the woman that has stolen the heart of my best friend. I can see why she finally switched teams." She wiggled her eyebrows and nudged Ally. Sydney smiled courteously and shifted uncomfortably.

"Shall we get going? We don't want to fall into traffic on I90, the toll way is a bitch this time of day if we don't get moving," Tracey explained, putting their bags into the trunk of her car.

"Oh, God, I don't miss the traffic around here, that's for sure." Ally grasped Sydney's hand and they walked around the car. Sydney took the backseat as Ally took the front.

"So, how was the flight?" Tracey inquired.

"It wasn't too bad actually, thank God. I hate flying. I'm sure Syd's hands are still sore from the landing."

"I think the blood has finally returned. Don't worry about it, honey." Sydney smiled and patted her lover's shoulder from the backseat.

Tracey and Ally chuckled. They chatted until they reached the end of Ally's street, where Ally could feel her nerves set in like a stampede of horses over her body. The sweat beaded on her brow. Without a word, Sydney reached her hand over the seat to softly caress Ally's shoulder. She moved to the edge of her seat to reach Ally's ear to whisper to her.

"You're gonna be great, sweetheart, I'm right here for you. If you want to cry, it's okay, you can have my shoulder," Sydney comforted.

Tracey fidgeted, trying not to overhear the sweet reassurances between Ally and her new lover. Ally reached up and squeezed Sydney's hand in thanks.

Ally had never felt so grateful; it was wonderful to have someone in her life like Sydney right now. Warmth swept through her as they entered her driveway. She instantly felt her parents with her and hoped they would stay until her visit was over.

"Wow, baby, your home is beautiful. You never mentioned how expansive the landscape was. God, it reminds me of home. This is simply gorgeous."

"Thanks, sweetheart. Yeah, Mom loved this house and it took Dad almost ten years to realize what he had," Ally said. "He didn't want to move here, but Mom wanted to be in the area. It's very private and quiet. A lot like Eddi's except we don't have horses." Ally leaned back to speak to Sydney conspiratorially. "We have a pool though, I think you'll enjoy your stay here. Wink, wink, nudge, nudge." Tracey put the car in park in front of the garage.

Sydney stepped out of the car, took a deep breath, and was pleased that their travels were over for now. She looked over the two-story Victorian house and was in awe of its beauty. They grabbed the luggage and, after Ally found her key to the house, entered her childhood home.

"Smells musty. I'm going to open some windows as soon as we get our bags upstairs." Ally said, heading for the staircase.

Sydney noticed her lover's slow glances around the quiet home and watched her facial expression change from indifference to sadness as she walked up the steps.

"Hey, I gotta get back to work," Tracey quietly said. "I think she's gonna need you right about now. Tell her I'll be back later on tonight, okay?"

"Sure. I think it'll take a bit of getting used to for her to be here without her parents. I'll let her know you'll be back," she responded.

"Thanks for being here for her Syd, she's very lucky to have you."

"I'm the lucky one," Sydney corrected.

"I'll see you later. It was great to meet you. You have a wonderful accent, did you know that?" Tracey smiled.

Sydney rolled her eyes and smiled. "I don't have an accent, you do! What is it with you women?" Sydney and Tracey laughed, and Sydney walked Tracey to the door.

Sydney walked upstairs and tried to guess where Ally had gone. There were several rooms upstairs to choose from. She sat and listened to see if she could hear her lover. She found Ally in what she assumed was her parents' bedroom. She was sitting on their bed holding a picture of her parents. The young woman stared at it, idly stroking their faces with her finger.

"Hey," Sydney said softly.

"Hey." Ally pushed out before letting the tears loose that she had been holding in since she walked into the house.

"Come here." Sydney put her arms around Ally's shoulders and pulled her to an embrace. Sydney felt Ally's sobs wrack her body. She held her tightly and was determined to stay like that for as long as Ally wanted.

"God, I miss them so much, Sydney." Ally sobbed.

"I know, honey, I know," Sydney soothed. "Shhh, I'm here, I gotcha. Let it all out, baby, I'm right here."

"I'm so glad you're here, God, I love you." Ally said before she could stop herself. She felt Sydney gasp and her heart rate increase.

"I know you do..." Sydney said, continuing to console her lover. She knew that Ally had heard her gasp at the revelation of Ally's love. It wasn't as if she didn't know, it just hit her hard hearing it for the first time. She wasn't sure if she ever wanted to hear anyone say that to her again. If love meant the treatment that she'd gotten from Sharon, then she wanted no part of it. She found herself in a very bad situation. She wanted to run away, but she knew that Ally needed her more than ever at the moment. Thinking of Ally first, she stayed right where she was.

                                        ಐ   ಞ

An hour or so later, Ally had finished giving Sydney the nickel tour of her home. Sydney was amazed at the size of the house and wondered why Ally hadn't mentioned her family's wealth.

"My father was a Psychologist and *he* had money. I mean I'm only twenty years old, well I will be in a week or so. I never thought of myself as wealthy because I didn't earn all this," Ally explained. "Hopefully my journalism degree will change that, and with the money they left me, I may have a chance at finding out what making a good living is all about."

"I have no doubt about your writing talent. Um, back up a sec, did you say you would be turning twenty in a week?"

"Yeah, September twenty-first. I don't know why I never mentioned it before. I'll be twenty, almost legal." Ally smiled and nudged Sydney.

"Like I was worried. Well, fair is fair, I'll be twenty-five in April."

"You know, I never asked you how old you were. I guess it didn't matter to me, but now that I know, I should have guessed that we were close in age. You don't look a day over twenty-three," Ally said playfully.

"Oh, thank you, may I take that as a compliment?" Sydney retorted.

"You can do whatever you like," Ally smiled.

"Oh really? Anything?"

"Should I be afraid now?" She backed up a few steps as Sydney prowled closer to her.

"Oh, definitely, be very afraid, Alicia," Sydney purred as she swept Ally into a soaring kiss that knocked out Ally's knees from under her. Sydney caught Ally and held her tightly until their kiss tapered off.

"That was incredible," Ally gasped. "God, where did you learn to do that?"

Chuckling, "I'm glad you liked it," Sydney answered, wiggling her eyebrows.

They moved upstairs and began to unpack some of their things. The window in Ally's room had been opened and Sydney took the opportunity to look out into their backyard. She took in a breath of fall air coming in from the screen and exhaled softly.

"You know, one of these days, I think I'll take you home to my Sydney. You'd love it there. It's very quiet, much like the ranch, but my God, it's gorgeous." Sydney turned to look at Ally's loving gaze

"You miss home don't you?" Ally asked softly.

"Mmhmm, very much. I haven't been home in what…six years?" Sydney paused reflecting. "My brother Tim is such a clown, you would love him. I thought that he would decline my offer of the sheep station when I was deciding to leave Australia, but he didn't. He was excited to have a part of our family in his life."

Sydney paused, but Ally waited and listened. Sydney rarely spoke of her past and she wasn't going to butt in now.

"He says that things are going well and I'd be happy with the way he was running things. I'm sure I would be. He taught me everything I needed to know, well everything that my dad didn't." She smiled. "Anyway, when Sharo...when I decided to leave home I never thought I'd miss it so much. So I can understand why you miss your home so much." She still had a hard time even speaking Sharon's name.

Ally didn't miss the slip and she hoped there would be more of them on their vacation together. Hopefully this trip would open Sydney up to Ally and she would finally understand the pain in the older woman's heart.

"It's the part of you that's the most you," Sydney said, gently stroking Ally's cheek. "Does that make any sense? I mean only being here for a little over an hour, I see so much of you in this house."

"You can see that simply from being here?" Ally asked, green eyes open and curious.

"Oh yeah," Sydney told her. "The warmth of the decor of your bedroom is so you. The openness and brightness of your reading room is unmistakably you. There are so many little things I see in this house that are...you."

"Wow, you are so incredible. I truly mean that," Ally said, wanting to tell her again how much she loved her. She decided that a hug would suffice for now. She walked up to Sydney and wrapped her arms around the taller woman's body.

"Mmm, I like it here. I like you here, too." Sydney said, running her fingers through Ally's silky golden hair. She ran her hand up and down Ally's back unconsciously and Ally let out a moan of content, bringing a smile to Sydney's lips.

"It's still pretty warm and musty in here don't you think?" Sydney nodded and released Ally's hold.

They went back downstairs and Ally walked through the living room, dining room, family room, kitchen, study, and sunroom, opening every window, letting in as much air into the stuffy old house as possible.

Ally found Sydney sitting on the leather sofa in the family room in deep thought. She didn't want to pry but she wanted Sydney to open up to her. *Soon, I hope.* "So, Syd, when did Tracey say that she'd be back?" Ally asked, perching on the arm of the chair Sydney sat in.

"Ah, she said that she had to go back to work and that she'd be back later on tonight. She wasn't actually specific with the time."

"Hmm, I wonder if she wants to do dinner with us this evening." She checked her watch and realized that she was still on Montana time. She moved her watch forward and then saw that it was technically close to mealtime.

"Did you remember to change your watch? I almost forgot," Ally said nonchalantly, fixing her watchstrap.

"Yes, I did already. I did it on the plane," Sydney replied. "I didn't want to get screwed up later on." She turned a warm smile toward her lover. "So, when do we get to try out that pool of yours?"

"You get a sudden urge to go swimming or something?" Ally asked, one eyebrow rising slightly.

"Maybe…" Sydney said with a bit of a grin on her face.

"I'll have to see if the pool was set up for the summer. I don't know if it was even filled this year. So much was going on when I came home, I didn't even notice. Let's go out back and check, you'll love it out there. Dad had the best garden, he had the most beautiful roses, I wonder if he groomed them before…" She trailed off as Sydney softly caressed her cheek.

"Let's go see." She said as she pulled the younger woman close and kissed the top of Ally's head. She took her arm and they walked through the patio to the pool area.

The roses were as beautiful as Ally remembered. There were rows and rows of roses in the garden adjacent to their fence.

Sydney simply marveled at Ally's face when she saw them. She took a look for herself and was amazed at their beauty. "My God, they're gorgeous," Sydney said in awe. "You were so right, Alicia. Your father definitely had a green thumb. I don't think I've ever seen roses like this before." Sydney's eyes scanned the colorful area.

"I don't think you'll ever see any like this anywhere. He truly made it an art." Ally explained proudly.

There was still a cover on the pool and Ally walked into the pool shed and opened the door to flip a switch. With a click the electronic pool cover slid open and revealed a full swimming pool. Ally looked up at Sydney and smiled.

"I bet I know who's responsible for this."

"Edna?"

"None other. I bet she called ahead and had the service come and take care of this. She's too much. We have to remember to call her tonight and thank her."

"Absolutely. She's such a wonderful woman. You're very lucky to have her as a part of your family."

"She's your family, too. I know Eddi thinks of you as family. She's said as much many times. I think you're the daughter she never had. I always hoped that I was that girl, but I think that she feels that way about you. She loves you, you know."

"Yeah, I do, she's one in a million. She took me in after Sharon and I split up…" Sydney realized a second too late that she had finally mentioned her ex's name to Ally fully for the first time.

Ally tried to control her excitement at Sydney's disclosure. She played it cool, not wanting this conversation to end. Sydney's body had panic running rampantly throughout it after her slip up.

"Anyway, she truly helped me get my head together. I'll be forever grateful to her for that."

"That's our Eddi; she'll stop at nothing to help people in need. God, I miss her already!" Ally laughed at herself.

"With me here? What am I, chopped steak?" Sydney shrieked in mock outrage.

"Liver, honey, chopped liver," Ally giggled.

"Ew, I hate liver, I'd much rather be steak," Sydney grinned, her dark mood evaporating.

"I love steak, it's the most delectable of meats I think. I could eat steak all the time." Ally said in her sexiest voice.

"Really? I think you get your share of...steak...don't you think?" Sydney whispered, playing along with their analogy.

"You can never have enough steak, especially when it tastes as good as it does." Ally said seductively, enjoying Sydney's mood.

"You love the flavor...you love the juice when you poke your fork into it for your first bite. The anticipation of the dripping morsel hitting your taste buds...it's intoxicating isn't it?" She rumbled into Ally's ears, sending her into fits of arousal.

"Yes, it is...and it's a good thing that I'm not a vegetarian. Don't you think?" She gulped as she saw the dark desire forming in her lover's eyes.

"Yes, I do...come here, Alicia...I need to kiss you..." Sydney commanded in soft humming tones.

Ally moved within reach of Sydney's lips and the passion from one kiss was astounding. She wanted Sydney to take her right then and there. That was when she heard someone clearing his or her throat behind them.

Looking up startled. "Tracey! My God, you scared the hell outta me!" She screamed at the smiling curly-headed woman.

"Yeah, you looked scared...hey Syd, how are ya?" Tracey smirked.

"Fine thanks, you?" Sydney said, trying to hide the blush she felt creeping up her neck.

"I'm good. Damn hungry though. You guys up for pizza?"

"God, Tracey is that all you still eat?"

"Hey, it's a fine meal," Tracey retorted. "You've eaten plenty of them with me if memory serves."

"Ha! Don't I know it. You know, Trace...you could take us to the bar tonight, if you wanted." She wiggled her eyebrows at Tracey who in turn raised hers high on her forehead.

"THE bar? You want to go there? God, I never thought I'd see the day! Man, Syd, I don't know what you've done to her, but I like the results."

"Hey! I went to plenty of bars at school. I just never wanted to go to a gay bar before. Now I think I'd love to enter a club on the arm of this beauty." Ally winked at Sydney whose body immediately reacted to the comment.

"Umm, could you two excuse me?" Sydney said, practically running up to the house.

"What was that about?" Tracey asked.

Ally shrugged her shoulders, "I have no idea. Let me go see. I have got to find out what's bugging her. She's been so strange since we left Montana. I'll be back in a few. Sorry, hon. " Ally squeezed her friends forearm and ran to the house in search of her love.

Sydney quickly found the bathroom. Her body was shaking from the stabbing pain in her gut. "She's not Sharon, Sydney, she's not Sharon. She wouldn't treat me like a prop. She's not like that!" her head was rumbling in a mantra. Her body continued to tremble as another wave of nausea hit her hard. This was going to be a long night indeed.

Ally ran into the house shouting Sydney's name and got no response. Only after seeing Syd exit from the bathroom, her face pale, did she calm her bellowing.

"Honey, are you ill? You look so pale." She ran up to Sydney and placed the back of her hand her cheek. "You're warm. Come on and sit down in here." Ally said, walking Sydney back to the couch. "Relax a bit. I'll get you some water." She softly caressed Sydney's ashen face and then went to the kitchen to retrieve a glass of water.

Tracey came back into the house and saw Sydney on the sofa in the family room. Her head was resting on the armrest of the sofa and she looked as if she was crying. Tracey heard Ally in the kitchen and decided to find her first.

"Hey, is she okay? She looks like she's crying over there." Tracey said sympathetically.

"I don't know. Do you mind if we take a rain check tonight? I think she has airsickness or flu or something." Ally explained.

"Sure, babe, tomorrow is Friday anyway, maybe we could go to the bar then, I mean if you guys are up to it."

"Thanks, darlin'. I have lots of packing to do here and hopefully I'll get that done during the day so we can play after dark!" Ally said, smiling at her friend.

"I've missed you, girl," Tracey cried, hugging her buddy.

"I've missed you, too. Have a good night."

"You too, hon."

"I have a feeling it's going to be a long one."

"Well, hopefully not too long. You look like you could use some sleep. Those eyes of yours need some shuteye."

"Yeah, I know. I haven't been sleeping all that well lately," Ally admitted. "I was hoping coming home this time would cure me of my night demons. Lots of bad dreams... Syd usually cuddles me close and I calm down." She laughed.

"God, you guys are sickening," Tracey said. "I'm glad you're happy though, Ally. She is gorgeous! And my God," Tracey lowered her voice. "How do you not faint with that accent calling out your name? Don't tell me she doesn't do that either. I know my talks with you taught you something!"

"Christ, Tracey!" Ally shook her head. "It took awhile not to blush whenever I heard her say my name, for sure, but I'll never tire of it. Not from that mouth or with that voice. God, she could melt butter with that voice." Ally said proudly. "Speaking of meltdowns, I think I need to get back to her. See you tomorrow?"

"You bet, babe, night." Tracey kissed Ally's cheek and headed to the door. She stopped, waved good-bye to Sydney, bidding her a goodnight as well.

☯ ☾

Ally returned to Sydney's side with some water. She gave her the glass and watched her pale partner slowly drink the contents. Sydney sighed softly and looked into Ally's eyes.

"I'm sorry, honey," Sydney apologized. "I guess I'm just not feeling that well. I don't like to fly, and maybe it finally got to me," she lied, with a sincere smile.

"That's all right, sweetie," Ally told her. "Just lay here." She shifted so Sydney could lie on the couch with her head resting on her thigh. She stroked Sydney's long dark hair and started to knead the knots from her lover's neck and shoulders. She could feel the stress beginning to melt away.

"God, Syd, you're so stiff and balled up with tension. Are you sure you're okay?" Ally asked, hoping that Sydney would finally open up to her.

"Yeah, baby, I'm feeling better being here with you. Sorry your first night home turned into a bust," Sydney said sleepily.

"Spending time with my best girl is never a bust in my eyes," Ally said. *I love you, you big goof.* She wished she could say it out loud. "There isn't anything I wouldn't do for you, Sydney. I hope you know that."

"Mmhhmmm," Sydney mumbled as she began to drop off into a restless sleep.

Ally continued to rub Sydney's head as she felt the long, sleek body relax and her breathing deepen. She sat there and held her love, trying to soothe whatever evil spirits may have invaded Sydney's soul. She shifted a little and felt Sydney's grip on her legs tighten.

"Shhh, don't worry, love, I'm not going anywhere," Ally began whispering to her slumbering companion. "I love you, Sydney. You don't know how hard it is for me not to tell you that," Ally continued rubbing the dark head in her lap. "You've helped me so much in the last few months. You've helped me to deal with the biggest loss in my life. When my parents were killed, I never wanted to know love again. I didn't want to hurt like that ever again and loving you sets me up for that. I don't care though, you brought out the person in me that I was afraid to know was there. I was afraid of knowing the person inside of me because I knew I was different. You showed me that loving a woman is no different than the love my father showed my mother. I know who I am for the first time in my life. I'm not afraid of the future because I know that I'll have you at my side."

Ally swallowed around the lump in her throat. Her hand continued stroking the long, dark hair spilling over her legs. "It makes me sad that you won't tell me what's bothering you so much," she told her sleeping partner. "You know you can tell me. You know whatever you say to me won't change the way I feel about you; nothing will. I only know that whatever it is that other woman did to you, will make me feel that much sorrier for her. She lost her chance with you, and you're mine now. It's bad enough I can't even compliment you without you thinking that's all I love about you. God, you aren't a trophy or a possession." Ally gazed lovingly at the quiet face under her hand.

"Sydney, you're a gorgeous woman, that's just the facts. Your physical beauty, though, doesn't even compare to the woman you are to me." Ally sighed and wiped a stray tear from her cheek. "I love you, baby, I love you with all of my heart." Ally finished and leaned her head back into the couch.

Sydney lay in Ally's lap with one teary eye opened, not knowing what to say to her partner. *Do I let her know that I heard most of what she said? Or do I lie here and pretend to be asleep? God,* Sydney marveled. *She is the most wonderful person I've ever known. She has a heart that parallels no other. I do love you, Alicia; I wish I knew how to say it to you. I want it to be more than just words, especially with the love I feel for you. I truly hoped that I could have forgotten about Sharon, because I never wanted to talk about her again.* Sydney gulped at the familiar ache settling in her chest. *She just won't let it be, though. Now the memories are so present again. Damn her! I just want her out of my head and out of our lives, forever.* Sydney felt her reserve returning. But the old fear kept her courage at bay.

I promise I'll tell you everything. I need the courage, help me find that courage, Alicia. Only you can help me to find that strength. I truly hope it's not too late by the time it arrives. I couldn't bear the thought of losing you. Ever, Sydney nonchalantly shifted in her so-called sleep to wipe her tear-stained face.

Twenty

Sydney extracted herself from Ally's hold on the couch and decided she needed to deal with some of her fears. She looked down at the sleeping woman and knew in her heart that she would be safe from harm. *What am I doing? She's done nothing even remotely close to hurting me. It's time I thanked her properly for loving me. I know she trusts me, now I need to show her I trust her as well. I don't want there to be any question of that any longer. She means too much to me.* Sydney pressed a soft kiss to Ally's forehead and made her way into the kitchen.

"Keys…keys…where would they have kept…" she paused, seeing the key rack next to the door. "Ok, I have keys, now where the hell do I go?" She opened a few cabinets in the kitchen until she found the phonebooks. She grabbed the yellow pages and leafed through them until she found what she was looking for. Picking up the phone, she dialed the number and politely asked for directions. Hanging up the phone, she walked back to Ally and noted she hadn't moved an inch.

"I'm pleased you're such a sound sleeper. Be back soon, baby." Sydney kissed her forehead again and left the house through the front door. She opened the garage and saw a silver BMW 325. "Nice," she said to herself. Next to the Beemer was a dark blue Camry. "I think I'd feel more comfortable driving that one," she said, trying the different keys in her hand and finally opening the locked door of the Toyota. She made her way into town, looking at the directions she'd written down.

Ok, Sydney, you can do this. Ally deserves a wonderful evening after what happened this afternoon. She's going through too much right now not to be able to lean on you. Give her yourself, all of yourself. You know she deserves at least that. Let her feel all the passion inside of you. Show her what you can't say…you love her. Sydney listened to the voice inside of her on the way back to Ally's home. She collected what she needed for Ally's big surprise.

"*I do love her. She needs to hear it, too. I need to tell her.*" Sydney turned the corner onto Ally's street and her heart raced in anticipation. "*God, I'm pathetic. I need to get past this...tonight.*"

Sydney placed the last of the accouterments next to the pool steps and wondered how Ally was going to react. *If she's not into it, then I'll just go to plan B...whatever that is.* She took one last look around and mentally patted herself on the back. "She's going to love this. I can't wait to see the expression on her face." Sniffing under her arm, she grimaced, "Whew, first things first, though," she said while heading toward the upstairs shower.

Ally awoke to find Sydney gone from her lap and the couch. She got up and walked to the kitchen, but the room was dark. She managed to turn on the lights in the hallway and head up the stairs. She found her bathroom door closed and then heard the shower turn off. She tapped lightly on the door.

"If you're a 5 foot 4 inch blonde-haired beauty, you may enter. If not please go away, my girlfriend will be up soon," Sydney said as she grabbed a towel and began to dry herself off.

The door opened up and the chilled air ran up her semi-wet naked form. Sydney grabbed Ally and quickly ushered her inside to close the door. She embraced her in a full bear hug and relaxed when she felt the smaller woman's hands on her.

"When did you wake up, honey?" Ally asked hesitantly.

"A couple of hours ago. Did you have a good rest?" Sydney pulled back to gaze into her lover's eyes.

"Mm, yeah I did. I didn't even know I was tired. Must have been the traveling. I'm going to be up all night now." Ally pouted.

"Ooh, I hope so. I'd hate to think that I'd be up all by myself in this big house. I might get scared," Sydney joked. "Besides, I have a surprise for you."

"A surprise? For me? Why? What did I do?" Ally's green eyes opened wide.

"You're simply you, baby, that's why." Sydney smiled and looked at their reflection in the semi-fogged mirror.

"Well, where is it?" Ally asked.

"It's downstairs. You want to see it?"

"Sure, in a sec," Ally said, hugging her tight again. "First, I want to know if you're feeling better." She pulled back to study Sydney's relaxed expression. "Your color is much better."

"I feel one hundred percent better, sweetheart," Sydney said, pulling the young woman into another hug. "And it is because of you and your TLC. Thanks for taking care of me."

"Aw, sweetie, it was nothing. I like taking care of you. I hope to do it for a long time." Ally smiled sweetly.

"Me too," Sydney agreed, brushing her fingers against Ally's soft face. "I'm hungry," Sydney said, grinning. "Let's go downstairs."

"Ohhh, the surprise is food-related?" Ally grinned impishly.

"How else would I thank you appropriately?"

"Lead the way!" Ally said excitedly.

Sydney grabbed a T-shirt and shorts from their room and led Ally downstairs, through the sunroom, and out toward the pool. As they reached the patio, Ally stopped in her tracks.

"Oh, Syd..." Ally gasped at the sight in front of her.

The perimeter of the pool was illuminated by candlelight. Sydney had set up a table with several entrees of Ally's favorite delicacy, Chinese food.

"How did...this is beautiful. How did you do this without me knowing?"

"I found the keys to one of the cars in the garage, found a phonebook, and I'm not above asking for directions." She smiled triumphantly.

"You are incredible! Thank you so much, God, you're so thoughtful," Ally said, capturing Sydney's lips in a deep sensual kiss.

"Mmm, you're so welcome. I know how much you wanted to spend your first night with Tracey, so I wanted to make up for it somehow," she said guiltily.

"Oh, Syd, you don't have to make up for being sick, it just happened. Don't think that you have to make up for that."

"Ally...I..." Sydney began softly.

"Hmm?" Ally asked.

"Nothing, I just wanted to tell you that I'm really happy you brought me here," she said, releasing a breath she didn't know she was holding. *You are pathetic*, she chastised herself, again.

"Me too, sweetie, I'm so glad that you're here with me." Ally scanned the delicacies on the poolside table. "Are you hungry?" she asked excitedly.

"Sure, let's hit it. Now remember, no swimming for at least an hour after eating."

"Oh, sweetie, I think they've pushed it down to a half hour now," she answered mischievously. She sat down and started spooning out little portions of everything that Sydney had ordered for them. "Ooh, can you pass me an egg roll?"

Laughing, Sydney complied with the request. "You know, it's still such entertainment for me to watch you eat. Between you and your aunt, I think I've found the two most adoring eaters on the planet. It's really something to watch," she said, putting a forkful of Cashew Chicken in her mouth. "Mmm this *is* good," she mumbled.

"It is. Oh, you've got to try this," Ally told her between mouthfuls. "God, I've missed this place. They just don't have this in Montana," she swallowed her bite and continued. "So um, did you venture around town?"

"Yeah, I did a little," Sydney admitted. "I didn't want to go too far without a chaperone."

"Did you like The Square? Isn't it like a little town of make believe?" Ally inquired.

"Yeah, it was like... what was that guy's name that had a children's show on television here in the States, a Mr. Robinson, or someone?"

"Ha, I think you mean Mr. Rogers. Yeah, he had a show for kids, 'Mr. Rogers' Neighborhood.' It was one of my favorite shows as a kid. I see your point; it's a little like that. You should see it around Christmas; they really do a wonderful job decorating every single tree in the square. The lights are just fantastic!"

"Even the huge one near the fountain?"

"Especially that one. It's really something to see."

"You know what?" Sydney said, staring at her lover.

"Hmm?" Ally replied in-between bites.

"You looked about twelve years old just then. I don't think I've seen that look in your eyes until you spoke of Christmas. You're so adorable, baby."

"You're just biased," Ally replied shyly.

"No, I just call them as I see them." Sydney said, winking at Ally.

೫ ೦೩

"Oh, Syd that was just wonderful. God it feels good to have food in my belly. I didn't want to eat too much, because I really want to get in the water. I don't remember September being this warm."

"It seems a little out of season, but I agree it is quite warm out; it's so beautiful though. The sky is clear and you can see lots of stars, but you're right, you don't quite see as many as you do at Edna's," she said, pouring more wine for herself.

"I'm glad that you're feeling better. What do you suppose hit you? Air sickness?"

"Well, whatever it was, I'm glad it decided to leave as quickly as it arrived."

"Me, too." She smiled, gesturing to Sydney to fill her glass as well. "You know, you could get arrested for aiding in the delinquency of a minor."

"Yeah well, I think they could arrest me for more than a drinking violation. Certain acts of love are illegal here in the States, no?"

Thinking about what Sydney said brought a flush of acknowledgment to what acts she was talking about.

"You're so beautiful when you blush. I'm a lucky woman."

"I'm the lucky one." She leaned over and kissed her partner.

"Mm, do you want to try the pool yet?" Sydney asked hopefully. "There's a little more to the surprise for this evening."

"Oohh there's more? What could you possibly have done in two hours?"

Sydney smiled innocently.

"Should I be afraid?"

"Yes, be very afraid. You left me on my own for a couple hours, be very afraid, Alicia," she purred in Ally's ear. Ally gulped audibly, feeling Sydney pull her to her feet.

"I don't think you'll be needing these." Sydney said seductively as she began to remove Ally's shorts. Sydney pushed the unwanted clothing to Ally's feet followed by her underwear.

The warm air felt wonderful on Ally's aroused skin. Sydney slowly unbuttoned Ally's shirt as she maintained eye contact with the smaller woman. She gently brought the garment over Ally's shoulders and down her arms, revealing well-tanned, delectable skin that she needed to taste. After her shirt fell to the ground with the other items of clothing, she removed the final piece of apparel, unleashing Ally's beautiful breasts.

Sydney just stared at her lover as she gently cupped Ally's breasts and began to brush her thumbs across Ally's already erect nipples.

"You are such a sensual person, Syd, I just love it. I never knew that making love could be this incredible. You never leave me wanting for more. You satisfy every need I thought I'd ever have. Sometimes you satisfy wants that I didn't even *know* I had."

"Good, I'm glad. I hope that you like what I've planned for you for tonight then," she said, capturing Ally's wanting mouth with her own. She let her tongue linger inside Ally's mouth as they exchanged gentle touches and caresses. Ally tugged on Sydney's shorts and pulled away breathlessly from the kiss.

"These have to go as well."

"Oh, that's not a problem, I want to feel your body against mine. I love the way our bodies feel when they are together. It's like we were made to fit perfectly with each other. We must've been, considering the differences of our heights."

"Mmmm, I love your body and the way it feels. I bet it'll feel even better in there." She said, gesturing to the water.

"Come on, let's get wet."

"Too late for that, my little country mouse. I've already reached that point. I don't think I'll ever have to worry about that being a problem as long as you're in my life." *I hope it's a long time.*

Sydney chuckled at Ally's admission.

The two women slowly entered the candle lit pool by walking down the stairs at the shallow end. Ally held onto the metal railing as she stepped down, letting the temperature of the water wash over her skin. Sydney dove under the water and came up like a goddess as the water cascaded down her tanned muscled form. Ally watched Sydney like a child in awe of a phenomenon. The desire she felt at that moment challenged any emotion she had ever had, and won.

Ally dove in toward her lover and surfaced in front of her. The taller woman wrapped her arms around the smaller form in front of her. Their bodies were warm and wet and glistened in the candlelight.

"You know, the only other time I've been naked in this pool was with Tracey. We got drunk and went skinny-dipping a couple summers ago. I thought *that* was fun. It doesn't even hold a candle to this...sorry, no pun intended."

"You and Tracey, huh? Should I be jealous?"

"Oh, God, no! Tracey's my best friend. I think that sex is the only thing we haven't shared. Did I tell you that she was the one that told me I was gay? I thought it was wishful thinking. She just knew me better than I knew myself. Still does sometimes. Other than you and Eddi, I've never trusted anyone, as I trust her. She's the best friend ever."

"She seems like she really cares about you. I think I'll like getting to know her," Sydney said, leaning over and gently nibbling on Ally's neck. She felt Ally's body shudder and moved her lips over to Ally's throat and began to gently kiss and suckle at it.

"Mm, no more talk about Tracey," Ally panted, claiming Sydney's mouth again. As she thrust her tongue deep inside Sydney's mouth, she felt feverish with the passion running through her body. Sydney reached down and started massaging Ally's bottom and she rewarded her with a hungry growl.

"Oh yes, Syd, God, you're so incredible," she gasped.

"Come on, here's where the surprise comes into play, and I do mean play. Do you trust me?" Sydney added, in response to the look of uncertainty on Ally's face. *Please say yes.*

"You know I do." *I don't care what it is. You need to know that I'd do anything for you. I trust you with my life. Once more, I trust you with yours. I know you won't hurt me.* "What did you have in mind?" Ally asked. Half of her was nervous, while her other half was on fire.

Sydney led them back to the pool stairs. She sat Ally down on the top step leaving her upper body exposed to her. She knelt between Ally's legs. Ally reached out and pulled Sydney into a lustful kiss. Their tongues battled for control inside their mouths while their bodies began to move against each other in a rhythm of desire. Sydney leaned over and reached for the towel she had resting poolside. She opened the towel to reveal a pair of handcuffs. Sydney pulled back slightly and raised her eyebrow in question. Ally's eyes widened in surprise and uncertainty.

"You game?" Sydney asked, dangling the cuffs from her finger.

"I've never been handcuffed before. Where did you want to cuff me to, the water?" Ally chuckled nervously.

"No, I thought this would serve us well." She clanged the cuffs against the railing next to the stairs.

"Oh, um, I sense a well thought out plan. Remind me to leave you alone more often." She smiled confidently at her lover. *She won't hurt me. She needs to see the trust I have for her.*

Ally leaned back and reached up so her hands were on either side of the railing. Sydney reached over and locked the cuffs to each of Ally's wrists around the railing. She ladled some water in her hands and poured it slowly over Ally's breasts watching the droplets of water return to their origin. Ally's nipples were fully erect and Sydney was eager to taste them. She leaned into Ally's body and captured a nipple with her teeth and gently stroked it with her tongue, eliciting a pleasurable moan. She looked up. Ally's eyes were closed; she moistened her lips with her tongue.

Sydney climbed a little further up Ally's body and whispered in her ear. "How far do you want to go?"

"I'd go anywhere with you." *Please believe that.*

You would wouldn't you? "All right. Then I want you to tell me how you feel about this." She smiled and lifted a candle and poured a little drop of wax on her palm and showed Ally. "You want to play with fire, scarecrow?"

"Go ahead, Sydney, you won't hurt me." Ally said confidently, watching Sydney raise the candle over her chest. She painfully waited in anticipation as the wax slowly ran from the candle onto her chest. "Oooh..." She hissed.

"Did that hurt you?" Sydney asked sincerely.

"No, it felt really umm...I don't know how to describe it, but it definitely didn't hurt."

"The journalist doesn't know how to describe something?"

"You've won this time; take it while you can."

"How about I take you instead?" She whispered sensually, allowing another few drops fall onto Ally's chest. A drop of wax rolled to her nipple before it hardened making Ally pull against the restraints. Her body was reacting to the stimulus with a ferocity she didn't expect. She was fully enjoying Sydney's little surprise. Another flow of the wax fell onto her and it landed directly on her nipple, making her cry out. Sydney dripped some water from the pool on the same spot and the combination of hot and cold made Ally shudder with desire.

Sydney drew patterns on her lover's chest and abdomen with the wax until she wanted to do much more than watch her lover squirm; she wanted to take Ally over the edge of reality. She wanted the screams; she needed to hear her name called into the heavens. She ladled more water over Ally's body and rubbed her chest until all the wax fell off her body. The exotic massage had Ally writhing with need. Sydney brought her hands lower to feel Ally's excitement. Not even the pool could wash away her lover's wetness.

Sydney played in Ally's folds of skin and slowly entered her with one teasing finger.

"Oh, sweet Jesus!" Ally screamed out.

Sydney began to thrust slowly into her lover as her thumb stimulated Ally's clitoris. She added another finger to the assault and felt Ally's body grind into her. Her arms were pulling hard on the railing wanting to be free to pull Sydney into her. The excitement of the restraints was almost unbearable...almost.

Sydney slid down and raised Ally's legs over her shoulders. She leaned back pulling on Ally, making the rest of Ally's body buoyant. She kissed her inner thighs and looked into Ally's eyes knowing that it wouldn't take much to bring her to release. Sydney had never seen a more beautiful sight in her life. She leaned forward and licked Ally's sex from the base of her anus to the tip of her clitoris. Ally's body started squirming from the welcomed invasion. Her breath was coming in short pants and Sydney heard her name coming from deep within Ally's throat. Her tongue rapidly moved against Ally's clitoris bringing her closer and closer to release. She drove her fingers deeper inside of Ally as she moved her tongue faster.

"Oh my... Syd...!" Ally shouted out as her release flooded through her body. She hung on to the railing as Sydney continued her assault on her body. Her body shook with every touch from Sydney's mouth and fingers. When Sydney knew her lover had had enough, she slowly lowered Ally's legs back into the water and pressed her body against her. Ally leaned her head against Sydney's head and shoulder in an embrace.

"Please...Sydney, can you take these off now? I need to hold you." Ally pleaded.

"Yes, sweetheart, of course." She reached up to the towel and found the key, releasing Ally's spent arms. Ally brought her arms around Sydney's strong form and held her as tightly as she could.

"That was so amazing," she whispered out. "You're really an incredible lover," she said softly as her emotions came over her.

"Shh, it's okay, sweetie, I've gotcha. Shhh. It was wonderful for me too, baby. To feel you lose all control like that, watching your expressions change, feeling your body finally giving in to me. Jesus...there's no other feeling like it. You're quite a gifted lover yourself." She said, gently kissing her lover's forehead.

೮ ೞ

"I thank God everyday for bringing you to me," Ally crooned, snuggling closer. "You're the most important thing in my life. I don't know what I'd do without you."

"Let's not think about that. Hopefully we won't ever have to find that out." She squeezed Ally to her. "Let's think about something much happier, like your birthday."

"What about my birthday?"

"Is there anything special you want or want to do?"

"I haven't really thought about it. I'm sure you'll think of something though. You, I've found out, are very resourceful." Ally smiled into Sydney's strong embrace.

Yes, I am, and believe me, between Tracey and me, you're going to have the best birthday ever; just you wait. Sydney thought.

☯ ☪

The first night sleeping in Ally's house was a quiet one for the two women, especially Sydney. Even though they fell asleep in the wee hours of the morning, she still woke up with the birds. She wasn't quite sure what to do with herself, since this was the first morning in nearly three years that she didn't have to tend to the horses in Edna's stables. Edna would often ask her to take a vacation, but Sydney would always politely decline.

Sydney decided to get up from under the warm assault of Ally's body. She managed to sneak out of the bed without waking her. There wasn't an easy way to awaken Ally, so she knew she could escape without disturbing her.

She walked downstairs and started to clean up the mess they had made the previous night. The sight in front of her made her smile. Her little surprise had paid off in spades. They had both had a wonderful time, but Sydney still felt a little guilty for not telling Ally everything she'd wanted to. Sydney knew she would probably feel better, but she couldn't stand the thought of what Ally would think of her after she knew what was done to her. She didn't want pity, she just wished all of the past and all of her thoughts of Sharon, would go away.

☯ ☪

Ally opened her eyes and noticed right away that she was alone. At first she was a little unnerved by this, then she figured that Sydney had probably gotten up at dawn as usual.

"Does she ever sleep?" she asked herself, still groggy.

Ally got up and put a pair of shorts on and one of Sydney's large T-shirts and stumbled into the bathroom. After she finished with her morning necessities, she went downstairs in search of Sydney. She found her poolside sunning herself. Ally took in the breathtaking sight before her.

Sydney had donned her black bikini and gone out for a morning swim. She did a few laps then relaxed in the lawn chair to get some sunshine. She felt Ally's presence before Ally even said anything to her.

"Good morning, gorgeous," Sydney greeted.

"How do you do that?" Ally marveled.

"I have many hidden talents." She smiled and squinted up at her friend.

"Yes, and I believe you've shown me some of those." Ally smiled back. "Did you sleep okay?"

"Mmm, yes I did. Your bed is quite comfortable."

"Yeah, I'd forgotten what it felt like," Ally admitted. "I think last night was the first night in weeks that I didn't have a nightmare." Ally gazed lovingly at her partner.

"I was going to say something about that but I didn't want to jinx anything."

"Thanks for noticing."

"Hey, when you're concerned, I always notice," Sydney told her honestly. "In a room of thousands, I'd know if you were missing."

"You are sweet," Ally said, putting her arms around Sydney's neck from behind her chair.

"Yeah, but don't let that get around. I've got a reputation to uphold," the dark-haired woman murmured, stroking the slender arm under her chin.

"Ooh, right, right. Sorry." Ally kissed her cheek.

"Are you hungry, sweetheart? I imagine you've worked up quite an appetite from last night."

"Yeah, and whose fault was that?"

"Oh, I'll take full responsibility for that, with pleasure," Sydney said, giving a full smile to Ally.

"God, you're so beautiful."

"So are you, baby. So are you," Sydney said, caressing the cheek of the face looking down at her. "Let's get some breakfast."

"Sure. You up for going into town? I really don't want to cook."

"All right, let me put something on that's not so revealing, and we can go," Sydney grinned.

"There is a place called The Harbor that I know you will love. They only serve breakfast and lunch, but it's the best food around. They'll make you any kind of egg you can think of. It's great stuff. Ooh, I can't wait," Ally said, clapping and skipping up to the house. Sydney just watched the childlike antics with a huge smile.

Twenty-One

Ally drove into town as though she were visiting for the first time. Her memories of life with her parents seemed so long ago. This was a whole new chapter for her. She was just grateful that Sydney was there with her. They pulled into the small shopping plaza and parked near the restaurant. Ally couldn't believe she was home again.

"God, Sydney, it feels like I've been gone a lifetime. It's so strange to be here again. I didn't get a chance to drive around when I was here last."

"I bet, honey. Did you want to go in?"

"In a sec, I just want to look around for a minute."

Ally walked through the tiny plaza gazing in every window to see if they had changed as much as she had in the last few months. She came across a tiny clothing shop and smiled at Sydney.

"They have the best cashmere sweaters in this place. Mom got me one for Christmas last year that's fabulous."

"Did you want to browse for a while before brunch?" Sydney asked, looking at her watch.

"Nah, I just liked reminiscing," Ally said. "We can go. I'm truly starting to get hungry."

"Okay. I hope there isn't a long wait."

"Hopefully not, but unfortunately this place is usually packed around lunchtime. Lots of business people come from all over just to eat here. It's really great."

"Can't wait, let's go and get our name in." Sydney smiled indulgently at her young partner.

Looking up from her menus, the hostess asked, "How many?"

"Just the two of us," Ally replied.

"Name?"

"McKenna."

"McKenna?" the hostess repeated.

"Yes, Ally McKenna."

"Wow, you probably don't remember me," the hostess began. "Melissa Milo? We went to the high school together."

"Oh, yeah, Melissa," Ally answered. "How are you?" she asked, giving the woman a bright smile.

"I'm doing well. I heard about what happened to your parents," Melissa said sadly. "I'm so sorry. Your father helped a lot of this town's 'Most Stressed.'"

"Thanks. It's been a rough year but I've had a lot of love and support from some really wonderful people. My dad loved what he did and really cared about his patients. I know a lot of people will miss him."

"Yes, that's true," Melissa agreed solemnly. "Umm," she said, scanning her list. "The wait will only be a few more minutes."

"That's all? This placed is jammed." Ally said, looking around the restaurant.

"I'll get you in," the hostess said, winking at Ally. "I've a little bit of an edge over these people."

"Thanks, Melissa."

"Sure, Ally, take care."

"You too, good to see you."

"You too," Melissa replied, walking toward oncoming guests.

"She seemed nice," Sydney commented.

"Yeah, she was extremely quiet in high school. You could be guaranteed a smile from her though if you said hello." She and Sydney moved toward the bench where other patrons waited to be seated. "She was one of those people who you knew would be a loyal friend. You know?"

"Yeah, so why didn't you hang with her?" Sydney asked, relaxing against the leather bench.

"We were in different circles I guess you could say. Funny, I don't really see or talk to any of those people now. My only constant has been Tracey."

"They say people change their ways in time. Those others weren't meant to be your friends," Sydney said quietly, stroking Ally's arm.

"I guess not. I didn't even hear from a lot of them when my parents died."

"That's terrible. I'm sorry."

"What for? I'm much better off without them," Ally said confidently.

A voice came from the front counter. "McKenna, party of two."

"That's us, come on!" Ally jumped from the bench.

"Right behind you." Sydney chuckled at her obviously hungry partner.

The two women were seated in a large booth in the upper level of the restaurant. Sydney looked around in disbelief at a place being so crowded that only served two meals out of the day.

"It's really nice in here," she told Ally.

"Yeah, like I said a lot of people come here from all over," Ally said, scanning the patrons around them. "I think some spend most of their lunch hour in the car to get here."

"Wow, it must have a great reputation," Sydney added.

"Yes, it does and it seems to be growing."

A waitress arrived at their table, "What can I get you ladies? Anything cold to drink today?"

"I'll just have water," Sydney said.

"Will that be bottled, filtered, mineral, carbonated, caffeinated or tap?"

Sydney just stared at Ally with her mouth open and eyes wide. She then returned her stare to the waitress. Ally had to stifle a laugh with her hand.

"Umm, I guess tap is fine."

"Lemon or no lemon?" the waitress asked, scribbling on her notepad.

Christ, I just want a glass of water! She thought to herself. "No lemon...thank you."

"And you miss?" The waitress turned to Ally.

"I'll have what she's having." Ally said.

The waitress flipped her pad closed, smiled, and walked to get their innocuous beverages.

"Oh...my God. All I asked for was water. I never really thought about how many different ways people would drink it. Jesus!" Sydney said, still wide-eyed and chuckling.

Laughing with her, Ally agreed. "I know, I wasn't sure if I should stop her to take a breath or not. Nothing is simple anymore, you know? Not EVEN water." She said, looking at her menu, "What are you going to get?"

"God, I've no idea. If ordering water was this much trouble, I'm afraid to order anything of substance."

Giggling, Ally nudged her gently. "Don't be, just get what you want. I'm sure they can make anything that you like."

"We'll see." Sydney said smiling.

The waitress came back with their glasses of tap water and opened her pad up to take their orders. Her eyes widened with the amount of food that Ally ordered. Sydney struggled through the ordering process and hoped to get her food the way she liked. Ally seemed confident that she would.

"Would you excuse me, Ally," Sydney said a few minutes later. "I'm going to visit the ladies room. Where is it, do you know?"

"Umm...yeah... it's over by the kitchen area," Ally said, pointing discreetly. "See the arrow?"

"Yeah, thanks, baby. See you in a bit."

"Okay." Ally answered, grabbing a package of breadsticks and dipping them into the butter. "Mmm, God, I'm so hungry," she said to the empty seat across from her.

☼ ☾

Sydney walked into the ladies room and used the facilities. She walked out of the stall and began to wash her hands and face at the sink. She rinsed off her face and felt a towel being held out to her. She accepted it and dried her face.

"Thanks..." Her words stopped cold when her eyes met with familiar dark brown ones.

"Hello, Sydney. My, my, my, what a small world it is," Sharon chuckled.

"What the hell are you doing here?" Sydney nearly spat trying to control her emotions.

"Now, Sydney is that anyway to treat an old friend?" Sharon crooned.

"You are NOT my friend. Have you been following me? First the airport and now here? What the hell do you want from me? Answer me!" Sydney sputtered impatiently.

"Following you? My aren't we the arrogant one? Don't flatter yourself darling, I'm here on business."

"Business? You mean you aren't here because of me?" Sydney said in disbelief.

"No, darling. Daddy's little company is planning a merger with one of the big boys of the Midwest. He sent me to..."

"To use your only attribute? He wanted you to seduce the big boys into seeing things *your way*? Right?" Sydney growled disgustedly. "You make me sick!" She tried to push away from the platinum blonde invading her space.

"Oh, Sydney, you can't still be angry with me, can you?" Sharon crooned, sending Sydney's stomach rolling.

"Look, I don't feel anything but pity for you. Is there anything else?"

"Yeah, you can tell me the name of that fine little thing sitting with you. She's the one from the airport isn't she? She was the reason for your teary good-bye, wasn't she?"

Sydney couldn't control her temper any longer. She threw Sharon up against the wall and pinned her forearm under the blonde's throat. "You even *breathe* on her and I'll rip you apart with my bare hands. Do you understand me?"

"That's all right, Sydney, I know all about young Alicia," Sharon taunted her. "Shame what happened to her parents. Tsk, tsk...I bet she's in desperate need of comfort. I'm sure I could..." The cold woman's speech was cut off by added pressure of Sydney's arm at her throat.

"You know what? You have about two seconds to shut the fuck up before I kill your whoring ass," Sydney hissed at the blonde's grinning face. "Leave her alone you psychotic freak or I swear to you..."

Laughing through her gritted teeth. "Oh, Sydney...God, I forgot how sexy you are. Especially when you get angry. Does she see that angry side of you, Sydney? Hmm? Does she know what a bad ass you are Sydney? Does she know about Billy? I bet you didn't tell her about that, did you?" Sharon paused and watched proudly as her words dug into Sydney like daggers.

"Does she see that aggressive sexual side of you? Does she like it rough like I did, Sydney?" The blonde murmured. Sydney's breath was coming in short gusts of emotion. Sharon just laughed and smiled. "Hmm?"

"You stay away from her Sharon. She is NOTHING like you! You harm one hair on her head, I swear to you; I'll make my purpose in life to make yours a living hell. And if you even SPEAK my brother's name again, I'll be your greatest nightmare. I promise you that," she snarled into Sharon's ear.

"Ooh baby, I'm getting so hot. Talk to me some more," she said, licking her lips.

"God, you're disgusting!" Sydney spat, releasing her hold on Sharon. She pointed her finger in warning. "If you do anything or say anything to her, I will come after you," she said and walked out of the ladies room, leaving an amused Sharon behind to straighten her suit. Sharon smiled victoriously at her reflection.

"Oh, Sydney, you ain't seen nothing yet." The blonde woman smiled with aplomb.

ಶ ಛ

Sydney stormed out of the ladies room and stopped to collect herself. She stood behind the wall separating the restrooms from the main room of the restaurant. *This is never going to end is it? God, this is a nightmare!* After taking a few breaths, she made her way back to the table where Ally was seated.

"Hey, sweetie, are you all right? You look a little pale." Ally observed.

"Ally...I..." Sydney started as she sat down.

"Here we are..." The waitress came just as Sydney began to tell Ally what had happened.

"Scrambled eggs, bacon, toast, and an English muffin with strawberry jam." She said, putting Sydney's plate down in front of her.

"And for you, we have a three-egg, four-cheese omelet, a side of bacon, a side of sausage, a small stack of blueberry pancakes, hash browns, an English muffin with grape jelly, a glass of milk, and two glasses of orange juice. Honey, I don't know where you're going to put this, but bon appetit," she said, sauntering off to another table.

"Ooh, look at this! God, I'm so hungry. Dig in, sweetheart," Ally said excitedly as she began to eat as if she hadn't in a week.

Sydney watched the younger woman consume huge amounts of food as she sat and stared at her full plate.

"Shydnee, are yooo k?" Ally said with a partially full mouth as she noticed Sydney not eating.

"Yeah, um, I think I lost my appetite," Sydney said nervously. "I'm not feeling that well all of a sudden. Maybe it's a little flu left from last night." She lied.

"Oh, honey, I'm sorry. I forgot about that. God, I'm so sorry. We can take this to go so we can get back home." Ally compromised.

"NO!" Sydney snapped, then softened her tone. "Please, finish your meal. You know how much I love to watch you eat." Sydney tried to smile sincerely but it just wasn't happening, and Ally saw right through it.

"What's wrong, honey? Please tell me." Ally almost pleaded.

"I'll tell you, but just not here and not now," Sydney promised shakily. "When the time is right, Ally, when the time is right," Sydney explained.

"Okay, I'll hold you to that. You can tell me anything. It won't change the way I feel about you, nothing could."

"Thanks, sweetheart, I don't know what I would do without you." She reached across the table to hold Ally's hand.

Sharon strolled out of the ladies room and glanced up at Sydney. They made eye contact; Sharon winked at her, smiled, then strut out of the restaurant. Sydney swallowed her emotions, watching Sharon leave. She gently caressed Ally's hand. Ally looked up from her meal and smiled at Sydney. She continued to devour the food in front of her until there was nothing but crumbs left. The waitress came by, stared in disbelief, and took Ally's empty plates. She tossed away Sydney's uneaten eggs as per Sydney's request. *Who likes to eat reheated eggs anyway?* Sydney thought.

Ally and Sydney walked up to the counter and Sydney insisted on paying for their meal. With a final huff, Ally agreed to let her pay and they left the restaurant. The two were quiet on the way home and Ally couldn't help but wonder what had set Sydney off. *She's never like this,* Ally thought. She looked over at her partner and saw the lost look on her face as she stared out the window.

What's going on with you, baby? God, I wish you would just tell me. It can't be that bad. It can't be... Ally continued her contemplation as they pulled into her driveway.

Twenty-Two

Ally went into the garage to get the last of the boxes to pack up the rest of her things. She'd decided with Edna that the best way to handle all of the furniture in the house was to have an estate sale. Whatever she could sell she would and whatever she couldn't she would donate or throw away. She had gone through quite a bit before moving to Montana, but there was more than ten years worth of stuff here. The service Tracey hired had been a huge help.

Her mother's jewelry and clothing had been sorted and given away. What people hadn't wanted she'd donated to the Salvation Army. She'd kept her mother's wedding ring set for herself. It was always a favorite of hers and she knew her mom would have wanted her to have it. There were a few items of her clothing that had extreme sentimental value to them, so she kept those as well. Her mother had recently gone to Paris and had brought back some wonderful perfume, Boucheron. On days when Ally really missed her, she would spray it into the air just to have her mother's scent nearby.

Ally cleaned out her parent's room in a few hours while Sydney decided to take care of the living and dining rooms downstairs. Sydney took this time to wonder why Sharon was in town and how she knew about Ally. She was shaking with feelings she hadn't felt in a long time. She was angry, nervous, and most of all, she was in shock. Seeing Sharon was not on her things-to-do list and the confrontation was still playing with her head.

God, what the hell is she doing here anyway? Sydney wondered. *How does she know about Alicia and what happened to her parents? It's not like she gives a shit about the human race, well only if she gets to sleep with them. Uugghhh, why the hell did she have to show up again and here of all places?* Sydney's mind was reeling as Ally walked downstairs to meet her.

"Hey, baby, feeling any better?" Ally asked sympathetically.

"Yeah, I guess a little," Sydney lied.

"Are you hungry? I could make you something to eat since you didn't get anything at the restaurant."

"No, sweetheart, that's okay, I don't really feel up to eating. Did you talk to Tracey? Does she want to go out this evening?"

"I did get a chance to talk with her briefly after lunch but her new girlfriend wants to spend time with her. So, I guess it's just you and me tonight."

"Ohh, new girlfriend eh? Is she cute?"

Ally wiggled her eyebrows. "Well, according to Trace, she's a 'hotty'. I guess they finally had sex, which is weird, I think."

"Sex with your girlfriend is weird?" Sydney quipped, one eyebrow drifting upward. "Um, I think you had better talk to mine then, 'cause she kind of likes that."

Laughing, Ally poked her playfully. "Ha, ha. No, I mean it's kinda soon for Tracey. She's the type to wait a while before making that kind of commitment. She's only known this woman, um, Char I think her name is, for a couple weeks."

"Alicia, I hate to break it to you, but you and I made love within days of knowing each other," Sydney reminded her.

"I know, but I'm not Tracey, nor do I think it is the same. Char, is a business associate of Tracey's. They've only really seen each other a few times."

"Oh, so she's isn't from around here?" Sydney asked.

"No, I think she is on the West Coast somewhere," Ally stated. "LA maybe? I don't remember. Anyway, she just arrived and is actually staying for a week or so this time, so maybe we'll get to meet her."

"Great, maybe we can get together or something with them for dinner or what not."

"I think that's a great idea. I really want to meet the woman who made Tracey's morals go right down the crapper!" Ally giggled with a large smile.

"Well, I'm sure she is something else if she broke down Tracey's walls so easily."

"Well, I guess we have to wait to find out."

"Yep," Sydney agreed. "Ah, I got most of these rooms in boxes for the sale. Did you want any of these knick-knacks?" she asked, indicating the collection. "There're some really nice porcelain statues and things here."

"No, I pretty much went through and kept all that I wanted to keep, as did Edna," Ally said. "The rest of the family really didn't come around that much so I don't plan on giving it to them. I think I'd rather sell or donate the rest. Mom used to give to Good Will all the time. I'm sure they'll take most of it." Her green eyes scanned the room. "It looks so damn empty in here. It's like someone else's house."

Sydney wrapped her arms around her partner. "I know, baby. How are you holding up? Can I do anything for you?" Sydney asked sincerely.

"You being here with me is all I'll ever need," Ally told her. "Thanks for coming here with me. I'm not sure I'd be this together had you not."

"Where you go, I go, get used to it," Sydney said. .

"That's easy enough." Ally tightened her hold on her. *I love you, baby.* She thought to herself.

ONE WEEK LATER

"So, everything is a go for tomorrow night?" Sydney asked Tracey, speaking into the phone quietly. She checked the hallway for her young lover.

"Yes, I've called all of our friends and Edna should arrive early tomorrow morning. I'll pick her up from the airport and keep her with me until the evening. Are you sure our little friend has no idea?" Tracey inquired insistently.

"No, Tracey," Sydney assured her. "She hasn't the foggiest. I can't wait! This is perfect. I think a night spent with old friends in celebration will be exactly what she needs to give her some kind of closure here. And Tracey?" Sydney prompted.

"Yeah?" She responded.

"Thank you for this. You are truly a good friend. I can see why Ally speaks so highly of you."

"Right back at'cha, babe. She's so crazy about you. And I've never seen her this happy," Tracey said sincerely.

"I really care about Alicia," Sydney said soberly. "I wouldn't hurt her for anything in the world. I'd rather...spit on the Pope than break her heart."

"That's a lovely visual." Tracey's laugh floated over the line. "But I get your meaning."

"All right then. I guess the last thing is to make sure we have enough to drink, the catering place knows the time and place," Sydney decided. "This is going to be a night that we all will remember, for a long time."

"I hope so, Sydney."

"Me too. I've gotta run. Ciao." Sydney hung up abruptly.

"Ciao?" Tracey smirked, hanging up the phone. "Ally, you've got yourself an incredible woman," she said, snuggling up to Char. "And so do I." Tracey kissed the smiling face looking up at her. "Babe, you're going to love Ally and Sydney. They are so awesome. I can't wait. Ally is going to be so surprised!"

So is Sydney, Sharon thought with a smirk. "I can't wait to see her expression! God, how I love surprises." Although it was Sydney's surprise Sharon was after, not Ally's.

"Me too, Char, me too."

☼ ☾

Tracey had met Char through Backburn Inc., a small software company looking to expand to the Midwest. Char had come into Chicago to make a play for Tracey's company. Tracey, as one of the research managers had decided to meet with the saleswoman to talk about the woman's father's ideas about expanding to the Midwest. They'd met a few weeks earlier and had seen each other a few times to discuss their companies and what they might offer one another. At a restaurant the two women discussed many things outside of work. They discovered they both enjoyed the company of women and so they made a point to see each other the next time Char came into town. Tracey couldn't wait. Char was a beautiful woman, blonde hair, deep brown eyes, and a beautifully shaped mouth. She stood about five feet eight inches and had absolutely no body fat. To Tracey, she wreaked perfection.

Char increased her trips to Chicago to check the status of their merger and, of course, to see Tracey. The two were fast becoming more than friends. The distance was the only thing to come between them. Tracey and Char consummated their relationship after Char's third visit to Chicago. Tracey was not one for casual sex, but there was nothing casual about Char. She was extraordinarily exciting.

Everything about her was a mystery to Tracey. She seemed very elusive about her past, it was obvious she'd been hurt and did not want to reopen old wounds. After Tracey had unsuccessfully asked her about it, she decided to leave well enough alone. She just wanted to enjoy what little time they had together. Tracey was so excited about her enigmatic lover; she couldn't wait for Ally to meet her. Tracey had phoned Ally to tell her about Char the day they'd met.

"Hello?" Ally answered.

"Hey, baby!"

"Trace! How are you, honey?"

"I'm really good. How are you doing?" Tracey asked tenderly.

"Things are all right, Tracey. They get better each day," Ally told her friend. "Sydney has been a great support to me. I can't wait for you two to meet. You're going to love her!"

"Well, I have some news myself," Tracey announced.

"Do you? Who did you meet and where?" Ally laughed, knowing full well it had to be a woman.

"Ally, God, she is such a hotty!" Tracey gushed. "She's like five-foot-eight, blonde with brown eyes, and a body to die for. There is no pinchability on this woman. The girl is tight!" she said exuberantly.

"Wow, Trace, she sounds fabulous," Ally said. "I can't wait to meet her. Where'd you guys hook up?"

"Wanna hear something funny?" Tracey giggled. "We met at work. I was just saying how horrid it was working here since there was no eye candy, then in walks Char. God, she took my breath away. Girl, she is soooo sexy. She could turn any straight woman, I'm sure of it. Goddamn!"

"Trace, sounds like you've got a keeper there," Ally laughed. "So, have you gone out yet? Like on a date or anything?"

"Well, that's the problem. We went out once to a restaurant after one of our meetings and we just clicked. We talked about everything," Tracey told her. "I talked about you and Sydney and how long you and I have known each other. I mean we just talked and talked. I haven't met a woman who could hold a conversation like that in a long time. I was ready to swear off intelligent women because I didn't think they existed anymore!" The two friends chuckled to each other. "No, seriously she is really amazing, Ally."

"I'm so happy for you," Ally told her friend. "But wait, you mentioned a problem?"

"Oh yeah, um well, she lives in California," Tracey admitted. "She works for a small software company that wants to move to the Midwest. So we're looking to do a small expansion to bring them over here. Blah, blah you don't need to hear that part; that's the boring stuff. So she came out here to talk to some companies and she found us. The rest is history," Tracey raced on, then paused a moment. "So the problem is, she lives across the country. I don't know if I'm up for a long distance relationship. I mean, part of me says 'Man, go get her.' then the sensible part of me says 'No, it'll be too hard on you.' I don't know what to do, but for right now, she's all I can think about." Tracey's voice eventually wound down.

"Well," Ally started to suggest. "See what happens the next time she comes into town and play it from there."

"I guess you're right, but man! My luck, huh? I finally find a 'Woo!' girl and she lives two thousand miles away."

"I'm sorry, Trace. Um, on a happier note, I'll be back home soon to pack up the rest of the house."

"Really? That's awesome! I'll get to spend more time with you this time."

"Yeah, I can't wait. You'll get to meet my girl, too!"

"Kick ass! I can't wait to see you. I can't wait to meet Sydney. She sounds wonderful."

"She is, Trace, she is. But ah, I gotta get going so I'll call you with information and flights, okay?"

"Okay, hon, take care of yourself. I love you," Tracey said.

"I love you, too, Trace. I'll talk with you soon. Bye."

"Bye."

ಬಿ ಛ

"Who was that on the phone, hon?" Ally asked a startled Sydney.

"Um, it was Tracey, I thought you were going to take a nap?" Sydney quickly replied.

"No, I couldn't sleep. What did she want?"

"Well, she wanted to see what we were doing tomorrow night. I guess she wants to introduce her new girlfriend to us."

"Oh, cool! I should call her back," Ally said excitedly.

"No!" Ally raised her eyebrows at Sydney's tone of voice. Thinking quickly Sydney softened her voice, "Um, well she said they were going out and she'd call you in the morning or something."

Sighing, Ally acquiesced. "All right, I guess I'll talk to her tomorrow then." Then she took a look around and realized the entire downstairs had been cleaned. "My goodness, Sydney. Look at all the work you did. This place is immaculate. You can actually hear an echo now. Thank you so much for all of your help. I couldn't have done all of this without you."

"You're most welcome sweetheart," Sydney told her, rubbing Ally's back gently. "I just want everything to go smoothly and as pain-free as possible for you. I know how hard this must be. I remember when we had to pack up my mom's belongings. It was really hard on my brother and me. She was all we had left after dad and...um...well after he died. I can't imagine what you must be going through. I, at least had Tim."

"Well, Miss Sydney, I have you, Eddi, and Tracey. So I think I'm doing just fine. Thank you for your concern though," she said, circling her arms around Sydney's larger frame and laying her head against her chest.

"You're welcome, baby." Sydney murmured into Ally's hair. They sat like that for several minutes and enjoyed the peace that passed between them.

ೞ 03

Sydney couldn't wait for the festivities to begin. She was determined to make this the best birthday Ally ever had. She was fighting a mental battle with herself and decided that she was going to bite the bullet and tell Ally that she loved her tonight.

Sydney had purchased Ally's birthday present when Ally was sleeping in, having found her way into town and to the jewelers. Her eyes had immediately fixated on a simple gold band with several tiny diamonds embedded in it.

"Oh, I like that one, may I see it please?" Sydney had pointed inside the glass case.

"Absolutely, it is quite an eye catcher." The jeweler had opened the case, taken out the ring, and handed it to Sydney.

Sydney fingered the small band and decided it was simple yet classy, just like Ally. It was perfect.

"Can I have it engraved today? I need it for tonight."

"As luck would have it, my engraver is working today which is rare for a Saturday," the jeweler told her. "Let me ask him if he has anything else lined up." He had smiled warmly at his customer. "Just give me a minute, I'll be right back." He took the ring in question with him to the back of the store. He went into the storeroom and looked for his employee.

Several moments had passed when the stocky man returned with a smile on his face.

"Well ma'am, you're in luck. He said he would take care of this for you while you waited. Do you have a few minutes?"

Excitedly, Sydney nodded her head. "Yes, I do, thank you so very much. This will mean a great deal to a very special person." She gave the man a dazzling smile, which appeared to hypnotize him.

Shaking himself out of his reverie, the man began filling out the invoice. Sydney gave him Ally's ring size and what she wanted engraved. Within a half-hour she had her gift and was on her way home.

"Now if I can keep my courage up, I'll give it to her tonight," Sydney thought, driving back to the house. "I don't know what I'm worried about," she chided herself. "Alicia is nothing like Sharon. I just have to keep reminding myself of that. They are nothing alike, thank God," Sydney breathed, pulling into the driveway.

She parked the car in the garage and went into the house to wake her sleeping woman. She walked up the stairs and into Ally's room to find a breathtaking view. Ally had rolled onto her stomach and was clutching her pillow. The lovely, naked form was covered only from her waist down. One knee was sticking out of the sheet and hanging slightly over the bed's edge. Golden locks spilled down the slender back and shoulders with a few stray strands falling over the young face. The vision was absolutely beautiful. Suddenly Sydney's fears all seemed to disappear. Seeing this angel before her completely dissolved any reservations she'd had in proclaiming her love.

After taking a moment to memorize every curve of Ally's lithe form, she decided to kick off her shoes and curl up next to her.

Ally immediately felt Sydney's presence and rolled her back into Sydney's front. Sydney's arm draped around Ally's waist in reflex and the rest of her body spooned into Ally's back. It was a perfect fit.

Sydney just lay there, enjoying the wonderful scent that was Ally. Her hair smelled like flowers and her body emitted a fragrance that was crisp and clean. Sydney would have stayed like that all morning, but Ally stirred awake and rolled towards her.

"Mm, good morning, sweetheart," Ally sleepily said.

"Good morning, sleepyhead. Did you sleep well?"

"Mmhmm, I did. I've slept so well since coming home," Ally yawned. "I hope I don't get spoiled by this."

"I think you've just been really tired. We've been doing a lot since we got here. You're just tuckered out." Sydney stroked the soft blonde hair.

"Perhaps. Have you been up long?"

"Nah, just an hour or so. I couldn't resist coming back to snuggle with you. You looked so damn cute."

Ally just buried her nose into Sydney's chest and inhaled deeply. She loved the way this woman smelled. She had a wonderful musk about her that was all her own. It was intoxicating as well as arousing. She was aware of Sydney's fingernails moving up and down her back and she felt the gooseflesh rising. The touches became more urgent as did the need to be one with each other.

Ally tilted her head up and captured Sydney's wanting mouth with her own. Their tongues instantly sought out the others. They tenderly stroked each other's tongues and nipped at each other's lips. Ally caught Sydney's bottom lip and began to suck on it. She pressed her mouth fully against Sydney's again and felt a bolt of desire wash over her. Sydney caught Ally's moan in her mouth and immediately wanted to be naked against this woman.

Ally looked into deep stormy blue eyes and knew that breakfast was not going to be an option this morning until much, much later.

☙ ❧

"Okay, Edna, I'm gonna take her out for about an hour, I'll make something up," Sydney into the phone spoke quietly. "I know, I'll make her take me to the beach. She wanted to go there yesterday, and I wasn't in the mood. So I'll make her take me there while you guys pile into the house." Sydney spent a moment scanning the part of the house she could see. "The caterers will get here shortly after we leave. We just need to check on the beverages. I ordered a bunch from Terry's Liquors and we just need to pick it up," she said into the phone again. "I couldn't very well bring a bunch of alcohol into the house without explanation. After we surprise her, I'll run out and get the drinks. Sound like a plan?"

"Okay, Syd, this is going to be so great," Edna's warm voice came through the receiver. "It sounds like you have it planned and ready to go. She's going to be so surprised! Tracey and I'll be around the corner. We'll watch for your car to leave and we'll pull up, so make sure you don't forget anything, okay?"

"All right, Edna, I'm so glad that you could make it," Sydney told the older woman. "You being here will make it all that much more special for her. She loves you so much."

"I know. I can say the same about you dear," Edna replied.

Sydney could feel the blush creep up her neck. "Thanks for saying so, Edna. I'll see you all in about two hours. Hey, is Tracey's girlfriend coming too?" Sydney asked as an afterthought. "I know that Ally is really looking forward to meeting her."

"Yes, she will be there later," Edna assured her. "Tracey said she had some things to do beforehand, so she wouldn't be able to make it in time for the surprise."

"Well, at least she's coming. Okay, let me think here for a sec," Sydney paused a moment to do so. She let out a short breath. "I do believe that's everything. I'll see you soon, Edna."

"Okay, dear, make this work, dammit. I didn't make this detour for nothin'!" she kidded.

"No problem. Ally has no idea. I gotta run...she's out of the shower, the water just turned off. Bye," Sydney whispered quickly and gently hung up the receiver.

Sydney took one last look around and saw that none of the party favors were in sight. She smiled to herself and went upstairs into Ally's bedroom to change and wait for her love to exit the bathroom.

The door opened and steam billowed from the bathroom. Ally walked into her room to find Sydney dressing and smirking at her with her jeans part way open.

"Well, don't you look like the cat who just swallowed the canary? What's up with that smirk?" Ally teased.

"Nothin, baby, you just look so damn sexy, I can't help myself," Sydney purred.

"Mmhhmm, whatever you say. You look great, Sydney. Are we going somewhere?"

"I'm not sure yet, but I thought you liked it when I dressed like this," Sydney smiled at her lover.

"When you wear those black jeans, you have the greatest butt in the world. It makes me want to squeeze it!" Ally grinned devilishly.

"I think we have squeezed enough body parts for one day, don't you?" Sydney laughed, batting Ally's hands away from her behind.

"Says you! I could do it all day long. You must be getting old."

"Old my ass, I'll show you old!" Sydney laughed and threw Ally on the bed and began tickling her mercilessly. Ally tried really hard to pretend that it had no effect on her but she couldn't fake it for long.

"I GIVE!" Ally panted. "Please...oh, Syd...stop...please!" She managed to get out between giggle fits.

Sydney ceased her attack and gently kissed Ally's cheek. She helped her up and walked to the closet to look for an outfit for Ally to wear. Ally jumped into the bathroom to dry her hair and apply a small amount of makeup to her face. When she was finished she went back to her room and found Sydney holding up some clothing.

"I'd like you to wear this tonight," Sydney said, her blue eyes soft.

"Sydney, what's going on? Are you taking me to dinner?"

"Mmmaaaybe," Sydney drawled out. "We haven't heard from Tracey yet about her meeting up with us, so I figured we should get ready anyway. If she doesn't call we'll go out, just the two of us. If she does call, we still go out. Sound good?"

"Sure, I never knew you liked these pants so much. I'd have worn them more often," Ally purred seductively.

"Well, speaking of nice butts, yours looks fabulous in those black slacks. I like the vest with that shirt, too." Sydney pointed as Ally dressed under instruction for the first time since the first grade.

"Shoes, Miss Sydney?" Ally asked in a very young voice. "Which shoes?"

"No shoes, wear your black boots. That will finish it off just right." Sydney said, watching Ally put the finishing touches on her outfit.

"See now? You've brought a little bit of the country home to you. You are beautiful, Alicia." Sydney said, kissing her gently on the lips.

Ally turned around in the mirror to see what Sydney saw in her. She had on a pair of black pants, a long-sleeved, white, collarless shirt with her sleeves rolled up, a black vest and black boots. "I look like an outlaw," she joked. "All I need is a black cowboy hat and a trusty steed and I'll be on my way!"

"You look very sexy, trust me," Sydney told her. "Although, seeing you on a horse always has been a favorite of mine. It must be looking at your legs straddling something that really gets me going."

"You are incorrigible, Sydney Thompson!" Ally laughed heartily.

"Always. Now let me get finished here."

Sydney went to the closet again and pulled out a finely knit, gray, cropped V-Neck short sleeved sweater and pulled it over her head. It fit snugly against her muscular torso and showed her belly when she raised her arms. She wrapped a black, braided belt through her belt loops and looked for the right shoes. She slipped on a pair of black loafers and brushed her hair so it loosely fell across her back. She added a little color to her lips and eyes and she was ready.

Ally took a breath and slowly let it out. Sydney's raven hair along with her cerulean eyes and dark clothing made her look like nothing Ally had ever seen before. Sydney was stunning.

"I thought we could take a drive down to that beach you wanted to show me," Sydney said. "I'll bet the colors down there are beautiful this time of year."

"Oh, Sydney, that would be wonderful. It is gorgeous around this time. You really want to? It may get a little chilly," Ally warned.

"Well, that's why I'll have you on my arm, to keep me warm," Sydney answered before she gave Ally a full smile that melted the young girl's heart. "Come on then, let's get this night underway."

"After you, my dear." Ally gestured towards the stairs.

The two walked arm in arm down the stairs and grabbed their jackets. They got into the car and pulled slowly out of the driveway. Once they'd rounded the corner, Tracey and Edna pulled into the driveway and headed up to the house. There was a lot to do in the next hour to make this a night to remember.

Twenty-Three

Ally drove down the winding road toward the beach. The steep incline made two cars passing one another nearly impossible. Ally could tell Sydney was a little unnerved, so she held onto her hand until she felt the taller woman calm.

"It's okay, hon, I've driven down here a million times. Relax," Ally soothed.

"It's just such a sharp curve on such a hill," Sydney said through gritted teeth. "It's kinda scary, don't you think?" Sydney asked, peering out the window.

"Yeah, at first I'd always make Tracey drive because I was afraid I'd hit someone. The more I drove it, the more at ease I became," Ally explained.

"Well, I, for one, am glad that you're driving. I think I'd be too preoccupied with the view." She turned her attention to the scenery outside. "This is really pretty, Alicia."

"It should be, they spent over eight million dollars on the restoration of it," Ally remarked dryly.

"Eight...million...dollars?" Sydney gasped.

"Yeah, see what happens when you get a roomful of bored, retired, millionaires together? They even made the city pay for it. Like they just couldn't reach into their little mad money jars and pay for it themselves. Some of the people in this town make me crazy."

"Wow, I can see why. Why did your parents stay here? I would have been dying to get away from here."

"It was a safe place to bring up children; there isn't much crime here. My dad's practice was here, and mom liked to golf at the club, which is only a mile or so away from home. They had a good life, why would they leave?"

"I guess you're right. Did you like this place growing up?" Sydney asked.

"It had its moments, but all in all, I've always liked this place a lot," Ally admitted. "It's very beautiful here, and how many towns are there, where it's safe to walk just about anywhere, without being bothered by someone? It's really expensive to live here, though. I'm very lucky that my parents were able to give me the life that I had."

"It's nice that you see that," Sydney told her. "Some people, when they are born into money don't feel quite the same way as you do. A lot of people expect to be catered to or just don't know how to do anything for themselves." Sydney smiled at her partner. "You're so not like that. I can't tell you how happy that makes me."

"I'm glad, Sydney. I don't know if I could ever be like that." Ally shook her blonde head slightly. "My whole high school class seemed to be filled with people like that. Let's just say that I'm very happy I didn't turn out that way." Ally paused when she remembered something from her past. "You know what? Okay, these are the kind of people that I went to school with, ready?"

"Sure, tell me," Sydney said with amusement. She shifted in her seat to watch Ally's face become more and more animated.

"I had a locker that was next to one of the more popular girls in my grade. I think her name was Jordan DuBois, or something ridiculous like that. Anyway, she would keep an extra outfit in her locker, just in case someone was wearing what she had on that day," Ally finished and Sydney's eyes shot wide open in disbelief.

"You have GOT to be kidding me," Sydney squawked.

"I wish I was, but that isn't even the horrible part," Ally laughed, a bit embarrassed herself.

"Oh God, there's more?" Sydney groaned.

"Yeah, so brace yourself." Ally giggled.

"Okay," Sydney said while smiling and gripping onto the dashboard.

"One day, I was in the commons area and I was near the phones. I saw Jordan on the phone and she was starting to raise her voice. Well, being the nosy body that I am, I slowly walked over to the phone next to her and pretended to use it. You know, just so I could listen." Ally paused and Sydney nodded in acknowledgment.

"So anyway, she was talking to her mother and she was bitching about the fact that someone had on the same outfit she had on. Well, her mother said to change into her other outfit. Jordan said that she had done that already, and it was her second outfit that this person was wearing. So she asked her mother to bring her a *third* outfit so she could change."

"OH, MY GOD! My mother would have laughed at me and hung up the phone."

"Yeah, no shit, so guess what?"

"I'm afraid to know anymore," Sydney replied while chuckling through hands that now covered her face.

"Well, you guessed it, her mother came to school and dropped off another outfit for 'Miss Priss' to wear!"

"I cannot believe that!" Sydney's voice rose in surprise.

"Yeah well, believe it, because it's true," Ally said without humor. "And I think she bitched at her mom because it was wrinkled or some shit, and her mom apologized and promised to take her out to the mall after school."

"Jesus! That's exactly what I'm talking about! You're so lucky that you didn't turn out that way. I may have had to kill you." Sydney growled jokingly.

"Believe me, I would have killed myself," Ally agreed and slowed the car into a parking space.

Ally and Sydney walked to the brick path just short of the sand leading to the water. They stood next to each other just admiring the view. The sun had begun its descent leaving a beautiful trail of color its wake. The water glistened with the light of the upcoming night's sky. It was truly a sight to behold. Ally had never seen a sky like this one. She felt as if it were smiling upon her. She felt a warm calm wash over her and goose bumps trail up her arms. She took in a sharp breath of air and suddenly tears began to roll down her cheeks. Ally smiled at the sky knowing her parents were the cause of this phenomenon. Sydney looked away from the view, saw Ally weeping, and wrapped her arms around her.

"What's wrong, baby?" Sydney asked, kissing the top of Ally's head.

Sniffling, Ally whispered. "Sydney, I just felt my parents surround me. It was like all of a sudden I couldn't breathe, and then a warmth ran through me. Then I took in a quick breath and I could faintly smell them." She hugged Sydney tighter. "It probably happened in like two seconds, but my God, Sydney, I know it was them," Ally sobbed into Sydney's embrace.

"The people who love you will always be with you Alicia," Sydney gently told her. "Death doesn't even stop that; at least *I* don't think so. I believe in souls, I believe in angels, and I do believe that you're watched by loved ones who have passed on. It doesn't surprise me that you felt them. You must have fond memories of the beach with your folks," Sydney said, stroking Ally's hair with her fingers.

"I do. They used to take me here all the time in the summer. I'd swim, and mom would help me build sandcastles, and then dad would let us bury him occasionally," Ally spoke quietly, then took a deep breath. "They were the sweetest people Syd. My mom was the most wonderful woman that I've ever known. I could only dream of being the mother she was."

"Alicia, you have the biggest heart I've ever seen. There is no doubt in my mind, that if you have children, you would be a wonderful mother," Sydney assured her. She gently took Ally's face in her hands. "I feel lucky to have met you, Alicia. There aren't many hearts like yours. I feel honored that you chose to share some of it with me."

Ally looked up into the deep pools of blue and felt the love pass through them. Sydney had to fight back the tears threatening to blow her cool exterior. She resumed her hold on Ally and felt the younger woman snuggle back against her chest. Sydney hoped that Ally didn't hear her racing heartbeat. She was so scared about her feelings towards Ally. She loved this woman with her entire being and she was going to tell her tonight.

Tracy and Edna were racing around the kitchen finding bowls and platters for the caterers. The food came on time and so did most of the guests. The family room was filled with people who loved Ally and a few that just liked her a whole lot. There were people she hadn't seen in a long while; some since before her parents died.

Tracey was a wreck; she wanted everything to go well. She wanted her friend to have the best birthday ever. Edna just sat and watched as Tracey continued running from room to room making sure everything was perfect.

"If anyone sees headlights, let me know. Everyone is here except for Ally and Sydney. So shush everyone when they arrive." Everyone looked at the crazed woman and smiled. Tracey ran around again to double and triple checking everything, making sure that nothing was left undone before they arrived. The house was ready for Ally. She was going to have the best birthday party ever, if Tracey had any say in this matter at all.

Sydney continued to hold Ally as the rest of the daylight was engulfed into the lake. She knew tonight was going to be something special, but she couldn't erase the fact that Sharon was around. Business or not, she hoped that the evil woman would be leaving shortly. *How does she know about Alicia? Why was she here? Why did she follow me?* Sydney's brain hammered nervously. *How does she know of her parents' death? She had just better stay away from her,* Sydney thought angrily. *She's a selfish, money hungry bitch that knows nothing of the value of the human heart—especially a heart like Alicia's. She'd just better stay away.* Sydney's body stiffened while thinking about Sharon. Ally looked up at her lover with concern in her eyes.

"What is it, honey? You seem very uncomfortable. Are you okay?" Ally asked.

"I, ah, I was just thinking, baby, I'm sorry. I was thinking of my past and how lucky I am to have you," Sydney improvised. "Sometimes I look back at the person I was and then I look at you, and wonder if I really deserve you."

Ally straightened herself in Sydney's hold and held Sydney's shoulders to gain her full attention.

"Now you look here, Sydney Thompson," Ally said seriously. "Don't you ever let me hear that out of your mouth again. You deserve to be happy and to be loved by someone. Everyone deserves some kind of happiness in life. If I can be the one to give you that love and happiness, then I'm going to do just that. Why would you say something like that?"

Sydney just shrugged, "I guess I'm waiting for all of this to blow up," she admitted. "I've never felt about anyone the way I feel about you, Alicia. I never thought I was worthy of such a gift. The last woman I was with…" Sydney stopped, not wanting to bring all of this up on Ally's birthday night.

"Come on, Sydney, I know you're holding something back from me. You have to know by now that you can tell me anything." She looked up into troubled blue eyes. "And I know you feel you will shatter me with whatever it is that you're keeping to yourself, but please know that whatever it is, we will get through it, I promise you," she pleaded with Sydney to understand.

"Don't make promises you can't keep, Alicia," Sydney murmured, her tone hesitant.

"I've never made a promise to you that I didn't keep. I never intend to break any promise that I've made to you, ever." Ally's tone was firm.

Sydney's gaze was fixed on the lovely scene before them. Finally she met her partner's soft green eyes. "All right then, I'll tell you as much as I can for right now okay?"

"Whatever you'd like to share is all that I ask, Sydney. I just want to help you with these demons that seem to be plaguing you."

"You are such a find, Alicia," Sydney said somewhat awed. "I can't tell you that enough."

Ally hugged Sydney one more time and they walked to a nearby bench. Sydney really didn't want to spoil Ally's evening, but to deny this woman anything was something Sydney didn't want to do, either.

Sydney took a deep breath and started to tell her tale of woe.

"Well, as you know, many years ago, my parents died. What I didn't mention to you was that I had a brother."

"Tim? Sydney, you've told me so much about Tim."

"Alicia, if I tell you this, it will be much easier to just say it and have you ask questions later, is that all right?" Sydney said in a strained voice.

"All right, honey, I'm sorry," Ally conceded. "Go on. Please."

"Tim is my brother, yes, but I had another brother, Billy, who died about two years after my dad did." She paused to see the sadness in Ally's eyes. It was sadness for Sydney that Ally felt. Sydney took another breath and continued. "Anyway I was an angry person after my dad passed away. I didn't understand why people that we loved had to leave us. It didn't make sense to me and I became very angry and I hung out with a bad bunch of people," Sydney said, her eyes lowered to the ground beneath their feet. She kept her hands on the edge of the bench.

"They made me feel like I belonged to something, that we could do anything, that we were in control, and nothing could hurt us. I guess I needed some reassurance that I'd never be out of control again. This I could handle, and no one was going to take that from me." Sydney's voice turned defiant.

"If there were people out there that challenged us and the way we thought, well we would just change their minds. I'm sure you know they weren't peaceful negotiations that took place." Sydney stopped to register Ally's reaction to her admission. Ally just studied Sydney's face and wondered how she changed so much in ten years.

"Anyway, like I said," Sydney went on. "I was a very angry person back then. When Billy died, I turned into something even worse. I was my own worst enemy. Everything I touched, everything I loved was leaving me and I only knew one thing that would release the pain that I felt. It was pure violence. Everything that I did was nothing short of...psychotic." Sydney's hands moved to her lap, the fingers twisting together. "I didn't know the person I used to be. I just became this...thing that destroyed or abused anything or anyone that got in my way of thinking or feeling or doing." She raised one hand to her forehead, as if to rub away her painful memories.

"Then when my mom died it finally hit me; I had no control over anything." Sydney's hand dropped back into her lap, the fingers twisting together again. "All the people that I'd hurt, all the damage I'd done was all for nothing. So I guess it was at that time when I finally realized that all I'd done for the past four years was become a stupid, worthless bully. I had no self-respect anymore. I didn't like the person I'd become. It was truly time for a life makeover." Sydney took a very deep breath. "So, that's when I made up with my brother and decided to go to University and work on the sheep station." Sydney paused to let Ally soak in everything she had told her. She knew that she needed to finish her tale, but she just wasn't sure if she could muster the courage.

"Sydney? May I say something?" Ally said, looking at the pained face of her lover.

"Sure," Sydney answered uncertainly, giving a half smile. She held her breath, almost dreading what Ally might say after what she'd just heard. She raised her eyes to meet the girl's green gaze.

"I know you think you probably just dropped a huge bomb on me and now is the time when I'll just run for cover," Ally paused, watching her lover intently. "Well, let me reassure you again, that I love you. I know it's hard for you to hear that, but sweetheart I can't hold it in any longer. I've never loved anyone the way I love you. You make me a whole person. In a sense you complete me. I know that there is more to your story, and I will listen to every word you speak, but please know that I'll never stop loving you."

Ally stopped to brush the fresh tears that were falling freely down Sydney's cheeks. She took the cherished face in her hands and looked her square in the swollen blue eyes.

"I love you, Sydney." Ally said again and sealed it with a soul-binding kiss. "Know that I'll always love you. You don't have to keep anything from me. In fact I'd prefer that you didn't, but I know that you're hurting from something, and if you can't tell me now, I do trust you enough to know that one day you will." Ally waited for Sydney to regain her composure, to make sure the dark-haired woman understood her clearly.

"Now, if you want, you can keep going with your story. Or if you'd like to stop now, you can. I just want you to know that I don't want to drag any of this out of you, unwillingly. Whenever you're ready to tell me the rest, please do. Okay?"

Sydney's astonished gaze remained on her lover's face. Finally, she found her voice again. "Alicia...you are the most extraordinary woman I've ever met. You're such a gift to me. Thank you. Thank you for loving me." Sydney wiped the rest of the tears that had fallen down her face. She took a shaky breath and continued her story

"At University, I met a woman named...Sharon Harris." Even now, her very name brought a wave of pain to the tall woman's chest. "She was the first person that I thought truly accepted the dark side that I had possessed for so long. She and I became close friends. She would share stories of her life in the States with me, and I told her about my past. Mine of course were scary tales of angst and rage and death, while hers were nothing like that. She never flinched at any of the tales that I told. She would just listen, sometimes she would hold my hand, if any of the stories would get ugly, which they usually did."

Sydney paused, turning toward Ally slightly. She wanted her partner to understand how lonely she'd been and how much she'd wanted the relationship with Sharon to work. "She was the most comfort I'd had in almost five years. Tim and I were not close for a while, but that was my fault. After mom died, we finally reconnected. After all, we were what was left of our family, so we had no choice but to find each other again. He had gotten married and was on the road to starting his own family, but it was just nice to have my brother back." Ally's gaze was open and sincere; there was no judgment there, only silent understanding. Sydney turned away from the accepting expression.

"Anyway, about Sharon...God I hate thinking about her." Sydney paused and took a deep breath. "Sharon was a beautiful woman, she was tall, lean, and blonde. She had the darkest eyes I'd ever seen. She was everything I thought I was looking for in a partner. God, I was so wrong." Sydney's tone had turned bitter and loathing. "At any rate, Sharon and I became lovers. We spent all our time together. I told her everything about me and still she stayed, so I thought I'd found gold. Well, I found fool's gold, Alicia," Sydney told the younger woman. "Boy, did I find that out the hard way."

Ally simply waited, keeping her eyes on her lover's anguished face.

"Sharon asked me to move to the States with her after the school year had ended. God, I think I was about nineteen at the time. I was so in love, or so I thought, that I couldn't think of doing anything or being with anyone else. I told my brother about selling the sheep station, and he, thankfully, wanted to keep it going. That's when I packed up my life in Sydney and moved to Montana. Sharon and I stayed together for about three years I think it was."

Suddenly Sydney's voice cracked; a wash of pain swept through her very being. Ally wanted to wrap her arms around her lover, but she decided Sydney needed to get the story out, in order for the healing to start. The young woman clenched her fists in her lap...and waited. Finally, Sydney continued.

"One night, she called me from the office. She said she had a project that she had to finish. It was gonna take a few hours so she was gonna be late getting home. Silly me started to feel bad for her," she chuckled bitterly. "So, I decided to pack us a dinner picnic. I got some stuff together and put it in a basket and took it to her office."

Sydney paused to gain control in her voice. It had begun to quiver as she started talking about that night. She regained her breathing and started again.

"I walked into her office and there she was at her desk. Well, I should say, on her desk."

Ally's heart began to hammer in her breast as she sensed what the next episode of the story would be. "She was having sex with her secretary, Tina," Sydney blurted out painfully. "Isn't that the oldest cliché in the book?" the dark-haired woman said, her voice hoarse with renewed pain. "She didn't even stop until she had a fucking orgasm!" Ally closed her eyes at the sight of her lover's anguish. When she heard Sydney continue, she opened them, her heart breaking for the older woman beside her.

"She then proceeded to tell me that I was a prize to her," Sydney went on. "A 'beautiful trophy'," Sydney spat out. "That she could come home to or she could have on her arm whenever we went to a bar or something. I was something that she could *show off*. I was a fucking possession of hers!" The tall woman's voice splintered. Her breath had turned ragged and uneven. Eventually, Sydney became calm again. The defeat in her voice made Ally's throat ache.

"Sharon had so many affairs behind my back. All of her compassion for me was just a lie. She didn't give a shit one way or the other for me. She liked my money and she liked the way I looked. Obviously, I was lacking in the sex department since she had sex with anyone she could get her fingers into. I should have told you this before, but she's been following me, Alicia. I saw her at the airport when you came here before. Then I saw her again just the other day," Sydney confessed.

"The other day!" Ally almost shouted in disbelief. "Sydney when did you see her?"

"She approached me when I was in the restroom at the restaurant last week," Sydney replied in a very tired voice.

"Why didn't you say anything? God, no wonder you were so upset when you came back."

"I didn't say anything because I didn't want you to worry," Sydney said almost apologetically. "You've had so much on your mind, this would have only added to it." The tall woman paused, her jaw muscles rippling. "I literally almost killed her, Alicia. She brings out an anger in me I forgot I had."

"What happened, Sydney? Did she threaten you?" Ally asked, concerned.

"More like I threatened her. Somehow she found out about you and the fact that your parents were killed. I just don't know how she did it, I really think she's been following me. She said she was here on business for her father's company, but still," Sydney mused, almost to herself. Then she turned to Ally. "I swear, Alicia, I can't tell you how much I wanted to hurt her when she mentioned your name." Sydney's voice showed her own surprise at the depth of her anger. "It really freaked me out to see her again."

"Oh Sydney, I'm so sorry," Ally said, pulling her lover into her arms. "God, I wish you would've told me," she said, sitting back to look into Sydney's face. "I don't want you to ever go through anything like that alone again. Do you understand me?" The young woman's voice held an authoritative tone. "I want you to promise that you will ask for help if you need it. If something is bothering you, I want to know about it. Are we clear about this? We are in this together!" Ally said sternly, but her love was truly evident in her voice.

"Yes, Alicia, I understand," Sydney replied meekly. "Thanks. Your concern means the world to me."

"Okay, I'm sorry," Ally said, lovingly brushing Sydney's hair back from her face. "I didn't mean to jump in like that, but damn Sydney," the young woman's tone regained some of its stern quality. "To hear that you had seen her at the airport and then here, of all places!" The green eyes sparkled with certain anger. "I hope to God that I never meet this woman, Sydney. I swear to everything Holy, that I will punch her lights out."

"My hero." Sydney chuckled and pulled Ally close, kissing the blonde's temple. She sat back again, still holding Ally's small hand in her own. She let out a short, brisk breath. "So to finish this damn thing, I left her that night. I told her I didn't want to be found by her and that she shouldn't come home until the next day. I stayed with some friends until one of them told me about Edna needing a stable hand. I'd worked with horses before so I knew what kind of work would be involved." Sydney raised a hand and stroked her lover's soft cheek. "I called your aunt and we had a great talk. I came to the ranch and she showed me around. I loved it there and I really took a liking to Edna. She took me in and the rest as you say, is history. She is the dearest friend that I've ever had. She always knew what to say to make me feel better; she still has that wonderful quality. This is my third year there, and I couldn't think of any place else I'd rather be." Sydney smiled down at Ally, a wave of relief and exhaustion passing through her.

"What about Australia?"

"Oh, I miss home, there is no question about that. I even contemplated moving back after what had happened," Sydney admitted. "But, there were just so many bad memories there for me, that I thought I needed a fresh start. Sure, it didn't start out great in the States either, but I was already here, and

Edna had entered my life." Sydney lowered her eyes to the small hand captured in hers. "It seemed like it was meant to be. How else do you explain me meeting the woman of my dreams?" She returned her gaze to the soft green eyes fastened on hers.

"The woman of your dreams?" Ally shyly asked.

"You, Alicia." Sydney shifted in her seat to face Ally. She gently caressed Ally's face with the back of her fingers. "I do love you, Alicia. I love you more than anything I've ever known. That scares the hell out of me, but it's time that you know that I'm in this for the long haul." Sydney's breath caught when she heard Ally's do the same. "I swore to myself that I'd never love anyone again, but you've shown me a love I've never seen before. I know that heart of yours doesn't have a mean streak in it. I know my heart is safe with you. You've owned it since we met at the stables the day you arrived at the ranch. I love you, Alicia with all of my heart."

Ally began to cry softly when she finally realized that Sydney did, in fact, love her and now was finally voicing it. With a shaky hand, Sydney reached into her pocket and pulled out a small velvet box and held it to face Ally.

"Alicia, I want you to have this," Sydney said as fresh tears streamed down her face. "Although it scares me senseless, I want you to be with me forever. However long forever is, I want you to share your life with me. Please accept this gift and know that you encircle my heart with every breath that I take. I love you, Alicia," Sydney watched her lover's face as she accepted the special gift.

Ally opened the box to find the ring that Sydney had picked out earlier that morning. "Oh, Sydney, this is beautiful!"

"Look in the inside of it."

"Oh, an inscription...*Always, Sydney*." Ally put the ring on and brought her hand to Sydney's heart. "I love you, too, Sydney. Thank you so much."

"Happy Birthday, baby."

The two just held onto each other as the waves of sobs passed and resurfaced over and over. All of a sudden, Sydney realized their trip to the beach had lasted well over her time limit and she knew that she had to get Ally back to the house. There were festivities awaiting them in Ally's honor, and a very nervous wreck named Tracey.

Twenty-Four

The ride from the beach was filled with tender kisses and touches. Sydney had never felt so loved in her life. The love she had thought she had with Sharon was nothing in comparison to what she had with Ally. She felt like the luckiest woman in the world. Her fears were melting with every minute she spent with the woman sitting next to her. Giving Ally the ring had been such a cleansing for Sydney's soul. *I could fly right now if she asked me to.* She thought to herself. There was only one thing left to tell Ally about her checkered past and that, indeed, could wait for another time. *I don't want to spoil her entire evening. Besides, she may not be as accepting as she was earlier,* Sydney thought, staring at the profile of her companion.

"What's on your mind, Sydney?" Ally asked.

"Mmm, you baby. I'm so happy right now. Nothing could possibly ruin this night for us." Sydney said.

"I agree. It's been the best birthday that I've ever had," Ally said, squeezing Sydney's hand. "Thank you, Sydney, for so much. You've been so good for me. You've helped me more than you know. If you hadn't been around, I may have just withered away into nothingness after my parents died." Sydney smiled back at her lover. "I didn't know what or how to feel, or even if I could feel loved or give love again. You've healed my heart, Sydney, I can't thank you enough for that," Ally squeezed Sydney's hand again.

"You don't have to thank me, honey," Sydney told her. "You've been just as important in my own healing. I never wanted to love again. Love was the equivalent of pain for me, and you smashed right through that wall." Sydney stroked the soft skin she held in her palm. "I saw your heart from the very beginning and knew that mine would be safe with you. You have no idea what that means to me."

"Yes, I do," Ally told her, glancing away from the windshield to smile at her partner. "I can understand completely. We helped each other while helping ourselves, if that makes any sense whatsoever."

"It does, sweetheart, it truly does." She paused to sneak a look at her watch. "I think it's a good idea that we go back to the house and check to see if Tracey called," Sydney offered innocently. "I know she wouldn't want to miss your birthday."

"Well, I know she has Char in town for only a couple more days," Ally giggled. "So she may be preoccupied."

"But you're her best friend, Alicia," Sydney returned in mock seriousness. "Surely, you'd think she would celebrate that with you."

"I can hope. She is just so smitten with this one," Ally said warmly. "I've never seen her so over the edge for anyone." The young face scowled slightly. "This girl had better not break her heart, otherwise, she will have me to deal with."

"Remind me never to break Tracey's heart," Sydney chortled. "I don't ever want to feel your wrath."

The two women chuckled as they pulled into the driveway of Ally's house. Sydney had to try hard to keep her emotions in check. But she couldn't wait to see Ally's face when she walked into the house.

Sydney walked around the car and opened the door for Ally. She took her hand and they walked together towards the house.

ஐ ✿

"They're here!" Tracey shouted to the crowded family room. "No one make a sound!" She peeked again outside and saw the two women walking toward the front door. "When they walk into the room and switch on the light, shout surprise, but wait until she walks in here, don't shout it to the foyer!" She insisted.

Everyone rolled their eyes at their slightly frenetic friend, but nodded their acceptance of her orders. Edna smiled to herself, eyeing the doorway.

ஐ ✿

"Sydney, I can open the door, sheesh. I know it's my birthday, but I can open a door for myself. Hey, why is it so dark in here? Didn't I leave a light on?"

"I guess we forgot. I can get the one in the family room. I think I remember where all the lamps are."

"Oh no you don't. They are going to end up on the floor if you start feeling your way around. Let me."

"Have it your way," Sydney said to a smiling Ally.

Click

"SURPRISE!" The room shouted at a very startled Ally. "HAPPY BIRTHDAY, ALLY!" They shouted again.

Tracey came rushing at Ally with a huge grin on her face. Before Ally knew what hit her, she and Tracey ended up sprawled on the couch. Tracey was hugging and kissing her surprised and happy friend.

"OH...MY...GOD! Who did this?" A stunned Ally asked, looking up at Tracey then at a grinning Sydney.

"I should have guessed. I can't leave you two alone for two minutes." Ally laughed and managed to climb over Tracey to her feet.

"Can I get a hug from my best girl?" A voice came from across the room. Ally turned to find Edna smiling at her.

"EDDI! Oh my God! YOU TOO?" Ally jumped and ran across the room to hug her aunt.

"Guilty as charged, afraid to say. Happy birthday, sweetheart."

"Thanks, Eddi. It means the world to me that you came." She said as tears threatened to leak down her cheeks. She turned into her aunt's body and wrapped her arms around the stout woman again. "God, I can't believe you're here."

"Believe it, honey. I wouldn't have missed this for all the horses in Montana."

"I love you, Eddi," Ally said, squeezing Edna again.

"You too, kiddo. I bet there are a lot of faces here you haven't seen in a while. Boy, I wouldn't have missed that expression of yours for anything. It was beautiful."

"It sure was." A low and throaty voice came from behind Ally and arms soon wrapped around her waist.

"Oh you...you are in so much trouble. I can't believe you didn't let any of this slip. I was totally surprised," Ally admitted.

"Well, isn't that the purpose of a surprise party?" Sydney sarcastically responded.

"Okay, Smart-Ass. That's enough outta you." Ally's guardian spoke.

"Hey, Edna, nice to see you," Sydney said, releasing Ally to embrace her dear friend.

"You too, honey. I gotta hand it to you and Tracey. You definitely surprised the little one here."

"Yep, we sure did. In many ways in fact." Sydney smiled down at Ally who understood what Sydney was referring to. She immediately raised her ringed finger to show her aunt what Sydney had gotten for her.

"Oh, honey, that's beautiful! I knew she had good taste." Edna smiled.

"The best. Look who's wearing it." Sydney laughed and pecked Ally's cheek.

"Hey, you two, I gotta make some rounds. I gotta find Tracey and meet this new girlie girl of hers." Ally said excitedly.

"Char isn't here yet, darlin'. She said she'd be here a little later. Some business came up or something. She should be arriving shortly." Edna explained.

"Oh, well, then I'm going to chat with some people. I haven't seen some of them in years. This is turning into a night of firsts, that's for sure."

"Firsts?" Sydney asked.

"Yeah, first you giving me the ring. Then you telling me you loved me. Then this party, I haven't ever had a surprise party before. I can't even wait to see what the rest of the night has in store for me."

"It's gonna be a night to remember, baby. I can feel it." Sydney smiled.

"I think you're right. Remind me to thank you properly later," Ally said.

"I love you, Sydney." She said, pulling Sydney down for a short but passionate kiss. "It gets better... later." Ally promised.

"I can hardly wait. I love you, too, baby. Go on now. I gotta run to Terry's and get the rest of the alcohol."

"Okay, sweetheart. I'll see you soon." Ally stopped and turned to see a familiar face. "Oh my God, Rita! I haven't seen you in ages! How have you been?" Ally's voice faded and blended in with the rest of the room. Sydney walked toward the door. Tracey ran up to her and planted a great big kiss on her lips. Sydney just looked at her awestruck and smiled a crooked grin.

"Thank you, Sydney. This worked out so great! Did you see her face? God, she was so surprised! This is just so great!"

"Yes, we did well. I think we really got her. So um, where is your lady?"

"Oh, she should be here any minute. Are you off to the liquor store?"

"Yep. I figure it's probably a good time before it gets totally hopping in here. I should be back in less than an hour or so."

"Okay, great. Sydney, thank you again for getting all of that taken care of," Tracey sincerely said.

"Hey, no problem, you took care of everything else. I'll see you soon." She smiled and opened the door.

"Okay, Sydney, be careful. You do remember where you're going, right?" Tracey asked hesitantly.

"Yea, I've been there before. See ya."

"Byeee," Tracey sang. "Now it's time to partaaaayy!" She screamed, jumping into a dancing line. The women around her just laughed and danced with their friend as the music thumped around them.

ಲ ಲ

"Dance with me, babe," Tracey said, grabbing Ally's arm and pulling her into the middle of the family room.

"Christ! Do I have a choice?" Ally yelped.

"Nope, come on," Tracey giggled, starting to sway with Ally to the bass of the music.

The two started to get overtly sexual on the dance floor. Their legs were intertwined as they started their decent to the floor and back up again. Their hips were gyrating with the rhythm and their arms were flailing above them. They looked at each other and broke into a fit of laughter as the song ended.

"Should I be jealous?" A voice came from behind Tracey. Ally looked into deep brown eyes and smiled.

"You must be Char. I'm Ally, no need for worry here. We agreed a long time ago that we were best as friends and nothing more." She extended her hand to Char and they exchanged a jovial meeting.

"That's a relief. Hi, honey, sorry it took me so long." She directed her gaze at Tracey.

"Hi, sweets, I'm glad you got here. This is my best friend in the whole world," she said, hugging and kissing the top of Ally's head.

"Nice to finally meet you, Ally. Oh and Happy Birthday. Sorry I missed the surprise, but I had some things to tend to before I was able to get here."

"That's quite all right. I'm just glad you're here. Tracey has said so many wonderful things about you. I couldn't wait to finally meet you."

"Likewise. I've heard nothing but great things about you and Sydney for the last few months. It is wonderful to see you in the flesh."

"Thanks. How long are you here for?"

"Only a couple more days, unfortunately. I gotta get back to LA. I'm just about done with my business deal. I should know by tomorrow morning."

"I see, well I hope it works out for you."

"Me too. Shall we get a drink?" Char asked Tracey and Ally.

"Sure, I think there is still a bit of wine left. Sydney went to the liquor store to get the rest of it."

"Oh, what a dear. To the bar then?"

"To the bar!" Ally said, raising her fist. She walked arm in arm with Tracey and Char.

ಠ ಡ

"God, I hope I went the right way...oh here it is," Sydney rambled to herself. "Thank God. That's all Alicia needs is to get a smoke signal from me because I got lost."

She walked into Terry's Liquor's and waited in line. She approached the counter and watched the young man's eyes popped out of his head as he stared at her.

"Are you all right?" She teasingly asked.

"Uhh, y...yeah. Can I help you?" The tongue-tied clerk asked.

"Yes. I'm Sydney Thompson. I called a few days back with an order for a keg of beer and some other things."

"Riiiight, um, let me go in back and make sure we got it all together," he said before he practically ran into the stockroom.

"God, if he is twenty-one I'd be surprised," she mused to herself.

"Hey, little lady. What does a fine thing like you need with so much booze? You needing to share it with anyone?

"Excuse me?" Sydney asked incredulously while her eyebrow raised of it's own volition.

"I said..." He started to drool a bit as he was swaying from foot to foot. "Do you need some company to help you drink all that?"

"No, thank you." Sydney noticed that a policeman had entered the store and she motioned for him to come closer. "Hey bud, did you drive here?" She asked the obviously inebriated man.

"Of course I did, that's my ride right out front, do you want me to show it to ya? I could take us somewheres more private."

"No, that's okay, I'm sure you'll be quite busy the rest of the night." She chuckled as the police officer made his presence known.

Sydney amused herself watching the drunken idiot try to walk out of the liquor store toward his car. After seeing that the man was attempting to drive away in his intoxicated state, the policemen arrested him and put him in the back of the squad car. Walking back into the store, he approached Sydney.

"Thanks, Miss," the office told her. "I appreciate you giving me the heads up with that one. I'm surprised that he didn't kill himself or someone else on the way here."

"That's no problem. A good friend of mine lost her parents to someone like him. I couldn't let that happen again to someone else's loved one," Sydney explained.

"I'm sorry to hear that. If more people like you made it their business to help, we may not have as many fatalities as we do. Thanks again, I do appreciate it." The officer smiled a bright toothy grin at Sydney.

"It's the least I could do. Have fun with that one." She shook his hand.

"Oh, we will. Have a good night now."

"I will. Goodnight." She watched the squad pull out of the parking lot. She decided to find the little salesman and see what was taking so damn long with her order.

"Excuse me?" She said, knocking on the backdoor. The same man exited the door.

"I'm sorry, ma'am. I'm just uhh, well I can't get the keg out of the back and I'm alone in here..."

Sydney stopped the kid in mid panic. "Where is it?"

"What?"

"Show me where it is and I'll help you."

"Ma'am you won't be able to lift it. It's really very heavy." The boy explained.

"Just point me in the right direction. I'm sure I can help. If I can hog tie farm animals, I certainly can roll a keg out here."

"Uhh, this way." He led Sydney into the refrigerated locker. She easily got the keg from its resting spot as the young man looked on in awe. She put the keg on a two-wheel cart and wheeled it out into the front of the store.

"Now if you can get the rest of my order together I may have enough time to enjoy my girlfriend's surprise party," Sydney deadpanned.

The young clerk just stared at her. "Tonight, would be good." She broke him out of his reverie.

"Yes...yes...sorry. I just...never mind... I'll be right up with the rest of your order," he said as he scurried into the back again.

After a few minutes the young clerk returned from the abyss with the rest of her supplies on her list.

"I think this just about covers it. You do know that you need to put a deposit on the tapper for the keg?"

"Yes, I was informed of that. You do take cash I assume?" She said, raising a quizzical eyebrow at him.

"Of course." He blushed. "I'm sorry, I've been a little out of it," he bashfully admitted.

"It's all right. Now, if you can carry the bags and the tub to the car for me, I'll handle the keg." She smiled her brightest smile at him. He jumbled the bags but agreed to help. *This poor kid needs to get laid and fast.* She rolled the keg to her car and placed it in her back seat. The clerk placed the rest of the bags in her trunk with a few extra bags of ice "on the house."

"Thank you for your help, umm..." She stopped and looked at his nametag, "Jimmy. You've been most helpful."

"Sure miss, anytime. Uhh, have a good time at your umm, party," he stumbled out.

"Thanks, my girlfriend thanks you, too. Bye now." She said, waving to him out her window and pulling out of the parking lot back toward Ally's house.

"My God, she has got to be the most stunning woman I have ever met," the young man said out loud to no one in particular. He turned and walked back into the store while glancing back over his shoulder for one last look.

ಬಿ ಆ

Ally was so happy. This was the best birthday that she could remember having. She had never had a surprise party before. Her parents would occasionally throw her a party for her birthday, but it had never been a surprise. She was really happy for Tracey, too. She'd never seen her so happy before. *This girl may just be the one,* Ally thought to herself, watching the interaction between the two women.

"Hey, Tracey? How long did Sydney say she'd be? I'm starting to worry." Ally questioned.

"Oh, darlin', she'll be fine. She said she'd be about an hour. It's almost that time now. Don't worry she'll be fine, babe." Tracey reassured her.

"You're right. I'm just being a worrywart. You're going to love Sydney, Char, she is just the best!"

"Oh, don't you worry. She and I will certainly have a spectacular conversation. You just wait." She smiled victoriously.

"Well, good. I know she's been looking forward to meeting you, as I have." Ally smiled.

"Thank you, the feeling is mutual," Char said with a smile.

☙ ❧

Sydney drove up the driveway to Ally's house and saw the people dancing through the main window. A smile came to her lips as she saw Ally and Tracey dancing together.

"She is just too damn cute. It looks like she is having a great time," she said out loud, parking the car into the garage. She walked around to the trunk, pulled out the bags from the liquor store, and headed up to the house. She opened the front door and walked towards the kitchen. She grabbed one of Ally's friends and asked him to help her with the keg.

"Sure, does that mean I get first pull from it?" A very thirsty Josh asked.

"Sure, cowboy, if you can tap this sucker, it's all yours." She smiled at him.

"Cool, I'm on it," he said as he grabbed the half-barrel out of the backseat. Sydney wheeled a handcart towards him and he just scoffed at her.

"I don't need that, just hold the doors for me."

"All right, studly, I'll lead the way." She winked at the young man, watching his facial expressions reach the crimson stage. "Are you sure you don't want the cart?"

"You know, I got this um, football injury and uh, it might be a good idea if I use that thing," he stammered.

"Sure, you're probably right. You don't want to aggravate your injury," she said while holding back a chuckle. "C'mon, we'll get this set up in the bar area."

"Okay, lead the way," an embarrassed Josh replied.

Sydney and Josh wheeled the keg into the bar area. She poured several bags of ice into the tub and watched as Josh tried to lift the keg alone. She handed him the tapper and together they lifted the keg into the tub of ice. Josh successfully tapped the keg and a line soon formed around that area. Ally was still dancing with Tracey, so Sydney decided to go into the kitchen and grab one of the bottles of champagne for her birthday girl. Sharon watched menacingly as Sydney walked into the kitchen.

"It's show time..." Sharon said to herself.

Twenty-Five

Sydney had her back to the doorway leading from the kitchen to the family room. She was trying to open the bottle of champagne she had bought for Ally, Tracey, and her new girlfriend, Char. She thought a toast would certainly be in order for this evening.

Ally got a glance of Sydney walking into the kitchen. She broke free from Tracey and headed towards the kitchen. "Hey, Trace, Sydney just got back. I'll be back in a sec."

"Okay, babe. Hey, if you see Char, tell her she owes me a dance, all right?" Tracey asked.

"Sure!" Ally replied. She saw Char follow Sydney into the kitchen and realized that Sydney had yet to meet her. *She is gonna love her!* she thought to herself. She picked up her pace so she could introduce the two women.

Sydney popped the champagne cork from its bottle and heard some people approaching. Char was standing behind Sydney in the kitchen as Ally walked in.

"Hey, honey, I want to introduce you to someone." Sydney heard Ally say.

Sydney turned around as if in slow motion, only to look into the eyes of her ex-lover and dropped the bottle of champagne. The bottle crashed onto the counter and glass particles were shattered everywhere.

"Sharon," Sydney said through gritted teeth.

"Hello, Sydney. Long time no see." Sharon smirked.

"Not long enough for me," Sydney retorted.

Ally's jaw dropped, hearing the exchange between the two.

"Sharon?" Ally whispered.

Sharon and Sydney turned to face Ally. Sydney's face was pale and drawn whereas Sharon's was flushed with excitement. Ally looked at them with so much confusion on her face.

"What do you mean? Sydney this is Char, Tracey's girlfriend."

"No, Alicia, this is Sharon Harris, my ex lover," Sydney corrected.

"What?" Ally said in disbelief. She suddenly found a rage building within her. She turned and got in Sharon's face. "You've got about five seconds to tell me why I shouldn't call the police and have them arrest you for trespassing."

"Oh, Sydney, you didn't tell me she had such spirit. I'd have looked her up her sooner." Sharon chuckled, staring at Ally's infuriated face.

"Don't you even think about it, Sharon," Sydney warned.

"Oh, don't worry, Sydney, it's not her I'm after. I came back to claim what you took from me." Sharon turned to face Sydney.

"And what did I EVER take from you?" Sydney spat at Sharon.

"You, my darling. I came back for you."

"You have *got* to be kidding me. I wouldn't go back to you for anything in this world!" Sydney shot back.

"Oh, Sydney, don't you remember how good we were together? We can have that again, Sydney. Just come with me and let's start our life over again," Sharon quietly spoke until she felt Ally grab her arm.

"Look here, Miss 'I-Lie-To-Everyone-About-My-Identity' Sydney is with me. She will ALWAYS be with me. There is nothing that you could say that will change that. What about poor Tracey? She has no idea of the lies you've fed to her. You're going to break her heart. But I guess someone that doesn't HAVE a heart wouldn't know what it feels like to have theirs broken." Ally paused to look into Sharon's unfeeling eyes. "Now, I'm going to ask you nicely one last time to leave my house. After that, I can't guarantee how it will come out!" Ally shouted.

"Oh, I think there is definitely something that I could say that would change Sydney's mind," Sharon threatened.

"Sharon, don't you dare," Sydney warned.

"What's the matter, Sydney? Are you afraid to tell your lover the truth? Afraid that she will see the monster you used to be? Or maybe you're still that person underneath that new exterior of yours." Sharon taunted. Sydney grabbed Sharon by her shoulders and put her face within inches of hers.

"Don't you dare say one word about my past. I've paid for everything that happened in that time. You of all people should know that!" She screamed, tightening her grip around Sharon.

"Oh, Sydney, how I've missed your arms around me. Don't think that I won't fight to have them back on a full time basis." Sharon smiled.

"What the hell does that mean? You will have to fight until hell freezes, Sharon. Our time together is over!" Sydney cried out, walking toward Ally.

"Oh no, no, no, my dearest. Our time is just beginning." She paused and looked at Ally. "Alicia? Has she told you about her brother, Billy?" Sydney whirled around and grabbed Sharon by the shirt.

"Shut the fuck up, Sharon, I'm warning you. You say one word disgracing my brother and I will drop you where you stand! Do you hear me?" Sydney hissed in her face.

"God, I've missed that fire. Remember how you used to take me after your nightmares, Sydney? Those dreams you had would wake you so abruptly. You were so filled with angst and rage. Do you remember that, Sydney? We could have that again, just say the word," Sharon continued to taunt as Sydney began to squeeze harder.

"Sydney, please...let her go." A soft voice entered Sydney's ears and she realized that Sharon was dangling under her grip. She slowly let her down and felt Ally's hand on the small of her back. One movement sent a calming sensation throughout her entire body.

"I'm so sorry," Sydney whispered to Ally.

Ally took Sydney's hand and walked her a few feet away from Sharon, who was smiling smugly .

"Sydney, what am I going to tell Tracey? I think she's in love with her. This is going to kill her."

"There is nothing that we can say that's going to lessen the blow from this one. She is an uncaring bitch. It doesn't matter to her who she hurts, as long as she gets what she wants," Sydney commented.

"Sydney, is there more to your story about Billy that I need to know about? I would much rather hear it from you than her," Ally said quietly.

"Yes, there is. I wish I would have told you the whole story, but I didn't want to upset you on your birthday. If you just go with the flow and pretend, just this once for me, I'll tell you everything. I can guarantee she is going to say it just to upset me. Please know that I love you, and whatever she may say, might not be the truth. So if you're confused or terrified by what may come out of her mouth, I'm sorry. I didn't tell you only because of everything you've gone through," Sydney tried to explain.

"What does that mean, Sydney? What more could have been in your past that would upset me now? I don't get it."

"What she means, brat, is that you lost your parents to someone like her. She killed her own brother. It was her fault that he died. Isn't that right, Sydney?" Sharon triumphantly stated.

"What?" Was all Ally could breathe out.

"You know that's not what happened! It's not true!" Sydney pleaded. She looked into Ally's eyes and could only read fear and confusion.

"Yes, it is, Sydney. You may as well have pulled the trigger yourself."

"Shut up, Sharon, I'm warning you for the last time," Sydney growled

"I...I don't know what to think here," Ally stammered. "I've gotta get out of here."

"Alicia, please. Don't go." She reached for Ally only to have her pull away. Ally ran out of the kitchen and went looking for Tracey and Edna.

Laughing, Sharon looked at Sydney with utter amusement.

"The little brat must be terrified of you now," Sharon chuckled.

Sydney stared at the floor listening to Sharon gloat, then she looked up to meet the eyes of the most heartless woman she had ever met. She swallowed a couple times before gaining the strength to speak coherently. She mustered a throaty one-word whisper.

"Why?" She asked through gritted teeth.

"Why not, Sydney? I came back for you and I'm not leaving without you," Sharon stated flatly.

"Why would you want to be with me? What part of 'I hate you,' don't you understand? I despise you more than I thought capable. You may have ruined everything that Alicia and I have built over the last few months." Her voice started to get louder. "What the hell did you possibly think I'd give you after you broke my heart the way you did over three fucking years ago?" Sydney started to pace through the kitchen. "I can't believe you! How could you? I want to know right NOW!"

Sharon laughed derisively. Sydney growled and grabbed the front of Sharon's shirt backing her up against the counter hard. "Not until you tell me why? NOW TALK!" Sydney demanded. "Tell me why you thought it necessary to ruin my life AGAIN!"

ಬಿ ೧೪

Ally ran out of the kitchen searching for Tracey and Edna. She found Edna talking to a couple of her friends. She rushed over to her and Edna immediately knew something was terribly wrong.

"What is it, honey? You look very upset." Edna said very concerned.

"I...I don't know what to say, Eddi. Sydney...she...oh my God..." Ally croaked out through her sobs. Edna pulled her into a hug as Ally quietly sobbed with onlookers giving them their privacy.

"What did Sydney do, honey? I can't help if I don't know what happened," Eddi comforted.

"Not here, let's go into the other room. Where's Tracey?" She asked.

"She's over there involved in a drinking contest. I think she's winning," she said. Ally could see Tracey pointing and laughing at her opponent on the floor.

"Oh no, that's just going to make matters worse," she said sadly.

"What? Girl, you tell me right now what is going on here?" Edna demanded.

Ally looked around and noticed that they were pretty much alone and decided it wouldn't make a difference if she told Eddi there or not.

"Sydney's ex-girlfriend is in my kitchen right now." She choked out.

"What? What are you talking about child?" Edna asked.

"Char, Tracey's girlfriend is really Sharon, Sydney's ex."

"Oh, my God."

"Yeah, I know. I don't know how I'm going to tell Tracey. She's really in love with this woman. I don't know how." Slowly, Ally's fears were replaced by anger at Sharon's accusations. "That woman is a total bitch. I was shaking in there I was so angry. Then she started talking about Sydney and how she killed her brother."

"Whoa, whoa, WHOA! Hold it right there. What's this about Sydney killing her brother?" Edna asked incredulously.

Ally relayed all of the information to Edna, who stared wide-eyed at her niece. Deciding they needed to find Tracey, Edna reached for Ally's hand.

"Come on, we have to tell Tracey before she finds out another way," Edna rationalized. "I think we need to sit her down and tell her before she is too drunk to comprehend what we're saying to her."

"Good idea, Eddi, let's go get her," Ally agreed.

They went over to the bar where Tracey was challenging everyone to a beer chugging contest. Ally walked behind her and tapped her on the shoulder.

"Tracey? I need to talk to you. It's really important."

"Can't it wait, Ally? I'm about to make fifty bucks off this guy." Tracey answered without looking at Ally.

Ally put her hand on Tracey's shoulder and made her look at her. "Trace, it's really important. Please," Ally pleaded.

"Okay, babe. What is it?"

Crash

"What the hell?" Tracey looked at Ally and Edna after hearing the crash and knew something was up. "Where's Char, you guys?" Tracey asked then ran towards the crashing sound from the kitchen.

"Tracey wait!" Ally screamed unsuccessfully. "Dammit. We've got to catch her!" Ally said to Eddi as they ran after Tracey.

ೞ ಚ

Tracey ran into the kitchen and was flabbergasted with what she saw. Sydney still had Sharon pushed against the counter. Edna and Ally soon followed into the kitchen.

"Holy shit! Sydney, what the fuck are you doing? Let go of her! NOW!" Tracey screamed and ran toward Sydney and Sharon.

"Tracey no! It's not what you think!" Ally tried to warn her.

Sydney half-turned to see Tracey coming after her. "Tracey stop right there. This is not the woman you think it is," Sydney attempted, feeling Tracey's hands on her shoulders.

"Tracey, no! Stop!" Ally screamed.

"What's your problem, Ally? She's attacking my girlfriend!"

"She's not your girlfriend, Tracey...she is my ex-lover, Sharon," Sydney said tightly. "I hate to have to tell you this, but she's been seeing you to get back at me."

"What are you talking about? Char, tell her it's not true," Tracey said looking up into her lover's eyes. Sharon looked at Tracey with a blank expression. "Char? Char, what's going on? Talk to me," Tracey said, releasing her hold on Sydney. Sydney backed away to reveal the woman that Tracey had grown to love. This time Tracey was looking into the eyes of a stranger. "She's telling the truth isn't she?"

Sharon didn't flinch or attempt to answer the question. Tracey, being more than a little tipsy, slapped Sharon across her face. "Why? Why would you lie to me like this? I thought you loved me." Blood trickled from Sharon's mouth and she licked it with her tongue and smiled.

"Oh, poor young, Tracey. I give you some sack time, which was mediocre at best, some warm embraces, and you think its love? You just kept me warm until I could have what I really wanted."

Tracey snarled, reached back to punch her only to have Sydney grab her arm.

"That's enough, Tracey," Sydney said quietly. She turned to Ally. "Ally, call the police. We have an unwanted guest here." They looked at Sharon who was just sitting on the counter staring into nothingness with a small smile on her face.

"Sharon, you've hurt my friends for the last time," Ally said to the numb woman. "I'm going to have you arrested for trespassing. " She looked at Sydney and mouthed, "I'm so sorry." Sydney walked over to her and put her arms around her.

"I'm the one who's sorry, honey. I shouldn't have kept this from you. I promise when all of this is over, I'll tell you the whole story."

"Okay then," Ally said, returning Sydney's hug. Right now, I have a phone call to make. I'll be right back." She turned to leave the room, looked into the bar area, and looked back into the kitchen. "You know, it's a good thing these people really like to party, because this would be hard to explain right about now."

Sydney looked over to Sharon's unbalanced expression and wondered what she'd seen in her. The beauty that once radiated there was now gone. Everything about her had changed for the worse. She knew now how lucky she was to have found Ally.

Tracey just sat at the kitchen table and stared at Sharon. What had just unfolded was unbelievable to her. The woman who had pretended to care for her for the last few weeks was nothing more than a lying sociopath. She buried her head in her hands and began to weep. Sydney walked over to her and put her hand on her shoulder.

"I'm so sorry I brought her into your life, Tracey," she whispered to the tearful woman. "I had no idea she'd do this."

Sharon slowly reached down to pick up a piece of the broken bottle from the counter. She had the glass in her palm and slowly slid away from the counter. Edna saw her move and motioned too late to Sydney. Sharon quickly raised her armed hand and rushed towards Sydney.

"If I can't have you, then no one can! Yaaahhh!" She shrieked, raising her hand to make the strike.

"Sydney! Look out!" Edna screamed.

Sydney whirled around and caught Sharon's raised arm before it made impact. Ally heard her aunt scream and ran into the kitchen. Tracey got behind Sharon and grabbed Sharon's other arm and shoved it behind her back.

"Drop it, Sharon, or whatever your name is!" Tracey commanded.

Sharon grunted and dropped the piece of glass on the floor. She started to kick and scream as Tracey threw her down onto the floor. Pieces of the broken glass dug into Tracey's knees and into Sharon's body. Sydney traded places with Tracey since she had a better advantage over Sharon.

"Sydney, are you all right?" Ally ran to her side.

"Yes, darlin'. We just need to wait for the cops now. We can add attempted murder to her sheet and she should be put away for a good long time. Maybe they'll put her into a mental hospital. I think she would benefit greatly from that." Sydney smirked, tightening her grip on Sharon's twisted arm.

"You think some shrink is gonna stop me from coming back to get you, Sydney?" Sharon spat onto the floor. "Think again. I'm going to haunt you until the day you die. You will never be able to forget me, I promise you that."

"You're right, Sharon, I won't forget you. I'll remember how you actually helped me to become a person again after Billy died," Sydney said plainly. "However, I know now what we had wasn't love. I'm glad that I know the difference," Sydney added sarcastically.

"Fuck you!" Sharon cried out.

"In your dreams, Sharon," Ally hissed.

Sydney got an idea and called to Ally, "Hey baby? Get me some packing tape will ya? I'd rather not have to sit like this all night."

"Sure, be right back," Ally answered, smiling down at Sharon.

Bringing Sydney the tape, they propped a struggling Sharon against the cabinets and taped her wrists and hands together. Sharon glared at Sydney and her friends.

"Now, don't even think about moving," Sydney warned.

"Hey! Someone called the cops!" a voice shouted from the other room. Ally shook her head and went to the door to welcome the arriving officers.

"Evening ma'am. We got a call that you had an intruder this evening?" One of the officers asked.

"Oh, how I wish it were that simple. Follow me," Ally explained with a grin on her face.

She led the officers into the kitchen. Most of the people had left the party already and the ones that remained just stared at the policemen.

"Well, what do we have here?" The first officer asked.

Sydney looked up and it was the officer from the liquor store. She recognized him and she smiled and rolled her eyes.

"Seems like you're doing our job again for us tonight. You're a busy woman." He smiled at Sydney.

"Again? Sydney?" Ally questioned.

"Long story," Sydney replied.

"Another one?" Ally teased. Sydney just raised her brow at Ally and grinned.

Sydney smiled victoriously at Sharon as the officers handcuffed her. As the second officer stood Sharon up and motioned for her to walk out of the kitchen, she turned to face Sydney.

"See you soon, my sweet," Sharon said.

"Not if I see you first," Sydney answered quickly.

Sharon was taken out of the house and placed into the squad car. The first officer questioned Ally and Sydney as to what happened.

"Long story short," Sydney began. "Her name is Sharon Harris. She's an ex-lover who's been following me. She lied her way into this house and then attempted to kill me with a shard of glass. I want to press charges on all counts." Sydney finished with her arms across her chest.

"Would you like to elaborate on any on this?" The officer smiled.

Sydney blew out a deep breath. "Okay, three years ago..."

Twenty-Six

Sydney relayed as much information as she could bear to remember. The officer was amazed that this woman hadn't been committed to a psych ward sooner. In his opinion, "She's a couple cents short of a dime."

"Thank you, Officer Randy, good to see you again." Sydney kidded.

"Thank you, Sydney. Ally, I'm sorry your birthday turned out this way, but rest assured, we'll take care of Ms. Harris. Have a good night, ladies. Well, what's left of it," he said as he checked his watch.

"Good night," both Ally and Sydney said in unison.

They closed the front door and realized that the four of them, Sydney, Ally, Edna, and Tracey, were the only ones left in the house. When the police showed up, the party pretty much broke up. They all took a seat at the bar and had a shot of Cuervo.

Ally had tended to Sydney's wounds and Edna to Tracey's. Tracey still hadn't absorbed everything that had happened that evening, but it would all sink in soon enough for her.

"God, I just can't believe all of this. What the hell would drive someone to that?" Tracey asked.

"I don't know, hon, I'm just glad that she didn't physically hurt you." Ally said, wrapping her arm around her best friend's shoulder.

"Sharon is sick, that's all there is to it. I can't think of any sane person that would do this," Edna threw in.

"Obsession is a scary thing. I hope this is the one and only time I get to be the subject matter." Sydney chuckled half-joking, half-serious.

"Well, kids, thanks for the excitement, but I have to go. I have to get my sorry butt to Indy!" Edna exclaimed. "They're having an auction there and I think I can pick up some equipment I need for the ranch."

"Aww, Eddi, are you sure you can't postpone your trip? Just for a day?" Ally asked.

"Honey, you don't need me here. This was just a detour. I wanted to see that face light up again. My limo is waiting for me outside. Besides, I do believe you have other plans for the rest of the evening. It's your birthday for cryin-out-loud! Have some fun tonight! I'll see you back at the ranch. Okay?" Edna replied.

"Thank you for coming, Eddi. It meant so much to me that you were here. I'm just sorry for the way that things ended. I only hope they lock her up for a good long time," Ally said as she hugged her aunt. "Have a safe trip Eddi, and please call me when you get in. You know how I am," Ally urged, pulling away from the hug.

"I love you, Ally. Take care of her," she said quietly, pointing to Tracey. "I think she's gonna need some TLC from you."

"I will."

"Edna, it was wonderful to see you again," Sydney said honestly as she hugged the older woman. "I know it meant the world to Alicia for you to be here for her birthday. I'll be back at work soon, boss lady," Sydney laughed. Edna laughed with her and then turned to face Tracey.

"Tracey, I'm so sorry, sweetheart. If there is anything that I can do for you, please, you know my number. Come here, child," Edna said, opening her arms to Tracey.

"Thanks, Edna. You seem to make things feel better with just one hug," Tracey said. "Take good care of yourself. Have a safe trip and good luck at the auction."

"Thanks, Tracey. All right, ladies, good night and take care. I'm off," she said.

She went upstairs to retrieve the remainder of her bags and Sydney helped her get them into the limousine. With one final kiss and a wave, Edna was gone and Sydney returned to the house.

ಬ ಡ

"Tracey, you know you can just spend the night here. It's late," Ally insisted.

"No, Ally, thanks, but I have so much to sort out. It's really hard for me to process everything that went down tonight. It's all just so surreal right now. I guess I'm still waiting to wake up from the nightmare."

"I know what you mean." The low sensual voice of Sydney came from over Ally's head.

"Hey you, did Eddi get off all right?" Ally said as Sydney hugged her from behind.

"Yeah, she did. Did I hear you were leaving, Tracey?" Sydney asked.

"I have to. I've got lots to think about. I appreciate the offer Ally, but I think I need to go home." Tracey reasoned.

"Let us drive you at least. You've had quite a bit to drink tonight," Ally compromised. Tracey knew not to argue this point with Ally.

"Okay, babe. You win. I know I can't win that argument," her friend acquiesced. "I'll get my stuff together. Be right back."

Ally turned to face Sydney. They studied each other for long moments before slowly embracing. The warmth and love they felt for each other came out in full force with this embrace.

"I love you, Alicia. I'm so sorry I wasn't completely honest with you. It almost cost me everything."

"Sydney, there's still a piece to this puzzle that I need to know about. Now, I also know that you'd never lie to me," Ally said, her green eyes open and honest. "I know there's a very good reason that you didn't tell me about the death of your brother. I'll just wait until we're alone and you're comfortable enough to talk more about it. I love you too, Syd. I always will."

"That's so good to know." She leaned down and slowly and tenderly kissed Ally's lips. The kiss deepened and the women found their embrace becoming more and more needy. Sydney's tongue demanded entrance and Ally didn't fight it.

Sydney's body pressed against Ally's and they began their private dance of desire. Ally pulled away suddenly and had a look of confusion on her face.

"Where's Tracey? I don't want her to find us like this. It may upset her with everything that's happened," Ally said, feeling her neck being nibbled on by Sydney. "Oh, God, that feels good. I totally know why Sharon wanted you back."

"Alicia, no more talk about that woman tonight, please?" Sydney asked softly but seriously.

"Deal, I'm sorry. I am, though, going to go upstairs to check on Tracey. She should have been down here already."

"I'll come with you," Sydney said.

"Is that a promise for later as well?" Ally said, wiggling her eyebrows.

"You're such a naughty girl. Come on. Let's see about your intoxicated friend upstairs."

"Okay, baby, after you."

The two women walked up the stairs hand in hand. They walked into Ally's room and there was no sign of Tracey. Ally turned and walked down the hall to her parents' room. She opened the door and looked into another empty room.

"Ally, I think I found her. Come here." Ally heard Sydney say. Ally ran down the hall to follow Sydney's voice.

"Syd? Where are you?" Ally called out with a bit of panic in her voice.

"Shh, in the guest room," she whispered.

Ally walked into the guestroom to find Tracey under the covers of the bed in the fetal position. She was lying on one pillow with another one in her arms.

"God, I feel so bad for her. On top of everything with Sharon, she's going to wake up with one helluva hangover," Ally commented sympathetically.

"Yeah, I don't envy the headache, she'll have. Come on you, I've got some 'splainin to do," Sydney said in her best Ricky Ricardo.

"Yeah, you do. Come on, Ricky." She giggled back and closed the door.

Back in Ally's room, they undressed and got into the bed. Sydney opened her arms for Ally to snuggle into. It was their favorite position to sleep in, and not to sleep in. They got themselves situated and Ally felt Sydney stiffen a bit and knew that she was ready to talk.

"Are you ready, sweetie? I just want this over with," Sydney asked as if to gear herself up.

"Sure, baby, whenever you are," she said, snuggling closer to her lover.

"Okay, what Sharon said about Billy was true at one time. I completely blamed myself for his death. I didn't kill him, so to speak, but I felt totally responsible for his death. We were having a brawl that night with one of the other gangs. He knew that they were going to be bringing some heavy stuff with them."

"Heavy stuff?" Ally asked.

"You know like guns and shit like that."

"Oh, I gotcha."

"Anyway, he begged me not to go that night. He was always the peacemaker. After dad died he tried to be the man of the family. He was such a gentle soul, but very passionate about family. He was really worried for me. He knew what we did and he hated that I was involved in it. He didn't understand why I needed to be with these people." Sydney stopped talking a moment, her blue eyes gazing quietly into the past. "Looking back," she commented softly, "I don't know what I thought I got from them either, but like I said, I was really lost at that time." She shook her dark head slowly. "Anyway, he had heard that the leader was gonna be packing guns that night. He urged me to stay home. I told him I wasn't going to change my mind. He just wouldn't listen. I told him to stay away if he didn't like it. He didn't.

"He showed up that night to try and talk some sense into me. Before I even saw him approach, he walked into a line of fire. Someone had shot him. Bullets were flying everywhere and all I could do was watch him fall. The cops came and everyone scrambled out of there. Billy bled to death in my arms." Sydney paused to control the emotions that were seeping through her pores.

"He told me that he loved me and that he would do it all again, if it meant keeping me alive. I didn't think I'd ever understand that kind of love. Family was the most important thing to him, though." Sydney swallowed hard, trying to keep herself together to get through the painful story. "He also said he knew how mom was going to react, boy was he right. She blamed me for all of it, which I don't fault her for. I was a terror at that point in my life. Timmy and I weren't speaking, and then of course he sided with mom, so my life was completely shit at that time. I wouldn't relive that time for anything in this world.

"There was no trial because the shooter's ass was covered by his people. His name was never even brought up. The cops had no the case because they had no suspects. Billy was just in the wrong place at the wrong time. Just like that, Billy became a statistic," Sydney said bitterly. Ally tightened her hold on her lover. "I miss him terribly," Sydney went on after a moment. "His death was very wrong, just like your parents'. " Sydney looked down at the young woman in her arms.

"I just didn't think the timing was right for me to tell you about him. I didn't want to upset you anymore than you already were. I wanted to give you as much time as possible to mourn the loss of your folks, before I laid this on you. I'm sorry, Alicia. I won't keep anything from you ever again. I promise you that."

"That's a promise that I'll hold you to, my dear, Sydney," Ally said, kissing the soft flesh beneath her lips.

"Mmm, I do believe it's still someone's birthday. You may have whatever you like," Sydney said in a low sexy voice.

"God, Sydney you give me chills when you talk like that." Ally shivered.

"Like what, Alicia?" She whispered into the younger woman's ears.

"You're such a tease."

"No, Alicia, I do believe a tease is someone that only pretends to offer something they have no intention of giving up. I have every intention of giving you whatever it is you desire tonight."

"Really? Well then, I take it back. You're not a tease."

"Thank you."

"You're a seductress."

"That, I cannot argue with." Sydney said, leaning and flipping Ally over onto her back. She kissed her soundly on the lips and their dance of desire played out once more. The kisses turned feral, the need to reconnect with each other was prominent with every movement. Sydney covered Ally's naked body with her own. She kissed and licked every inch of Ally's neck and throat. She nipped and suckled Ally's ears until every inch of Ally's body was covered in goose bumps. There was no doubt in Ally's mind that they would get through this.

∾ C&#x8;

Sydney looked up at her spent lover as she rested her chin on sweaty skin.

"Oh my God, Sydney," Ally panted out. "That was incredible."

"No, baby, you're incredible. I love making love with you. I can release myself, by just loving you. I've never been able to do that with anyone else."

"That does take talent," she giggled. "Hey, come up here, I want to hold you." Ally said, feeling her partner crawl up her body to embrace hers.

"God, this is home to me, Sydney. You, here with me, is my home. Some people think that home is a place. I think it could be a person. For me, that person is you, Sydney. I love you so much," she said, kissing Sydney tenderly.

Several kisses later the phone ringing disturbed the two women.

Ally grunted, "Who the hell could that be? It's almost the middle of the night. I'm just going to let the machine get it."

"Are you sure you want to do that? I mean, not to make you worry, but it could be Edna."

"Oh shit, you're right," Ally said, grabbing the phone off the nightstand. "Hello?"

"Alicia McKenna?"

"Speaking, who is this?" Ally asked.

"Hi there, it's Officer Randy. I just wanted to let you know that Ms. Harris is safely behind bars. May I speak with Sydney if she's there?" Ally could hear the hopefulness in his voice.

"Yeah, she is, hang on a sec'." Ally covered the phone with her hand. "It looks like you've started another fan club. It's Officer Randy. I think he has a crush on you." Ally giggled.

"Oh stop..." Sydney said, grabbing the receiver from Ally. "Hello, Officer Randy, how are you this morning?"

"Doing well, Sydney, how was the rest of your party?"

"Well, it kind of came to an abrupt halt. Gee, I wonder why." She smiled. Ally could hear the laughter coming from the officer and rolled her eyes.

"I'm going to get some water, Sydneeeey," Ally whispered tauntingly at her lover who was reaching for a pillow to throw at her.

ಬಂ ಅ

Ally walked down the hall toward the guest room. She checked in on Tracey and noticed she hadn't moved. Brushing some hair that had fallen into her eyes behind her ear, Ally gently kissed her friend's cheek. She tugged the covers up to her shoulders and smiled.

"Good night, sweetie," she whispered and walked downstairs.

Taking another look through her childhood home, tears mixed with sadness and joy rolled down her cheeks. The boxes lined against the walls held memories she would always treasure. Walking up to one of the unsealed boxes, she found a framed photograph of her and her parents. Picking up the photo, she outlined their faces reverently.

"I will love you both forever. I'm so sorry our time was cut short. I hope you'll be proud of the woman you raised. I'll do what I can to live my life they way you would've wanted me to. It's the least I can do."

Pressing her lips against the glass in the frame, she returned the picture to its box. Sighing deeply, she walked carefully into the kitchen, hoping not to step on any glass particles that may have missed in the clean up. Filling her tumbler with water, she headed back upstairs.

ಬ ಡ

"I also wanted to see if you would be able to come to the station tomorrow morning, or later today I should say, for questioning. We'd like to get a little more information if we could," the officer explained to Sydney on the telephone.

"Sure, we'll both be there as early as possible. I hope you won't mind if it's around nine or ten. It's a bit late right now."

"No problem, Sydney, thanks for your cooperation and assistance tonight."

"Sure thing. See you tomorrow. Goodnight."

"Night."

Ally returned with water in hand and sat on the rocking chair facing the window. She took a couple sips of water and stared out at the moon. "So how was the rest of the call?" she asked Sydney who was walking out of the bathroom.

"They found out that she'd taken the brochure from the airport with Tracey's information on it. I had no idea what had happened to it until now. I thought I'd thrown it out by mistake. She pretended to represent her father's company to get close to Tracey because of her connection to us. Apparently her father cut her off a while ago."

"Wow, so what was the deal with you? Why was she after you again?" Ally inquired.

"Just as I thought, she was after my money. She knew what I was worth after my folks passed away and she wanted it back. Her father cut her off so she went to the next best place she could think of, me. I don't think she expected the resistance I gave her. God, she really is a sick individual."

"Ew, that gives me the creeps," Ally said, shivering in her birthday suit.

"Hey, stand up for a second. I wanna do something," Sydney said, gathering a blanket from off the bed. Ally complied and Sydney sat down on the rocking chair, opening her arms. Ally climbed into her lap and Sydney cradled her like a mother would a child. She draped the blanket over their naked forms. Ally's head rested on her shoulder as she tenderly held the rest of Ally's body close to her own. The two women sat holding each other close as the rocking soothed any pain that may have been lingering.

"God, this is nice. I love feeling your arms around me," Ally hummed to her lover.

"Me too, baby. I wish we could stay like this forever. Away from crazies like Sharon."

"Mmm, me too," she agreed, yawning quietly. "Sydney?"

"Yes, sweetheart?"

"Thanks for my birthday party. Although Sharon may have ruined lots of it, it was still pretty cool. I don't think I'll ever have that kind of excitement again."

"God, I hope not. I've dealt with more than my share of that kind of stimulation."

"You should see the kitchen, Sydney. It is trashed. There are still some stains on the floor that Eddi and I couldn't get out. I'm glad we got all the glass up, though" Ally sighed. "Man, what a night."

"Yeah, when all of this is over and your house is sold, just think of the peace and quiet we will be able to have together."

"Mm, I can't wait. God, I want to be back at Edna's ranch. I really hate leaving Tracey here by herself after all of this, but... she's a big girl, I know she'll be all right." Ally's voice became nothing more than a whisper. Soon Sydney heard quiet snoring. She smiled and gently kissed the top of Ally's head. She tightened her hold on Ally, looked out the window, and stared into the night sky.

"You were right, Billy," Sydney whispered. "There really is no love greater than the one you have for your family. Ally, Edna, and Timmy are my family now, and I'll do everything that I can to protect them. It was a hard lesson for me to learn, but I think I finally understood what you were trying to teach me. I miss you, Billy, but I know that you'd be proud of the woman I am today. This little one in my arms is living proof of that."

A shooting star shot across the clear sky as Sydney finished her conversation with her brother. She smiled at his response and gently rocked her precious cargo until she, too, fell captive to the night.

DS Bauden

Born in Evanston, IL, Di has lived in the suburbs of Chicago her entire life. Today she resides there with her long-time partner, Lori. One of eight children, family and friends have always been the foundation for her life. When not writing, Di works in video production. She has done projects for theatre companies including Chicago's About Face Theatre, which produced the Jeff (Tony Award of Chicago) nominated show, "Xena Live - Episode Two - Xena Lives! The Musical." When asked to give advice to young writers she always says: "Make your dreams realities and never stop dreaming."

Would you like to write to Ms. Bauden?
Send your letters to:
Diane S. Bauden
PO Box 2408
Palatine, IL 60078
dsbauden@attbi.com
www.dsbauden.com

Of Drag Kings & the Wheel of Fate

by Susan Smith

An Excerpt

It was in the cemetery that Rosalind Olchawski first received the word on love. She was walking in Forest Lawn, seeking beauty where it was rumored to be found. There weren't many places in Buffalo she'd found to be beautiful, but she'd only been a resident for a few months. It was Rosalind's nature to try and be generous, with places and with people, and to find pleasing what was presented as pleasing. So she walked, and her accepting nature found the cemetery agreeable, the monuments somber and interesting, the trees stubbornly green against an early September sky.

Rosalind drew a hand through her hair, the strands mingling red and gold, the pale white of bleached bone, the yellow of saffron in a riot of color. Her eyes were a similar mingling, brown and gray and green, agate, like the edge of a mountain lake reflecting the changing leaves of autumn. Her face was that of an eternal youth, despite the fine lines that stress had started to carve near her mouth, around her eyes. At thirty-three, Rosalind Olchawski had the look of a perpetual teenager with the weariness of the aged.

Walking was an addiction, a time to put her seething brain on hold and let her body move without direction, a Zen exercise for a woman who lived too long and often in her head. In her own estimation, walking had saved her sanity during the writing of her dissertation. Having completed a doctorate, she was now convinced that no one went through the process and remained sane. She'd seen friends and colleagues succumb to their own brands of madness: fits of temper, drunken bouts, marriages thrown up on the rocks. Rosalind smiled, just a little, at that. Her marriage had already been shredded by the time she'd started writing, and over before she was halfway done. Poor Paul; he didn't even get the satisfaction of suffering grandly through her dissertation, claiming all the neglected spouse's privileges and sympathy. He'd been neglected long before, and taken his privileges elsewhere.

They had separated halfway through the first draft. The peaceful year that followed allowed her to write with a will, and only the awareness of how much she should have been suffering during the dissolution of her marriage kept her from speaking of it. A year of separation allowed him to dream of a reconciliation and allowed her to finish her doctorate in her maiden name. The degree and the divorce proceedings were born in the same month. By the time the divorce was final, she'd accepted a job teaching in Buffalo. The physical move from Ithaca over the summer was merely symbolic. She'd left long before.

Rosalind sighed and put her hands in the pockets of her jacket. It was an ungenerous memory, one that she didn't like to revisit. There was too much unfinished, too much inexplicable about the unraveling of her marriage for her to be settled with how it happened. Maybe no memory was easy until it was digested and reformed.

A car passed her on the cemetery path, moving at a stately pace. She stepped aside, wondering if they were visiting relatives, or were tourists. Rosalind ducked her head to acknowledge their potential grief, and hide the inappropriate thoughts she'd been thinking. She didn't know anyone who was buried here, but she could try and maintain a respectful air. A cemetery was a place for reflection, for communing with the divine. Her mind refused to get caught up in the rhythm of celestial time, and churned out thoughts that had no reflection of eternity. She held on to a hope that the beauty of the setting might change that.

An arrow of black tore across her vision, low and to the left. It took her mind a moment to recognize the shape. Rosalind watched as the crow back-winged and landed on a headstone some fifteen feet off the path. It arranged its feathers with a full body shake and turned, feet shuffling on the blue stone. One bright black marble of an eye found her. She had the oddest sensation that the crow was about to speak when it opened its yellow beak, but no sound came out. The silence was unnerving, as if she couldn't hear what was being said to her. The crow cocked its head, looked away, then was gone. The blue stone drew her eye. She walked off the path to get a better look.

It was unfinished. On the front was a patch smooth as glass, with writing inscribed. Not the name and date that Rosalind expected, but a quotation.

Love is the emblem
of eternity; it confounds
all notion of time
effaces all memory
of a beginning, all fear
of an end.

She reached in her pocket for a scrap of paper to copy it down. It was the kind of thing she'd love to recite, later, to a friend, to try and capture the moment of the crow and the gravestone. She wondered who slept under the stone, why they'd left no record of who they'd been, and when they had lived. A feeling of ineffable sadness gripped her, the weight of a grief she didn't possess. She interpreted the feeling as a stab of loneliness for Ithaca, for a familiar setting and familiar people. She was gentle with herself, letting the feeling pass. Loneliness was perfectly normal in a new town. She was starting a new job, which she had to admit she loved; she'd already made a friend.

Rosalind had had the impression, before she'd moved there, that Buffalo was a dying rust belt town, forlorn after the close of the steel mills, known only for chicken wings and bad football. She'd expected to find many sports bars, the truth behind all those snow jokes, and a monochrome city against a monochrome sky on the edge of a Great Lake. She'd consoled herself with thoughts of the two hour drive to Toronto, and all the theater to be had in that splendid Canadian metropolis. Ellie had shown her the way.

It was one of those getting-to-know-you department functions, the kind with nametags and plastic cups of juice. A chance, Rosalind thought very privately, for her to start practicing kissing ass. She remembered the very moment she met Ellie. She had to be from the Theater Department; her entrance was too perfect and too loud for her to be in English. The woman who entered wore black in celebration of mortuary finery. Black silk shirt, black leather jacket, black jeans over narrow black boots, all set against a curling array of ash blond hair. She sashayed into the room blowing kisses, just adoring everyone she came near in a manner too exaggerated to be real. Suddenly everyone else in the room was beige and wan. The woman poured herself a glass of juice, laughing with a mouth scarlet and brilliant.

Rosalind felt like she was back in high school. She wanted this woman to come talk to her, to laugh at her jokes, to turn the light of her attention her way. When the woman glanced at her and smiled, she nearly dropped her cup of juice. When the woman excused herself from an unfinished conversation and strolled over to her, Rosalind struggled to keep herself from looking over her shoulder to see whom she was approaching.

The woman stopped right next to her and leaned in as if they were the oldest of friends sharing a secret. "You look like you have a sense of humor. It's my duty to preserve that." There was such amusement in her tone that Rosalind found herself smiling in return.

"I like to think that I do," she said. It was the start of a conversation that hadn't ended for hours.

Ellie would like the quotation, she decided. The weight of grief she called loneliness shifted, she started walking faster. Maybe it was time to start unpacking her office.

"Dr. Olchawski?" The voice called from the partially open door, half shielding the office of the newest addition to the English Department at the University at Buffalo. The doctor in question, looking more like one of her students in faded jeans and a red t-shirt with a Shakespeare in Delaware Park logo, was lost behind a mountain of papers threatening to swamp her desk. She bravely held the trembling mass at bay, bracing an arm against it as she reached out with her foot, edging the door open.

"Incredible. I didn't think you were tall enough for that move, let alone limber enough. How can you have this much junk? The semester just started." Ellie's voice was rimmed with amusement. She sank into the empty chair at the corner of the desk, watching as the stack of papers started to teeter. The papers were given a firm shove back onto the desk, then a warning look.

"I'm still moving in," Rosalind commented to her reclining friend.

Ellie looked up at the picture over the desk, of Rosalind in Renaissance Festival wench's garb, a tankard in each hand, bosom straining against the low-cut gown. "You should put that thing away before your students start palpitating."

"This, from an actress. I thought you'd appreciate period costume," Rosalind said, sinking into her chair.

"Oh, I do. But you're lovely enough in your street drag. Put you in something low cut, and you're lethal," Ellie said with an appreciative look. Rosalind turned her agate eyes on her friend and narrowed them shrewdly.

"Thou dost protest too much. What's all the flattery for?"

Ellie's mobile face became the picture of innocence, a cherub out of Carravagio. "Can't I just appreciate my dear friend?"

"No."

"Oh. Well, Dr. Olchawski, I was wondering if I could trade sexual favors to get an A," Ellie said, brightly.

"Well, sure. I haven't had a date in months," Rosalind said immediately, putting her glasses on.

Ellie proceeded to look shocked and saddened. "Not my favors, unfortunately. I only wish I were gay; there are no heterosexual men in theater. More's the pity, Ros—you're a catch. No, I was thinking of a double date. Bill has a friend in Poetics, he'd be perfect for you."

Rosalind took her glasses back off, rubbing a hand across her eyes. "Oh, Ellie. No. School just started, I don't want to—"

"Ros. It's been final for nine months. You can stop mourning, it's the nineties. People do get divorced," Ellie said, taking the glasses away from her friend.

The truth was that Rosalind was not mourning, at least not her failed marriage. That she had expected from the moment Paul had proposed to her. There had been a warning voice in the back of her mind, saying *not a good idea*. She could never quite put her finger on why. He was a good man, pleasant to look at, good company, gentle in a fashion. They'd known one another forever, finally dating in their late twenties because everyone seemed to think they should. It wasn't regret she'd felt when he finally turned elsewhere to seek companionship, after she'd stopped sleeping with him. It was relief.

She hadn't even minded when he came home and told her about his affair. She'd accepted it with only a twinge of guilty pleasure, as if to say...*finally. We can admit that this was a mistake all along*. She hadn't chastised him for his infidelity, or turned down his offer of divorce.

It reduced him to tears that she didn't think enough of him to rage at him, strike out at him. *Why would I?* Rosalind wondered. She'd never hated him. That would require an intensity of emotion that didn't exist in her. She was a warm person, everyone said so, but hot, no. Not given to the fires of jealousy or rage, anger or revenge. Or, a small part of her admitted, love.

Paul had been good to her. She felt affection for his good heart, his simple masculine virtues and vanities, his dreams that seemed so manageable. All of this was coupled with a sense of superiority, a distance from the possessiveness he seemed to feel about her person. She really didn't care if he found someone else to make him happy, she just knew that she couldn't. It had broken his heart, finally, that she didn't love him enough to hate him.

"You're not normal, Ros. If I didn't know better, I'd say you were frigid. Or a dyke, but you never show any interest in girls either. You just don't get worked up over anybody."

She wanted to. In her heart, Rosalind yearned to be driven to distraction, to make every mistake a lover could, to lose herself in courtship's dance and retreat. To be out of control, to feel like there was nothing she wouldn't fight, wouldn't overcome to have...whoever.

That's where her imagination failed her. At thirty-three, nine months after her divorce from her old friend and erstwhile husband, she despaired of it ever happening.

I must be missing a piece of my heart, damaged in some way, because I've never felt it, she thought. *Shakespeare said that the poet, the lover, the madman are of imagination all compact...I'm not so sure.*

"Oh, Ellie. A poet. A blind date with a poet. Just what I need," Rosalind finally said.

"Look, I promise you it'll be fun. There's a drag show downtown at Club Marcella. I want to go check it out before I send my students to review it. You love that stuff—I've seen your notes for your Gender In Shakespeare seminars. You look like you need to have some fun, baby. Come out and play."

Hours later, in Rosalind's car on the way to the club, Ellie was still insisting that it would be a grand evening. Rosalind had insisted on taking her car as an escape valve. If the date went awry, Ellie could go home with Bill and she could slip away on her own.

"You remember my signal if he's boring the devil out of me?" she asked Ellie, not for the first time.

"You start choking on the little umbrella in your drink and fall off the chair. When you turn blue, I yell 'man overboard!' And drag you clear." She turned the rearview mirror so she could regard herself.

Rosalind turned the mirror back. "That's for driving, not looking at yourself. No, if I go like this, you meet me at the pay phone and we invent a sick relative."

Ellie nodded in a parody of comprehension. "The eagle flies at midnight. The crow is on the gravestone."

Rosalind looked sharply at her friend. After Ellie had surprised her with news of the double date, she'd forgotten about the quotation from the cemetery.

"Did I tell you about the crow?" she asked.

"You make this gesture..." Ellie said, demonstrating.

"No, not that. I spent the afternoon in Forest Lawn. I found this quote I wanted to read to you, something carved on one of the stones. I only noticed it because a crow flew down and landed on the stone." Rosalind left one hand on the wheel and reached in her pocket for the scrap of paper. She pulled it out, feeling a small thrill of triumph. "Read that."

Ellie did, squinting over Rosalind's handwriting. "How very Gothic and morbid. It's gorgeous. I didn't know you liked Madame de Staël. What had you haunting the cemetery this afternoon?"

"Just walking. I wanted to see Red Jacket's monument and the pond with the swans." Rosalind took the scrap of paper back and folded it neatly in half. "Do you believe in it?" she asked, casting a glance at Ellie. Ellie was fixing her lipstick, making obscene faces at herself in the mirror.

"Red Jacket, or the swans? I believe in swans, but they are a little suspect."

"Love." When Rosalind spoke the word, it took on the grandeur of Paris, the strangeness of Byzantium. She had added, without knowing it, a level of reverence that only those who had never visited could add to the name of a destination. "Love like that, that erases time."

Ellie stopped applying her makeup. "It's the blind date, isn't it. Look, I think he'll be a nice guy. Bill said he'd be perfect for you—"

"*Bill* said? You mean you haven't even met this guy?" Rosalind demanded, taking the corner sharply.

"I'm looking out for your best interests! Sweetie, you may not have noticed, but you are moping. I'm trying to get you out into the world."

"Ellie, I just moved here a couple of months ago. I'm starting a new job, getting to know the area, I don't have to start dating immediately," Rosalind said, indignant.

"Great excuse. I might even buy it, if I were an idiot," Ellie returned, smiling broadly.

It deflated Rosalind's small store of anger. She parked the car where Ellie indicated, sheepish. She picked up her purse, took a quick look at herself in the mirror, and saw the wary mix of despair and hope in her own eyes. She looked away, unable to face it. Life was much more bearable without the apparition of hope, whispering its sugared promises of paradise. That sort of thing happened to other people, people who were larger than life, like Ellie. She could see Ellie getting consumed with passion. Rosalind knew it was different for her. She'd been married, to a man she'd known most of her life. And wasn't friendship what all women's magazines recommended as the basis for a lasting relationship? She and Paul had been great friends. There hadn't been the bodice-ripping lust, but surely that was fiction. Warm affection was the reality. "It's a crime that women grow up reading romance novels," Rosalind said, halfway to herself.

"It's a crime that love does exist, and we are reminded of its absence. If anybody ever told the truth about love, the pages would curl and burn," Ellie said.

"I should be so lucky," Rosalind said. Ellie linked her arm though Rosalind's.

"Your luck is changing. Trust me, I'm an actress. We're superstitious about these things. I see great change coming your way, starting tonight."

Ellie had included Marcella's on her tour of small theaters, coffeehouses, and gay bars. Rosalind knew that Marcella's was a drag bar downtown in the Theatre District, firmly planted between the two largest regional houses, Studio Area and Shea's Buffalo.

Both theaters Ellie advised her to take in small doses. "They cater to the white white suburban tourists from Orchard Park and Williamsville. They'll get touring companies doing *Phantom*, *Grease*, and for a real big thrill, *Rent*. If you like your musicals white bread, go to Shea's. If you want to find some good stuff being done, hit the Ujima Company, Buffalo Ensemble, Paul Robeson—any of the small houses. The tourists would drop dead of fright to see what's really being done in Buffalo," Ellie proclaimed like a priestess giving the mystery to an initiate.

The Theater District was largely a marketing ploy on behalf of a dying downtown trying to lure new blood and money in from the suburbs. Businesses were dying by the day and residents had long fled, but a small strip of bars and clubs aimed at young people were thriving on Chippewa Street. The Irish Classical Theatre on Chippewa drew a mixed crowd, suits and hipsters, students and old guard, suburbanites who wanted to feel very adventuresome. The bars on

Chippewa had started a mini-revival, supporting a few restaurants, coffee shops and fast food joints mingled with the older businesses. The old shoe store was still there next to the new Atomic Cafe, the pizzeria still sat across from the porn shop that always had two huge cats sleeping in the window. Chippewa was alive with college students and yuppies.

An enterprising businessman from neighboring Rochester had seen the market and found it good. He'd purchased the space next to Shea's box office, a club space that he transformed into Marcella's. He'd named the bar for his own drag queen persona and set about making a success of it. Local gay papers carried ads of buff, nearly naked men holding up text detailing drink specials. He held contests, special parties, events, and finally, the first regular drag nights in Buffalo. Model searches encouraged the young to show off their assets for the chance at a calendar or poster of their own.

The front room of Marcella's had a long curved aluminum and glass bar, a dance floor with a DJ booth, and an impressive light system. Handsome young men with soap star smiles and lifetime memberships to health clubs gyrated and enticed one another. Shined, oiled, sleek and sexy dancers hired for their looks performed on the bar, on the dance floor, as bar-backs and bouncers. Marcella had an eye for beautiful young men and included them in the decor. The bar was quickly adopted by a contingent of straight girls in full makeup and tight dresses enjoying the display of splendid male flesh, enjoying the chance to dance and flirt with the boys in an atmosphere oddly safe. They could dance salaciously with gorgeous men, who then went home with each other. When the crowd from Chippewa started drifting in, Marcella's became a gold mine.

Everyone had thought that Marcella's wouldn't last. A gay club in the middle of the straightest, most touristy part of downtown? Madness. Yet, a strange synergy took over. The Theatre District embraced Marcella's. The crowds from Amherst and Williamsville, some of them at least, loved it. It was like visiting a foreign country, where friendly, colorful natives are eager to perform their folk dances for you, take your money, then disparage you behind your back.

Straight people brought cash, so Marcella's catered to them. The drag shows proved to be immensely popular and became a fixture. Ellie had told her about the drag shows, told her that the level of performance could be exceptional. She wanted to send her first year acting students to see the show. "I'd send them to St. Catherine's to see the lap dancing if I could get away with it. Now that takes energy, working with enthusiasm night after night, but I don't think they're ready for that yet," Ellie said, breezing past the bouncer, a three hundred pound man in a security guard's uniform.

He nodded to Ellie affably, then held his arm up, blocking Rosalind from entering. Ellie turned around, and frowned at the guard. "Tony, come on. You know me. Would I bring the unworthy here?"

"She with you? Okay, Ellie, but keep an eye on that one. She looks like trouble." He pointed to Rosalind, who promptly blushed.

Ellie led them past the dance floor, past the gorgeous men displaying themselves for one another. Rosalind did her best not to stare like a tourist on her first trip to a gay bar. Ellie was a performance in herself, moving across the floor, greeting other regulars, blowing air kisses to the dancing men. One of the men turned, saw Ellie pass by, and threw a smile of appreciation at Rosalind. She realized that she was being congratulated, and felt a flush of warmth at the assumption. That someone would think she could land Ellie was flattering. Rosalind stood up a little straighter and smiled back, enjoying the moment of notoriety. She was still smiling as she followed Ellie into the back room. She started looking around, checking to see if anyone else made the same assumption. It was like trying on another identity for the night. Her mind skipped off, picturing what the night might be like if it were just she and Ellie there to see the show. People would see them sitting together, alone, laughing—they'd assume they were lovers. Rosalind pictured Ellie ordering wine, narrating the finer points of the drag show.

The appearance of Ellie's boyfriend shattered her fantasy. Bill was almost colorless next to her, sandy hair receding, face as smooth as a boy's. He was quiet where Ellie was flamboyant, but Ellie found his presence comforting. He kissed Ellie demurely on the cheek and held out his hand to Rosalind. "I'd like you to meet Greg, my friend from the department. Greg, this is Rosalind." He stepped aside, and Rosalind got her first look at her date for the evening.

Whatever perverse hope had lingered in the secret chambers of her heart died on the spot. He wasn't a bad-looking man, with his longish hair and his goatee and his glasses. It was the way he turned to Bill with a self-congratulatory smirk, as if she couldn't see the exchange. He'd been expecting the worst, and seemed pleased with the sight of her. He stroked his goatee with one hand, a gesture she promptly hated. He took her hand, but managed not to say hello.

Rosalind smiled graciously and silently promised to get back at Ellie.

The back room at Marcella's had cafe tables in front of a proscenium stage. It reminded Rosalind of a high school auditorium, despite the loud music from the front room. A good rigging and lighting system had been installed, and occasionally a runway would be rented for fashion shows and special events. The stage had created, in the regular Friday night shows, royalty of its own. The audience knew the performers, many of whom worked every week, and had their favorites.

Miz Understood, a buxom blond, was the MC. Her routine had the snap of vicious stand-up, and the audience loved her. She would get them worked up between numbers, handle hecklers and intoxicated tourists, and keep the peace.

Ellie sat them down at a table right in front of the stage. Bill held the chair for Ellie, Greg sat himself, leaving Rosalind to select her own chair. Bill sat to her right, Ellie across from her. To her left was her poet blind date. Rosalind smoothed down her skirt, wondering if she should have dressed more dramatically. She loved simple clothes, plums and russets, deep browns and oranges. She took a quick look at Greg and tried not to sigh. He was stroking his goatee again, a gesture so reminiscent of Errol Flynn movies that she wanted to scream. What was she doing here, anyway? *He looks like a stereotypical poet*, she thought, with his nervous eyes and his ascerbic commentary on the denizens of the club. This had all the earmarks of a colossal mistake.

The warning voice in the back of her head chided her for being unkind. She hadn't dated in months, how could she reject this man out of hand? Calmly, reasonably, she told herself to engage him in conversation, get to know him, to find pleasing what was presented as pleasing. She'd had enough practice at that. So Rosalind smiled warmly and put on her most interested face.

A beautiful boy with a Caesar haircut wearing only leather shorts and a chest harness appeared at the table to take their drink order. "I'll have a Glenlivet, neat," Ellie said grandly, accepting the role of psychopomp for the night. Greg was looking like a lost soul; he'd need a guide through the underworld. He shook out his napkin, looking askance at Ellie as she warmed to her position as guide and mentor. She ordered Bill a gin and tonic without asking, and Greg ordered a Bordeaux. Ellie looked at Rosalind, knowing that she usually drank white wine. Something, maybe the setting, maybe the look on Ellie's face, the relaxation and self-knowledge, spurred her on. Rosalind resolved to make a real adventure of the night.

"Glenlivet, neat," she said, in a perfect imitation of Ellie's tone. Her friend laughed, delighted.

The bar back left, sliding between tables rapidly filling up with men in suits, women in cocktail dresses. Rosalind looked around the room at the difference in the back room crowd.

Male/female pairings dominated, with an occasional table of only men. The doors to the front of the bar were shut, closing out the techno pulsing on the dance floor.

"I thought this was a gay club," Rosalind said to Ellie.

"It is. This is the tourist room. Suburbanites just love coming to see the show. Makes them feel wicked," Ellie said.

"So, Rosalind, Bill tells me that you're from Ithaca," Greg said, looking her over very carefully. It made Rosalind wonder what he saw. It was clear to her that he had a certain dislike for Ellie. His mouth pinched in mild discomfort when she burst forth in laughter, when she waved enthusiastically to a drag queen she knew. Ellie's spontaneous joy looked a little too brazen, seen through his eyes. Greg was smiling at her, so what did he see? Someone more acceptable, quiet, attractive in a distracted academic way, without Ellie's fire and verve. The thought of such a comparison made Rosalind feel resentful and ornery.

"I did my Ph.D. at Cornell. But I'm originally from Poughkeepsie," Rosalind said, forcing herself to look directly at him. She noticed that he frowned when he looked around the room and didn't bother to conceal his distaste.

"Po-what? Never heard of it. One of those made up Indian names, right? Is that New York State?" he said, sipping at his Bordeaux. A drop of the dark red liquid spilled onto his shirt. He cursed and brushed at it with a napkin.

The lights in the room faded down and came up onstage. Miz Understood came out to the cheers of the regulars. She was a large queen in a short champagne skirt, a gold jacket and matching bustier. Candles on the tables glowed, the light reflecting off the sequins on Miz Understood's jacket. In her right hand she held a mike with a display of dexterity that Rosalind found remarkable, considering her three-inch fire engine red nails. For that matter, Rosalind admired outright the queen's ability to walk in five-inch spike heels, something she had only attempted once and nearly broken her ankles.

"Good evening ladies, gentlemen and the other way around. You know me, I'm Miz Understood. My husband doesn't get me. But if you come back to my dressing room later on honey, you'll get me." She picked out a tourist in a blue suit, sitting close to the stage, and pounced on him. She stopped dead, pointing. "Whoa! Lance, put the spot on him."

Miz Understood walked offstage, went right to the table, and sat down in the startled man's lap. "I'm the welcome wagon. Well, come on! Honey, she's not good enough for you. You need a lot of woman." Miz Understood indicated, with a wave of her red nails, the painfully thin woman sitting with the man. The man in the blue suit had the grace to laugh nervously, so Miz Understood let him off the hook. She rose and went back to the stage.

"He was a good sport. Send him a drink and my room key. We have something different tonight for all of you—Egyptia has a Special Friend performing with her." The queen paused, holding the mike out to the audience. Everyone oohed and ahhed in anticipation until Miz Understood took the mike back. "That's better. But before we bring out our own Queen of Denial—and I don't mean a river in Egypt, honey. I'd like to introduce my girlfriend Diva Las Vegas, doing what she does so well."

Ellie and Bill relaxed, enjoying the show. Diva Las Vegas slid onstage and right into a rendition of "I am Woman." Greg rolled his eyes. "Something bothering you, Greg?" Ellie asked, sweetly. She'd already decided that this blind date was a mistake, and knew that she owed Rosalind a debt of gratitude for seeing this through. Her friend kept smoothing her skirt, pushing her hair behind her ears, and ignoring the idiot at her elbow. *You are a trooper, Ros,* Ellie thought.

"Yes. The ridiculous insistence these people have on calling themselves 'she.' They've even got you doing it," Greg said, blotting at his beard with a napkin.

"There isn't enough royalty in the world, and not enough that we can disrespect it," Bill said.

Greg picked up his glass, and found it empty. "The boy in the daisy dukes will never make it over here to take my order," he said.

"Not during the show, no. You'll have to brave the bar," Bill said. Greg grumbled and left the table without asking if anyone else wanted anything. Ellie heaved a sigh of relief as soon as he was out of earshot.

"I've got a treat for you," she leaned over and shouted into Rosalind's ear.

"Greg's going home?" she asked.

"No, not that. The something special they are doing tonight? I think I found your Ganymede."

They had been in Rosalind's office, a few days after they'd met. Ellie was helping her move in, tossing books out of their cardboard boxes with abandon. She'd picked up Rosalind's *Unabridged Works of Shakespeare* and hefted it. "I feel the spirit moving me. Take this book, close your eyes, flip open to a page and point to a word. That will tell your fortune."

"You're kidding, right?" Rosalind had asked.

"You leave vibrations on your favorite book; it becomes attuned to you. You should try it with a dictionary, it's wild. Just close your eyes, clear your mind, and let the book tell you what you need."

So Rosalind closed her eyes, took the heavy book in both hands, and let it fall open to a page. She'd stabbed her finger down randomly, then opened her eyes. Ellie looked over her shoulder at where her finger had landed. "From As You Like It. Ganymede—the name Rosalind takes when she disguises herself as a young man, " Ellie had said.

"Great. I'm destined to crossdress and hide in a forest, " Rosalind said, putting the book down. She didn't know why fortune-telling irked her, but it always had, from Tarot cards to horoscopes. There were far more interesting things the book could have told her if it were true divination. It was proof that fortune-telling didn't work for her.

"You have to interpret the signs. The book is telling you what you need. Something that's a part of you, under a different name, maybe in a guise you wouldn't expect," Ellie had said.

On stage, Diva Las Vegas was finishing her song. The lights dimmed down, the Diva made a grand exit. Egyptia entered, a six foot two queen in a stunning platinum wig. Bill whistled in admiration. Egyptia had flawless chocolate skin set against pale green eyes, slim arms, and legs that went on for days. She jumped into her signature number, "We are Family."

Men ran up to the stage and handed her dollar bills. Egyptia flirted with them, making her favorites tuck the money in her plunging neckline. Rosalind asked Ellie, "Why are they bringing money to the stage?"

"Show of appreciation. You always tip your favorite queens."

Egyptia finished the number to loud cheers and hooting. A boy ran on-stage with a chair, and she favored him with a blinding smile. He grinned before vanishing into the audience. The lights dimmed down, leaving a single brilliant spot on Egyptia as she draped herself into a chair, beautifully alone.

From the darkness, a form started to emerge, walking slowly into the pool of light. Rosalind caught a glimpse of blue-black hair slicked back, smooth skin stretched over perfect cheekbones, a slim, broad-shouldered frame in a sleek black suit. She felt her heart start beating faster, like a sprinter off the block. When this vision paused and swept electric blue eyes over the crowd, Rosalind swore that they looked right at her, into her.

She could feel sparks jumping on her skin.

The illusion was perfect. Elvis gave a sleepy-eyed look at the audience, curled his lip, ran a hand through his black hair. Egyptia turned her head away, ignoring him. He moved closer to the chair, a sensual menace that Egyptia struggled to ignore. Music started, Elvis crooned in the background.

Are you lonesome tonight? The King sang, and the sex god in the black suit lip-synched to the sighing Egyptia. She tried to act aloof, but the sex god slid around the chair, easing a smile out of the pouting queen. Egyptia gave up the fight and melted, eyes adoring the handsome young man. He knew he'd charmed her, his smile grew, he added a shake to his hips as he sang.

"He's gorgeous," Rosalind breathed, unaware she was speaking aloud. Her heartbeat threatened to deafen her. Was this it, finally she'd be killed by a stroke in the middle of this splendid creature's performance? *With my luck, someone that gorgeous just has to be gay. Mother Nature does not love me-* Rosalind thought. Ellie smirked at her, drawing her eyes away from he stage for the barest minute. "What?" Rosalind asked, her eyes drifting back to the King.

"Yes. He is gorgeous, isn't she? Your Ganymede," Ellie said.

Bill looked like he was salivating, too, so Rosalind didn't feel quite as bad. Then it registered, what Ellie had said. "She. You said she," Rosalind repeated, trying to grasp something vitally important, despite the pain in her chest from the coming attack.

"You should say 'he,' hon. He's a male impersonator, who just started performing with Egyptia. A drag king. I think they're friends," Bill said, watching the sex god stroke Egyptia's neck with long fingered hands. Egyptia looked ready to faint. Rosalind thought she might follow her. The sex god in the jet black suit was a woman.

If you would like to read more of Susan Smith's *Of Drag Kings & the Wheel of Fate* contact your local bookseller.

Other books by
Justice House
Publishing

ACCIDENTAL LOVE, BL Miller

Accidental Love is a captivating story between Rose Grayson, a destitute, lonely, young woman, and Veronica Cartwright, head of a vast family empire and extraordinarily rich. What happens when love is based on deception? Can it survive discovering the truth?
0-9677687-1-3 $17.99

BLOOD SCENT, Patty G. Henderson

A story of obsession...
Love beyond the grave.

Blood Scent takes the popular trappings of vampirism, romance and the gothic; bringing them together in a modern tale of a young woman's journey into the dark side of her soul.

Set in fictional Bayton Isle, off the coast of Maine, Samantha Barnes, a successful cover artist for romance novels, must come to terms with her manic depressive past and her obsessive desire to find true love even if it leads her to the grave itself.

When Samantha suddenly finds herself attracted to a woman with a mysterious and haunting past, she is whisked into a nightmare world of vampires, blood and murder. Thinking that she has finally found the perfect lover in Lara Karnov, the unholy pact she forges with the vampire nearly costs her the lives of those who love her most. Samantha slowly discovers that the infamous Karnov Family is a savvy group of vampires surviving for centuries on the blood of those who served them. By the time Samantha comes to realize the truth, the trail of blood has taken a deadly turn.

The Countess Lara Karnov brings to vampire lore a new and surprising twist in an ending that will haunt you long after you've put the book down.

Blood Scent delivers a bold and daring look into our own darkest fears.   0-9708874-4-2 $14.99

COURTING DEATH, Maggie S. Schweitzer

J.Z. Mackenzie has been unlucky at love, though not for lack of trying on the part of her best friend, Samantha Devaraux. And things are about to take a turn for the worse. While Sandy Garrett seems warm, kind, loving, and reasonably well-balanced, the police seem to think that she murdered her ex-lover, prominent trial attorney, Chris St. James. It's always something. J.Z. learns of this startling development not long after sharing an intimate and passionate night with Sandy. So much for the warm afterglow. Sam, naïve creature that she is, has no doubt about Sandy's innocence. But then, Sam has never been overly concerned with logic or details.

J.Z., a private investigator by trade, has nagging doubts, despite the warm tingly feeling she gets when she thinks about Sandy. After all, the police did find Sandy's fingerprint, smeared in the victim's blood at the scene of the crime. Reluctantly, J.Z. agrees to investigate the murder, hoping to unearth the truth about the brutal crime. But will the truth reveal Sandy's guilt or innocence? Renowned criminal defense attorney, Mavis "Slick" Weathers, a brilliant legal mind in a disheveled package, takes on Sandy's case.

Along the way, we meet Ethel Hale, J.Z.'s feisty old neighbor who has trouble remembering who she is. Then there's Nealy Constantine, Sam's earthy significant other whose quiet and subdued manner belies her inner depth. There are plenty of other quirky characters, including J.Z.'s cats, Corey and Tasha, who have perfected the "happy tuna dance" and endless ways in which to torture each other.

Join J.Z. and her friends as they weave their way through the clues in this humorous romp.   0-9708874-5-0 $17.99

THE DEAL, Maggie Ryan

Laura Kasdan is cruising along as the News Director at the number one television station in Dallas. When a momentary lapse of control almost costs her a stellar career, she makes a deal to save her job and keep a promise and moves to a smaller station, where she meets a charismatic reporter who promises to turn her well-ordered world upside down.   0-9677687-7-2 $17.99

OF DRAG KINGS AND THE WHEEL OF FATE, Susan Smith

Elvis isn't dead, he's just in Buffalo—and he's a she. When Shakespearean scholar Rosalind meets Taryn, a young drag king, they invoke a karmic cycle that began with recorded history. Is their love strong enough to outwit fate and revise their destiny? *Of Drag Kings and the Wheel of Fate* is passion, mystery, and magic, just as you like it.   0-9677687-8-0 $17.99

JOSIE & REBECCA: THE WESTERN CHRONICLES,
BL Miller & Vada Foster

At the center of this story are two women; one a deadly gunslinger bitter from the injustices of her past, the other a gentle dreamer trying to escape the horrors of the present. Their destinies come together one fateful afternoon when the feared outlaw makes the choice to rescue a young woman in trouble. For her part, Josie Hunter considers the brief encounter at an end once the girl is safe, but Rebecca Cameron has other ideas....
0-9677687-3-X $17.99

KONA DREAMS, Shari J. Berman

Kona Dreams, the tale of a chance encounter between two mature women still looking for that special someone, unfolds on the beautiful Big Island of Hawaii. Freddie and Stephanie are in their sexual primes and self-aware enough to be able to laugh at themselves, but can they make an improbable relationship out of their newfound laughter and lust?

Freddie

Can love at first sight be trusted? Twice unlucky in love, Freddie is in Kona nursing the demise of her second marriage. Forlorn and frustrated among the honeymooning vacationers, she heads off the beaten path. When she sees Stephanie, her heart and soul turn somersaults. Life, as she has known it flips abruptly. Can she handle all of the acrobatics involved?

Stephanie

Healing from a break-up, Stephanie decides to console herself at the Kona Cantina. What she finds there looks like it could be the whole enchilada. Everything about Freddie is perfect, except Freddie's never been with a woman before! Freddie's excess baggage also includes a parade of visiting family members who add to the mayhem. Stephanie wants it all, but is that too much to expect from a straight tourist?
0-9708874-3-4 $17.99

HURRICANE WATCH, Melissa Good

Dar and Kerry are back and making their relationship permanent. But an ambitious new colleague threatens to divide them—and out them. He wants Dar's head and her job, and is willing to use Kerry to get it. Can their home life survive the office power play?
0-9677687-6-4 $17.99

LUCIFER RISING, Sharon Bowers

Lucifer Rising is a novel about love and fear. It is the story of fallen DEA angel Jude Lucien and the Miami Herald reporter determined to unearth Jude's secrets. When an apparently happenstance meeting introduces Jude to reporter Liz Gardener, the dark ex-agent is both intrigued and aroused by the young woman. A sniper shot intended for Jude strikes Liz, and the two women are thrown together in a race to discover who is intent on killing her. As their lives become more and more intertwined, Jude finds herself unexpected falling for the reporter, and Liz discovers that the agent-turned-drug-dealer is both more and less than she seems.

In eloquent language, author Sharon Bowers paints a dazzling portrait of a woman driven to the darkest extremes of the human condition-and the journey she makes to cross to the other side.
0-9677687-2-1 $17.99

REDEMPTION, Susanne Beck

Redemption is the story of a young woman who finds out that the best things in life are often found in the last place you'd look for them. Angel is a small-town girl who finds herself trapped within her worst nightmare, a state penitentiary. She finds inner strength, maturity, friendship and love while at the same time giving to others something she thought she'd lost within herself: Hope. It is the story of how Angel rediscovers hope blazing within the piercing blue eyes of another inmate, Ice.   0-9677687-5-6 $17.99

SEVERAL DEVILS, K. Simpson

What do you do when you live in the most boring city in America, you hate your job, and you're celibate? Invoke a demon to shake things up, of course. Join Devlin Kerry on her devilishly funny deconstructive tour of guilt, fear, caffeine, and suburbia.
0-9677687-9-9 $14.99

TRISTAINE, Cate Culpepper

Tristaine focuses on the fierce love that develops among strong women facing a common evil. Jesstin is an Amazon from the village of Tristaine who has been imprisoned in the Clinic, a scientific research facility. Brenna, the young medic assigned to monitor Jess's health, becomes increasingly disturbed by the savage punishments her patient endures at the hands of the ambitious scientist Caster, and a bond grows between the two women. The struggle Brenna and Jess face in escaping the Clinic and Caster's determined pursuit deepens the connection between them. When they unite with three of Jess's Amazon sisters, the simple beauty of Tristaine's women-centered culture weaves through the plot, which moves toward a violent confrontation with Caster's posse.   0-9708874-0-X $14.99

TROPICAL STORM, Melissa Good

Tropical Storm... Enter the lives of two captivating characters and their world that hundreds of fans of Melissa Good's writing already know and love. Your heart will be touched by the realism of the story. Your senses will be affected by the electricity, your emotions caught up by the intensity. You will care about these characters before you are far into the story... and you will demand justice be done.   0-9677687-0-5 $17.99

UNEXPECTED SPARKS, G.L. Dartt

Unexpected Sparks opens with a fatal fire for Sam Madison, Truro's local Lothario, as his insurance office burns to the ground. This arson and subsequent fires makes falling in love a little more complicated as Kate Shannon, forty years old, elegant and highly respected in the small Maritime town, finally surrenders to her growing feelings for twenty-six-year-old Nikki Harris, a country girl who has a habit of poking her nose in where it doesn't belong. Will discovering the unexpected sparks for each other blind these two very different women to the sparks set by an arsonist? Or will the new couple, working together, stop the killer before anything else goes up in flames?
0-9708874-7-7 $17.99

A YEAR IN PARIS, Malaurie Barber

When student Chloe Jones becomes an au pair, all she's looking for is an interesting year abroad in Paris, but she gets more than she bargained for in the mysterious Glairon family. While caring for sweet little Clement, Chloe begins to care a great deal for his beautiful but haunted half sister, Laurence. But not even the most romantic city in the world can help these two when the family's secrets threaten to destroy them all.   0-9708874-1-8 $17.99

Join the legacy of
Justice House Publishing

A<small>CCIDENTAL</small> L<small>OVE</small>, BL Miller   0-9677687-1-3 $17.99

B<small>LOOD</small> S<small>CENT</small>, Patty G. Henderson
0-9708874-4-2 $14.99

C<small>OURTING</small> D<small>EATH</small>, Margie Schweitzer   0-9708874-5-0 $17.99

T<small>HE</small> D<small>EAL</small>, Maggie Ryan   0-9677687-7-2 $17.99

O<small>F</small> D<small>RAG</small> K<small>INGS AND THE</small> W<small>HEEL OF</small> F<small>ATE</small>, Susan Smith
0-9677687-8-0 $17.99

J<small>OSIE</small> & R<small>EBECCA</small>: T<small>HE</small> W<small>ESTERN</small> C<small>HRONICLES</small>,
BL Miller & Vada Foster   0-9677687-3-X $17.99

K<small>ONA</small> D<small>REAMS</small>, Shari J. Berman   0-9708874-3-4 $17.99

H<small>URRICANE</small> W<small>ATCH</small>, Melissa Good
0-9677687-6-4 $17.99
   (Dar & Kerry Vol. 2, the sequel to T<small>ROPICAL</small> S<small>TORM</small>)

L<small>UCIFER</small> R<small>ISING</small>, Sharon Bowers   0-9677687-2-1 $17.99

R<small>EDEMPTION</small>, Susanne Beck   0-9677687-5-6 $17.99

S<small>EVERAL</small> D<small>EVILS</small>, K. Simpson   0-9677687-9-9 $14.99

T<small>RISTAINE</small>, Cate Culpepper   0-9708874-0-X $14.99

T<small>ROPICAL</small> S<small>TORM</small>, Melissa Good   0-9677687-0-5 $17.99

U<small>NEXPECTED</small> S<small>PARKS</small>, G.L. Dartt   0-9708874-7-7 $17.99

A Y<small>EAR IN</small> P<small>ARIS</small>, Malaurie Barber   0-9708874-4-2 $17.99

Printed in the United States
980700001B